Shadows
of Madness

Tracy L. Ward

Willow Hill House

Ontario, Canada

The Marshall House Mystery Series

CHORUS OF THE DEAD
DEAD SILENT
THE DEAD AMONG US
SWEET ASYLUM
PRAYERS FOR THE DYING
SHADOWS OF MADNESS

First Edition
ISBN: 978-09958914-2-5

Cover Art Copyright © 2017 by Jessica Allain

Edited by Lourdes Venard, Comma Sense Editing

This is a work of fiction. Any names, characters, places and incidents are either the product of the author's imagination or are used fictiously, and any resemblance to actual persons, living or dead, business establishments, events or locales is entirely coincidental.

For Mrs. Sandra Bethel,
who taught me to never strive for less than 100%

TRACY L. WARD

Prologue

Edinburgh, 1868—Blood has a peculiar consistency. It congeals and forms a layer, a semi-solid state, which if pushed aside reveals a deeper pool, untouched by air and its sometimes harmful additives. Surgeons like Jonas Davies know the substance well. It is the ever-present element of their trade, giving life or taking it away.

Bathed in the warm light of the morning sun, Jonas flexed his right hand and felt the blood, now cold and somewhat hardened, seep between his fingers. He knew it was blood. He could tell as much without having to open his eyes. This blood had been spilled on the floor for a while. The pool itself felt thin, the blood having spread out from its originating source growing thinner and thinner as it crept toward him.

His mind begged for more sleep, but his body ached to move.

Get up.

His bed for the night had been hard. His muscles were now stiff and his joints tender. He couldn't help but groan into the wood floorboards at his cheek as he forced his arm to move. His fingers touched something metal, something that spun freely in the sticky pool.

Get up, now.

His eyes shot open. His image of the world was marred by blood, a great lake of it starting inches from his face. The nearly solidified pool gave off a sheen like satin, reflecting portions of the ceiling as he eyed it from his place on the floor. He was not drunk or recovering from its effects. No headache greeted him, no nausea plagued him. It was just sleep that beckoned him.

His right hand began to tingle. The metal thing, twirling, tapped his finger, sending a rush of pulses down to his wrist. Instinctively, he grabbed for the metal object and recognized the feeling of the handle in his grasp. It was a surgical blade. He had one of his own in his medical bag.

Surgery, he told himself. You were performing a surgery.

But he hadn't performed any surgeries in the previous two days. As the pieces of his memory filed into their rightful place, a panic set in.

Get up, you fool!

This was his voice now, his own admonishment for not being able to pull himself from his hazy state. With a great concentrated heave, he pushed himself up from the floor and spied his colleague, Professor Frobisher, laying close by, a gaping wound to his abdomen, blood seeping out over his clothes and spilling out over the floor.

"No," Jonas said, looking to the knife in his hand. "Please God, no!"

Chapter 1

Ainsley couldn't stand the smell of the alcohol vapours, the microscopic miasma meandering in the air. The stench, once pleasant and desirable, turned his stomach as he made his way through the theatre lobby, which was so jammed with patrons he was forced to turn sideways to slide by. Everyone seemed pleased with the performance. Even Aunt Louisa and Ainsley's sister, Margaret, who kept close behind him, appeared to be in good spirits after the play despite the story's tragic outcome.

He could tell they wished to stay, to mingle with the others, perhaps enjoy a drink as midnight turned to next day but Ainsley felt an urge tugging at his throat and chest, a panic that had been needling him since the start of the fourth act. Something was wrong, deeply wrong, and he needed to get home.

"Peter, darling, perhaps you'd like to speak with the Driscolls," Aunt Louisa suggested from behind Margaret as he led them toward the front doors of the Royal Opera House. "I hear they acquired the house next to Marshall House for their son."

"I shall speak with them another time," he said unapologetically. When he looked over his shoulder, still walking in the direction of the doors, he saw Margaret's look of worry. This was very unlike him. Ainsley was not easily spooked and she knew this. Something was urging him on.

"Aunt Louisa, perhaps you'd like to stay for a short time," Margaret suggested, pulling the train of three to a stop.

Ainsley glanced to the doors, four paces away, and could feel the crowd of boisterous theatre patrons swell as they spilled out from the main gallery. The street out front was a quagmire of carriages and drivers, horse teams and their excrement, another maze to be manoeuvred in order to make their way home.

"We can send the carriage back for you," Margaret

explained, stealing a glance to Ainsley. A carriage ride for the two of them would allow him the freedom to explain his sudden departure from the theatre without their meddling aunt injecting her own thoughts on the matter. Clever.

Aunt Louisa looked about, pursing her lips as she surveyed the crowd. She swallowed hard before looking back to Ainsley. "No," she said at last, pulling her shawl higher onto her shoulder, "I shall come with you both. It seems whenever I lose sight of you calamity is sure to follow."

Ainsley was in no condition to argue. The feeling of panic pressed its way down to his stomach, wreaking havoc on the bile and what little he had had to eat. There was something amiss, something foreboding happening.

The smell of October rain greeted them at the front doors. A sudden blast of air whipped through their hair and left scarves, shawls, and coattails flapping in the wind. Jacob, the Marshall family driver, had done as instructed and waited with the team at the corner of Bow and Russell streets. While the other drivers huddled together, smoking and sharing sips from their flasks, Jacob brushed the horses and fed them treats, often speaking stories to them as if they were children enraptured by his yarns.

Startled by the family's approach, so sudden after the final curtain call, Jacob stood at attention and nodded to Ainsley before jumping to open the latch of the carriage door. As the door opened, the step mechanism was released, bringing two metal steps out from under the belly of the cab.

"Was it a good performance, sir?" he asked.

"As good as any, I suppose," Ainsley said. He stood on the other side of the steps and offered his hand to his sister and Aunt Louisa.

"Millie would enjoy it," Margaret said, knowing that by the end of the following week Jacob would wish to take his wife.

Margaret stepped in first, and Aunt Louisa after. Before Jacob could turn to his bench, Ainsley snatched his shoulder. "Fast as you can, Jacob," he whispered as he leaned in close.

A dutiful servant, Jacob nodded and scrambled to his

place while Ainsley slipped into the carriage and snapped the door shut. He took his place on the bench opposite Aunt Louisa and Margaret.

"Do you think it may be Lucy?" Margaret asked, her own voice sounding anxious and ill at ease.

Lucy was the five-month-old Ainsley had adopted as his own only two months before when both her parents had been killed.

"I'm not sure," Ainsley answered honestly. The panic he felt, dry and gnawing, couldn't be traced to a specific event or thought. There was something else, he reasoned, something ethereal. He wasn't a stranger to otherworldly interference. For the past year his mind seemed to teeter on the edge of realism and spiritualism, coaxing him, taunting him. For a time, he was in a state of denial, unable to comprehend what was happening. Even now, while the muffled whispers echoed from the recesses of his consciousness, he wasn't sure that it wasn't just his mind playing tricks on him.

By the time the carriage pulled up in front of the house, a grand three-storey terrace house in the heart of London's Belgravia, Ainsley was jumping out of his skin. He was the first to step out onto the pavement. Decorum demanded he remain to assist the women from the conveyance but he did so with apprehension, unease, and an unrelenting sense of urgency.

The street was dark. The gas lamps above shed little to no light and the cold kept biting at him as he stood beside the carriage steps. Only once all three were touching pavement did he turn to the cement steps that would take them to the front door of Marshall House.

A shadow moved beside them. Behind him Aunt Louisa gasped as Ainsley stopped suddenly. The shadow grew larger. Margaret clutched at his arm, more to pull Ainsley back than seek protection. Slowly, the shadow morphed into the silhouette of a man, broad and tall. In the lamplight, Ainsley could not see his face.

"Do not take another step," Ainsley commanded. Inside he shivered but he knew such emotions were never good to reveal. "Who are you and what is your business here?" He tried to shield Margaret and Aunt Louisa. Running for the front door was out of the question. There simply wasn't enough room between them and the man in front of them.

The horse team stomped impatiently at the kerb, and breathed a heavy sigh. Ainsley could hear the reins, clasps, and buckles clinking amongst the leather of the halters and bridle. He wasn't sure where Jacob stood but he hadn't abandoned them. The loyal servant either saw what Ainsley witnessed or was questioning the sanity of his lordship's son.

Ignoring Ainsley's command to stay, the shadow moved closer.

"Peter?" Aunt Louisa called but remained close to the carriage.

"Announce yourself!" Ainsley commanded, taking a half step forward. He wasn't in the habit of carrying a pistol as other men of means had been known to do. This was the first time Ainsley wished he had such a weapon to brandish, and perhaps deter any would-be bandits.

Ainsley watched as the form stopped a mere two paces away from them. There was something familiar in its stance, something Ainsley had not noticed until then. "Have you no patience," the stranger asked, "for an old friend?" The figure pulled at his hat and allowed the lamppost to bathe him in soft light.

"Jonas?" Ainsley stepped forward, a rush of relief giving way to joy as he took in the sight of his friend and medical school colleague.

Margaret pulled back on Ainsley but he ignored her.

With arms open wide for an overdue embrace, Ainsley stepped forward toward his friend but stopped suddenly at the sight of something black, no crimson, glistening over Jonas's white shirt.

"What's happened here?" Ainsley asked, afraid to commit to the embrace.

Weary and pained, Jonas looked to Ainsley, his eyes pleading. "You have to help me, friend," he said. "Something terrible has happened."

"What? What is it? What do you need me to do?"

Ainsley would have done anything for the man, his friend. While in school together, he regularly gave up sleep to help Jonas raid the country graveyards for fresh cadavers. The money they made by selling them to the very medical school they attended helped Jonas pay his fees. In truth, Ainsley, the second son and heir to the Earl of Montcliff, could have paid Jonas's fees ten times over had the man let him, which he did not. The cost of his schooling and his subsequent success as a surgeon was all due to the tenacity of Jonas himself.

This time Jonas did not readily accept Ainsley's offer of help. Jonas stood still for many moments. His face twisted into a painful grimace. His eyes unfocused. His shoulders slouched.

"Tell me," Ainsley pleaded. "I can help you."

Margaret came alongside Ainsley, pulling her shawl tighter over her shoulders. "What is he saying, Peter?"

Ainsley shook his head but did not take his eyes from his friend. Something wasn't right. This didn't seem like Jonas at all. "He isn't saying anything," Ainsley said. "I don't understand."

At the sound of Ainsley's voice, Jonas turned and started down the pavement, carrying his hat at his side.

"Jonas, wait!"

"What's happening?" Margaret asked, frightened. She clutched Ainsley's sleeve tighter, preventing him from running after his friend.

"He's leaving. Don't you see?" Ainsley finally looked to Margaret and saw the fear embedded in her eyes. "It's Jonas. He's right there." When Ainsley turned back, his friend was gone, swallowed by the black night of London.

"Let's get you inside and out of this cold," Aunt Louisa said, gesturing for them from the top of the front steps.

"Tell me you saw him," Ainsley said when he turned back to his sister. She had been standing at his side the entire time. She couldn't have missed seeing him. "Margaret?"

Margaret looked as if she could cry at any moment. Good-natured and kind, Margaret often took his side in family squabbles, even at times when she doubted his motives or questioned his means. In this moment she could not bring herself to lie, not even to him. "We"—she swallowed hard—"we don't see anything."

Ainsley stared down the now-empty street.

"It's getting late," Margaret said softly, taking his hand

and hinting toward Aunt Louisa. "You need rest."

☙   ❧

Ten minutes later Ainsley was in his room, dropping his favourite carpet bag on his bed and unlatching it. Since arriving home he had roused both Maxwell, their butler, and Cutter, their footman, with instructions to help him pack. Maxwell had disappeared into the basement with two pairs of Ainsley's shoes while Cutter headed into the attic to retrieve his trunk.

Appearing at the door with her arms crossed, Aunt Louisa looked on contemptuously as Ainsley tossed a few items in the waiting bag. "You'll be glad to know no one else saw your little performance," she said.

Ainsley eyed her from the other side of the bed. He was in no mood for another of her lessons on decorum and respectability.

"I've spoken with Jacob, who has graciously agreed that none of the events that transpired tonight will pass his lips, which is a blessing considering the track record this family has with less-than-loyal servants," she said, sauntering into the room. She stopped suddenly when she saw the carpet bag and her face blanched. "What are you doing?" she asked. "Peter, you can't go barrelling off into the night. We haven't the slightest clue what this man has gotten himself involved in. How on earth do you expect to help him?" She turned to Margaret, who stood just inside the door, seeking reinforcement.

Ainsley could tell by the look on Margaret's face that she was as equally worried for their friend's welfare as he was. Realizing she was alone in her protestations, Aunt Louisa waved a dismissive hand at Margaret.

"Oh fiddlesticks," she said. "You two are acting more with your hearts than your heads."

"I see nothing wrong with that," Ainsley said, feverishly pacing the room and scooping up anything he thought he may need.

"I know you believe these visions are real—"

"They are real," he said pointedly.

Aunt Louisa looked poised to laugh but merely closed her

eyes instead. "It must be a trait from your mother's side because I have never heard the like."

Ainsley had no need for her to understand. He knew a small part of these visitations, these spectres, were real in some way. He had ignored their warnings before, but now, in good conscience, he could not. Jonas was a good friend and had been for some years. If he was dead or at death's door, Ainsley needed to know.

"Peter, this is not wise," Aunt Louisa said. "Your brother will not—"

"My brother has everything well at hand," Ainsley said, angrily tossing a book onto the top of the bed. "He certainly has no more use for me, or Father, even though he lives. He may as well assume his position as head of the Marshalls and leave me to live my life as I see fit." He gave his aunt a pointed finger. "You would do better to do the same."

Ainsley, born Peter Benjamin Marshall, was the second son and heir to Lord Abraham Marshall, third Earl of Montcliff. Bedridden after sustaining a head injury, Lord Marshall, a once-commanding patriarch, had forbidden Ainsley's early pursuits into science and only relented to his medical studies when his son agreed to attend under his mother's maiden name, Ainsley.

Straddling two worlds, Ainsley was both gentleman and labourer, with equal footing in high society balls and the morgue room at St. Thomas Hospital in Vauxhall. Though somewhat tricky, the duplicity had become so ingrained in him that imagining a time without the delicate balance seemed incomprehensible. Many times it felt as if his life as a Marshall was more an act than his position at the hospital.

The room went quiet after his outburst. Ainsley rubbed his temples. "I'm sorry," he said after a time. "I'm just overwrought, tired, and pressed for time." Ainsley walked to his bureau.

"What exactly did you see?" Margaret asked.

"Don't encourage him, Margaret," said Aunt Louisa, who was still a bit sour.

"I saw Jonas plain as you or I. Just as he was the last time we saw him only ..." Ainsley was hesitant to say more for Margaret's sake. She had never been good at hiding her affection for Jonas.

"Tell me," she said.

"He had blood all over his shirt. And some on his hands."

"Was he hurt?" she asked anxiously.

Ainsley inhaled deeply but before he could answer Aunt Louisa chimed in.

"He's a surgeon, dear. It's more than likely your brother was only recalling what he looked like after some difficult procedure."

Ainsley shook his head. "No. In surgery we wear aprons and, while it's true we use our bare hands, this was different. There was something in his eyes." Ainsley tried to shake the image from his memory. "He looked afraid, truly afraid."

"Is he dead?" Margaret asked. Ainsley could see how her emotions threatened to spill over at the very idea of Jonas being killed.

In recent months Jonas and Margaret had developed a closer bond. For a time, Ainsley was sure they would marry. The only thing that seemed to stand in their way was Lord Marshall, who no doubt had expected to arrange a better marriage prospect, one with titles and riches befitting the daughter of an earl. There was one man, Blair Thornton, who fit the bill perfectly and had easily met the approval of Aunt Louisa. But Ainsley had seen how sterile Margaret was with him, how guarded her affections were. Mr. Thornton had no hope of the easy connection with Margaret that Jonas had.

As a doctor, a surgeon no less, Jonas was a tradesman with a tidy sum of money to live from but certainly no political connections or noble prospects. If Margaret married him she'd be downgrading considerably from her aristocratic upbringing. It was a sacrifice Ainsley wasn't certain she was ready to make.

When Jonas left for Scotland, shortly before their father fell ill, they didn't hear from him for two months. By the time Ainsley set about to write he worried his long silence would have a negative impact on the friendship they once shared. He did not know if Margaret wrote to Jonas. Ainsley had asked her once but his enquiry was met with hostility and then reminders of their father's illness. She had taken it upon herself to see to his care and that had left no room for ill-fated matches or secret sweethearts.

Margaret cared for him still, Ainsley knew that much. He could see it in her eyes as she looked at him from the threshold. If Jonas were dead, Ainsley had no doubt Margaret would be most affected.

"I don't think he's dead," Ainsley said, making sure he looked Margaret in the eye.

"How could you know?" Aunt Louisa turned to Margaret with arms outstretched. "It is best, my dear, if you just accept it now."

"He's not dead!" Ainsley yelled, forcing Aunt Louisa to stop midstep. "He is in trouble and I need to go to him."

"You are going then," Margaret asked, "to see if something can be done?"

Ainsley nodded. "Yes. There's an express train leaving in the morning and I intend to be on it."

"I'm coming with you," Margaret said, turning for the door.

Ainsley nodded, and turned back to his task.

"Have you both gone mad?" Aunt Louisa asked, dividing her attention between Margaret heading down the hall and Ainsley in front of her. "Blair Thornton is coming over tomorrow afternoon to take you to tea. Margaret!"

Margaret ignored her and continued to head for her room. Seconds later Cutter appeared with Ainsley's trunk and set it at the foot of the bed.

"Thank you, Cutter. Please check with Maxwell to find out if there is anything else he needs you to see to."

The footman nodded and left.

"What about Lucy?" Aunt Louisa asked when they were alone again. "You cannot leave her here, not with things as they are. It isn't safe for her or Cassandra."

If there was one thing that could make Ainsley stay it was the baby in the nursery down the hall and the woman he loved, who had been forced to take on another identity. Aunt Louisa knew the way to entice him to do as she bid was to bring these two people to the forefront of his mind. At the mention of them his resolve waned slightly and he was brought to a halt at his bookcase.

He wished Cassandra were there so he could ask her

himself. When she lived at Marshall House, as a lady's maid to Margaret, he had taken her near-constant presence for granted. She was always just a room or flight of stairs away and could be summoned easily at times such as these. Not that he summoned her often. Most of the time she found a way to come to him, sensing his need for her, he imagined. Now she lived outside the city and only made infrequent trips to see him as his aunt prescribed. It was for Cassandra's protection while they established her new life under an assumed name. Lucy was her orphaned niece and one of the reasons that Ainsley decided to adopt her. It was a forgone conclusion that eventually, after enough time had passed, he and Cassandra would marry and Lucy would complete their little family. Until then, the separation was nearly unbearable, especially when he had come so close to losing her forever.

A bottle of brandy sat hidden in his side table drawer, a remnant of darker days—a time when he had less resolve to better himself, the time before Lucy and Cassandra entered his life. It had been a month since his last drink. For the first few weeks without drink he counted the days, and never forgot to congratulate himself for another twenty-four-hour period without imbibing. Once his new sober state took a firm hold, he allowed the sense of accomplishment to diminish as the tasks of daily life took greater priority. At no other time during that month had he wanted a drink more than that moment. Even a half glass, he thought, would do much to suppress the shaking in his hands.

"Cassandra will understand," he said, resigning himself to the task before him. "I have to go to Edinburgh."

"Can we send a wire?' Aunt Louisa asked. "We could know the outcome in a few hours."

"Everyone is most likely asleep at this hour. By the time we get a response, good or bad, we could be halfway there." Ainsley turned from her and went for his medical bag. "I'd rather see for myself. I'll send a note to Inspector Simms. Perhaps the Yard can make sure to keep an eye on things while I am gone. Lucy is safe here. Perhaps Julia—" He stopped himself. "Perhaps Casandra should stay in the country until I return."

Aunt Louisa came to his side and placed a gentle hand on his arm. "Peter, I don't like this, any of it. When will you stop taking on all that ails the world?"

Ainsley smiled and placed a hand on top of hers. "I'm not taking on all the world. I'm just protecting what matters most to me in it."

Chapter 2

The train for Edinburgh was scheduled to leave King's Cross station at precisely 10:10 in the morning. Ainsley and Margaret made it to their platform with only seconds to spare. Travelling light, they had a trunk each, hastily packed up until the hour before, much to the dismay of Elmira, Margaret's recently hired lady's maid, who grew more flustered and sweaty as the morning went on. Cutter, who agreed to stand in as Ainsley's footman, appeared less frazzled and more accustomed to the Marshalls' sudden departures. Surrounded by their things, Cutter nodded to Ainsley on the platform, assuring him that the luggage would find its way on board before the final whistle.

"Come, Margaret," Ainsley said, ushering her for the door. Even as they boarded, Ainsley saw the porters rushing to aid Cutter in getting the parcels to the baggage car. "After you, Miss Elmira," Ainsley said, standing aside so the maid could follow her mistress into the passenger car.

His closed-mouth smile was met with a scowl as she shuffled by.

"Heaven knows why I took this position," he had heard her say once.

It was a miracle they were able to find anyone willing to align themselves with the Marshall clan. Dragged through the gauntlet of scandal in recent months, the topic of the gossip pages, and at the forefront of a capital murder trial and execution, Ainsley and Margaret were pleased to have anyone reply to Aunt Louisa's advertisement. They weren't about to be choosy.

Elmira was older, practically an ancient elder from the days of the Druids, judging by the way she slouched over the furniture as she moved about a room. Her hair was white and stringy with dozens of untameable strands that poked out from behind her ears and at the back of her neck. She wore a collar high into her neck and so tight that flaps of aging skin often dangled over the laced edge. Her voice was often shaky when she spoke but she said very little as she set about to help Margaret.

Ainsley had offered, on numerous occasions, to hire someone else, perhaps someone younger whom Margaret could better relate to, but Margaret would hear none of it. The prospect of interviewing and adjusting to yet another person in what had been a steady stream of newly acquired staff members was almost too much to bear.

The three of them made their way down the centre aisle of the train. The first class car was three cars from the front and so they moved from car to car until the plush red-and-gold carpet and fringed window coverings with tasselled drawstrings signalled they were in the appropriate car. They found two seats toward the centre. Elmira moved to place Margaret's valise beneath the small side table set next to the window.

"Thank you, Elmira," Margaret said. "I can manage."

The older woman nodded. "Very well, Lady Margaret," she said. "Mr. Cutter and I are only a car away should either of you need anything. I'll have a porter bring you and Mr. Marshall here a drink to start your journey."

Margaret nodded her thanks and took her seat just as the final whistle blew and the train jerked into motion. The table rocked. The fringe and tassels swayed. And Miss Elmira was nearly knocked off her feet by the sudden movement. Ainsley caught her and held her upright while she gained her balance.

"Shall I escort you to Cutter?" Ainsley asked, reluctant to let go of the woman's frail and boney body.

Forcibly, she pulled her arms away and slapped at his chest. "Heavens no," she snapped before making her way down the aisle, using the backs of each chair she passed to hold her steady.

Ainsley watched expectantly for some time until Cutter appeared at the car door and she was safely escorted to the next passenger car.

"I don't believe she likes me," Ainsley said as he sat down opposite his sister.

Margaret chuckled. "I'm not so sure she likes anyone."

"Perhaps we should have brought Prudence," he said, referring to one of the chambermaids who was still too young to be a lady's maid, but would have been more light and nimble. "She would have at least been better company for you."

"Certainly not. My patience is thin for anyone not my age or older," Margaret said. "Besides, I'm not quite sure anyone will be able to replace J—" Margaret stopped herself. "My previous maid."

Ainsley tried to hide his smile at the mention of his future wife. They had been meeting in secret over the past few weeks and biding their time until a formal engagement could be announced. They would marry, he had no doubt, but for the time being they had to be careful.

"You did tell her we were leaving the city?" Margaret asked.

"I sent a note this morning telling her where we were headed and why," Ainsley explained. "I had a mind to bring her along, and Lucy as well, but I'm not exactly sure what we are walking into. I think I will rest easier knowing they are both far away and safe."

Margaret licked her lips as she nodded. Her eyes had a far-off look to them. "Did you have a dream last night?" she asked, snapping her attention back.

"I barely slept," Ainsley answered truthfully. He glanced out the window as the train picked up speed in the outskirts of London. "He's not dead," he said, suddenly looking back at her. "I know that much."

"How do you know?" Margaret looked doubtful and reluctant to accept any hope he offered.

"I don't know. It's just a feeling I have."

Margaret found no comfort in this and said very little throughout the rest of their journey. The train ride would take up the greater part of the day and extend into the night, a ten-and-a-half-hour endeavour. Knowing this, they settled in for the long, cross-country journey north, with their eyes on the passing landscape while trying to keep their minds off the myriad of possibilities that lay ahead.

They disembarked in York sometime in the afternoon and were allowed twenty minutes for lunch in the station dining room. Both Ainsley and Margaret ate very little, to the dismay of the wait staff.

"Is there something wrong, Mr. Marshall?" the waiter asked after approaching their table.

"No, sir," Ainsley said, taking a final look over all that had been provided for them. Nothing was ordered specifically. All of it was brought once it was known who their father was. It was this sort of attention that Ainsley and Margaret were loathe to receive. It was conspicuous and uncharitable.

"Everything is wonderful," Ainsley said, unsure whether his words were perceived as sincere.

The waiter took a step back and bowed as Ainsley and Margaret stood up from the table and began making their way back to the train.

"For Pete's sake, I wish they'd just get on with it. Seems a right waste of time to stop here for so long," Margaret said, glancing about nervously.

"We shall be on our way soon enough."

As they neared their platform, Ainsley pulled their tickets from his inside jacket pocket. He felt Margaret pull closer as a gust of wind swirled around them, sending some dry leaves up into the air.

"Peter Ainsley?" A loud voice bellowed over the passengers who surrounded them. "Dr. Peter Ainsley?"

Ainsley and Margaret looked over to see a man about their age heading toward them with an overcoat draped over his bent arm. He had short, black hair, with a gentle curl to the ends. His smile was broad and his eyes were slits against his high cheekbones. He switched his newspaper from his right hand to his left and held out a hand to Ainsley, fingers like fat, rough sausages. "I knew it was you," he said, loud enough so that everyone in the immediate vicinity could hear. "What are you doing here?" he asked. "It feels like I haven't seen you in a dog's age," he continued before Ainsley had the chance to answer his question.

"Giles Grant," Ainsley said, taking the man's hand into his own.

"Eh, that's Dr. Grant to you," he said, with a chuckle and pointed finger.

Ainsley gave a forced laugh before seeing Giles's eyes

dart to Margaret beside him. "Allow me to introduce my sister, Margaret."

"Well, goodness me," Giles said, folding the hand with the newspaper over his stomach and bowing slightly. "It's a good thing you look nothing like your brother."

Margaret smiled. "I shall take that as a compliment," she said, nodding to acknowledge his bow.

"Absolutely, that's a compliment. Pretty as a picture. Jonas was absolutely right about one thing." He continued to smile as he looked at her and only looked away when Ainsley began to speak.

"We're headed to Edinburgh to pay a visit to Jonas."

Giles raised his eyebrows. "Are you? Won't he be delighted. We're flatmates, you realize?"

Margaret perked up. "Are you?"

"We share a house with a few others who work at the university. It's a nice house in New Town, one of those large homes no one wants anymore on account of needing too many servants. We manage well enough just ourselves and the housekeeper."

"Sounds lovely," Margaret said, squeezing tighter on Ainsley's arm.

Ainsley looked at her and realized he would never hear the end of it if he did not ask. "Would you know if anything had happened to Jonas in the last few days?"

Giles pulled his mouth and shook his head. "Everything was fine when I left, but that was three days ago now."

"You were in London?" Margaret asked.

"Yes. I was visiting my sister and her new wee sprite. I'm an uncle now," he said, spreading his arms out to exaggerate his point. "Can you believe it?"

Ainsley slapped him on the upper arm. "Congratulations are in order."

Giles nodded and his smile dimmed somewhat. "Yeah, it's quite a development. I can't quite grasp it myself." His eyes darted to the passenger car beside them, no doubt noticing FIRST CLASS in gold lettering painted on the side. "Last I heard you were at the morgue at St. Thomas."

Ainsley could hear the questions that went unasked. Giles wanted to know how a surgeon, a lowly tradesman like himself, could afford two seats in first class.

"We were turned around by the crowd," Ainsley said quickly. He pointed further along the train. "We're headed back that way."

Giles turned suddenly to look where Ainsley pointed. His newspaper hit Ainsley's hand and sent their tickets flying. In the commotion Giles dropped his newspaper in a puddle.

"Oh clumsy me," he said, scrambling to gather up the newspaper and the tickets that spilled out onto the concrete. "Forgive me," he said as he turned and handed Ainsley two tickets. "They have fared better than my paper I am afraid." Giles held up his soaked newspaper.

Tucking the tickets safely in his inner pocket, Ainsley stole a glance to Margaret, who clasped a gloved hand over her mouth to keep herself from laughing at the dripping newsprint.

"There goes my reading material for the afternoon," Giles said with a laugh before taking two steps to the bin to throw it away.

The first whistle sounded.

"Well," Giles said with a tight smile, "I guess I'm off to find a seat. It was nice meeting you, Margaret." He touched the brim of his hat, flashed a winning smile, and slipped into the crowd.

"He seems friendly," Margaret said as they watched him disappear. "A colleague, I understand?"

"He failed out of our class," Ainsley explained. "He was always pestering Jonas and me to tutor him more, but truly there was little we could do. He understood so little of the material." Ainsley glanced to the first class car. "If he's a doctor now, that means he passed eventually."

"Hardly instills confidence in the man," Margaret said.

Ainsley suppressed a laugh. "I could tell you a story or two, but it may prevent you from seeing a doctor ever again." He smiled when she looked to him with shock. "It will be all right. It's not like Giles Grant is the sort of physician employed by us Marshalls anyhow."

❧   ❦

When they arrived at Waverly Station it was dusk, with the final embers of sun giving a faint dusting of light over the lower edge of the night sky. Ainsley helped Margaret disembark before seeing Elmira and Cutter waiting on the platform alongside the locomotive. Cutter was gesturing for a nearby porter to bring the luggage cart to them.

"You look cold, Lady Margaret," Elmira said as she approached.

"I'm fine," Margaret answered somewhat curtly, her breath steaming up the air about them. It had been a long journey and Ainsley could tell she was anxious to find out what information awaited them.

"I'll secure a hansom, sir," Cutter said, after all their trunks and belongings were loaded onto a cart.

"Thank you, Cutter." Ainsley turned to Margaret and found her staring off into the distance. "You're tired, Margaret," he said, coming alongside her. "Let's get you to the hotel."

"I want to see Jonas," she said. "I need to know he is all right."

"I doubt he will be up for visitors at this hour," Ainsley said. He was just as anxious as she but he was also extremely tired.

Begrudgingly, Margaret allowed Ainsley to guide her through the crowded station. Passengers and waiting family members darted back and forth all around them, scarcely leaving much room for the trio to advance forward.

Ainsley felt Margaret clutch at his sleeve so they would not be separated. The crowd thinned considerably the farther they stepped from the locomotive and toward a handful of cart vendors selling newspapers, hot teas and pies, tourist pamphlets—anything disembarking passengers might need.

A beggar woman, hunched over and shuffling her feet under a tattered cloak, approached Margaret with an outstretched hand.

"Perfume for the pretty lady?" The woman grabbed Margaret's hand and pulled at something in her satchel. "Two pence. Two pence." The woman wore a pair of fingerless lace gloves which had turned grey with age and use, but her nails were kept short and clean. In her free hand the woman flashed a small bottle with a cork stopper. "Lavender oil is just the thing to induce calm."

Margaret pulled her hand away before a drop touched her skin. Ainsley pushed his way between them and guided his sister away. "No, thank you," he said over his shoulder as they sped along.

A few feet away they spied Giles Grant standing next to a brick pillar, a fat cigar drooping from the side of his mouth. He looked up as they passed. "Peter. Peter!"

Ainsley stopped and Giles pointed to the thin newsprint. "Did you know about this?"

In bold type on the first page a headline read: Local Doctor Arrested on Suspicion of Murder. Ainsley's heart leapt into his throat.

The first sentence of the article revealed the doctor in question was Jonas Davies.

Ainsley's first instinct was to hide it from Margaret, but when he looked to her he saw she had already seen it. She grabbed for the edges of the paper and pulled the article closer to continue reading the incredibly small typeset.

"This can't be," she said at long last. "Jonas would never—" She swallowed hard and reached for something solid to hold her upright. Elmira went to her side but was little help given her own frail state.

Ainsley used one hand to fold back the paper and slapped it back on Giles's chest.

"My apologies, miss," Giles said, stammering as he took in her shock. "I had not realized ... well, that is to say ..." The proper words failed him and soon he gave up trying to console her.

"Elmira, let's get her to the hotel," Ainsley said.

"No." Margaret grabbed hold of Ainsley's arm as he reached over to guide her away. "I need to see him."

"Margaret, he has been sent to jail," Ainsley protested.

"Take me to him."

Elmira grabbed Margaret's hand. "That's hardly a place—"

"Take me there, or I shall find my way there on my own," Margaret said, cutting off the words of her maid and ripping her hand away.

Ainsley and Giles exchanged glances.

"In Edinburgh, prisoners are taken to Calton Jail, miss," Giles explained. "But I do not think they accept women ...

women visitors, I mean." Giles wet his lips and looked to Ainsley. "Perhaps you and I should go. And see how we can be of assistance."

Ainsley knew there was no way Margaret would allow herself to be left behind. After his premonition the evening before and the anxious day-long journey to Scotland, she was more concerned for Jonas's wellbeing than anybody.

"No," Ainsley said after some thought. "She should come with us. Jonas will be glad to see her."

Chapter 3

The prison stood like a castle on top of a high hill overlooking much of the city. Constructed of limestone, the jail appeared as a fortress with a solid two-storey wall separating the main buildings from the road and surrounding landscape. The five-storey structure boasted ramparts along the roofline and towers placed haphazardly as if to showcase the institution's strength rather than its usefulness.

Ainsley's distress at the news of his friend's current state was only made worse as the hansom rolled up to the gate. The driver would venture no further. Ainsley hopped down from the door of the carriage and turned to assist Margaret. With her hand in his, Ainsley noticed her eyes forced upward at the oppressive structure. Her face looked frozen in fear, her mind unable to accept what they had just learned.

"It will be all right, Margaret," Ainsley said quietly so Giles behind her would not hear. "Jonas is a stocky sort."

She made no reply while her gaze trailed the arch that straddled the laneway.

Ainsley began to second-guess his decision to let her come. "I should have insisted you go to the hotel with Cutter and Elmira," he said. He gave a sideways glance but she did not indicate that she had heard him.

On the pavement, Giles adjusted his jacket and pulled his sleeves down over his wrists while the driver retrieved his small valise from the perch of the carriage. "Feels as if a dream, yes?" he asked, after he paid the driver.

"More like a nightmare," Margaret corrected him. She was the first to step forward away from the safety of the road and into the dark recesses of the prison yard. At the gate they were asked about the nature of their visit and were permitted through. A portly man at the front desk just inside the arched doorway, however, refused their admittance. He had a thick, black handlebar moustache but possessed very little hair on the top of his head.

"'Tis nearly ten o'clock," he said, aghast at their request. "We have rules, ye know."

"He was only brought here today," Giles protested, pointing to the article that had alerted them of Jonas's arrest. "Surely, he's entitled to visitors who are helping him formulate his defence."

"Defence?" The prison guard laughed, holding his rotund belly with one hand as if to prevent the buttons from popping from his uniform. After his merriment, he jerked forward, leaning his elbow into his desk and lowering his voice. "We found him, elbow deep in the victim's blood. He had some of the victim's belongings in his possession at the time of his arrest. And he can't recall a minute of the last two days to give his own account. I don't believe there's much of a defence that can be given for a situation like that." The guard leaned back in his chair, knitting his fingers together over his belly.

"But he is owed a fair trial," Ainsley sneered. "We are not barbarians."

"But it was a barbarian who did him in, wasn't it? Sliced open his stomach, he did. And as I understand it, the professor he done killed was going to be knighted a'fore long. Your doctor is cooked, if you ask me." The guard smiled out the side of his mouth and huffed.

Margaret stepped forward, pushing between Giles and Ainsley, and laid a gloved fist on the visitor's logbook in front of them. "I don't recall asking you for your legal opinion. This man was arrested only this morning and it's my understanding that we are permitted to pay for his release until such a time that a trial can be held. Now, are you going to start the paperwork so that my friend isn't expected to spend another goddamn minute in this hell or do I have to take the damn keys to his cell myself?"

"You will do no such thing."

A voice behind them bellowed through the cavernous hall. When the threesome turned they spied a well-dressed man with a slender dossier held at his side. He slipped his other hand into the pocket of his trousers in a nonchalant manner. Sporting a full beard and short haircut, the man was an imposing figure, made even more so by the darkness of the place and the overall vulnerable position Ainsley and Margaret found themselves in.

"Detective Inspector Bertram Hearst," he said, stepping closer. "Edinburgh Police." He did not bother to extend a hand in greeting.

Ainsley could smell a strong odour of whiskey emanating from the detective, a smell that nearly brought back all his darkest memories.

"We intend to punish your doctor friend to the full extent of the law."

"The punishment for murder is execution," Giles said hesitantly.

"I know." Hearst looked almost delighted at the prospect. "The governor, the procurator fiscal, and I are of the same accord on this. This is a very serious crime, which deserves a very serious punishment."

"Our friend is innocent," Margaret said, without the slightest quiver in her voice.

Hearst raised an eyebrow at her insistence, and gave a half smile. "Aren't they all? Young lady, your belief in him is commendable, sweet even, but terribly misguided. Dr. Davies was seen arriving at the university late last evening inebriated. At some point he encountered Professor Frobisher and, for reasons yet to be determined, he stabbed him to death. This morning, Dr. Davies was found alongside the body, the blood clearly evident on his hands. These are the facts, which cannot be argued. I should hate to see you waste your time defending a man who clearly cannot be defended."

Ainsley studied the man, allowing him to speak while trying to decipher his motivation for being so assured.

"We must see him," Margaret pressed.

The detective pulled a pocket watch from the front pocket of his vest. "I'm sorry but there is nothing that can be done, especially at this late an hour. You'll have to come back in the morning." He looked to the guard seated at the desk. "Angus, you'll see that these doors are locked once they leave?"

The desk guard sat up taller in his chair and straightened the ledger on his desktop. "Yes, sir."

Placing the watch back in his pocket, Hearst started to

walk for the door but stopped suddenly and turned to Margaret. "My apologies, ma'am."

The three of them watched as he made his way out the door and into the October night. Ainsley saw the look of pure anguish on Margaret's face, most likely spurred on by the inspector's smugness and arrogance. When Ainsley looked back to the guard, Angus shrugged and leaned back further into his chair.

"I only do what I am told," he said.

Ainsley found the remark laughable. "For six shillings a day?"

Angus furrowed his eyebrows and sat up straight, but said nothing to contradict Ainsley's claim.

"I'll give you a month's worth if you let me speak with my friend," Ainsley said, hastily reaching into his pocket to pull out all the coins he had and spilling them onto the man's logbook. He reached into his inner breast pocket and pulled out a few notes and slapped them down as well.

As Angus reached to snatch up the money, Ainsley slapped a sturdy hand over it all. The guard was too slow and for a second tried to pull Ainsley's hand away.

"Just a quick visit, that's all we ask. Tell me where he is."

Eying the loose bribe, the guard swallowed. "He's being held in the basement, second cell on the right."

Ainsley waited a moment, studying the man's features for sincerity before finally pulling his hand away. "You will allow us as much time as we need."

Angus nodded rapidly before looking down the hall as if to ensure they were alone. "Yes, sir. I'll make sure no one bothers you."

The hallways were dark but Angus lent them a single tin lantern they could use to navigate the stairwell. Ainsley couldn't help but be grateful for the darkness, knowing that beyond their light was the filth and squalor this particular jail was known for. Rats could be heard scurrying along the edges of the walls and every so often they could hear themselves stepping into pools of liquid, which could have been anything from blood or urine to stomach bile.

Margaret stayed close at Ainsley's side until they reached the stairwell that would take them down to the basement.

Giles's steps behind them had grown more distant as

they went. At the top of the stairs, Ainsley glanced back to ensure the man was still there. A look of abject horror washed over Giles as the light hit his face. His brow gave off beads of sweat that Giles tried to keep at bay with a wipe of his sleeve.

"What is it?" Ainsley asked.

Giles's gaze looked beyond them into the darkness, his expression betraying his fear. "My apologies," he said, "I cannot go any further."

Ainsley felt Margaret's hands gripping tighter around his arm.

"I'm sorry, Miss Margaret," Giles said, "I would have liked to offer you my support." He retreated slowly into the darkness, using one hand on the wall as his guide. "I'll wait for you both outside."

Neither Margaret nor Ainsley protested. They could not force him on further and were secretly glad for the privacy. Ainsley remembered Giles had always been weak in the stomach, never able to hold back as the cadavers in their classroom turned after weeks of dissection and exploration. He imagined the man retching out the contents of his stomach just as he reached the outside door.

"You have a stronger stomach, it seems," Ainsley offered when he looked to Margaret.

"Why is this surprising to you?" Margaret asked.

They made their way gingerly down the steps and out into a larger room. At first they could not see the cell bars and this forced Margaret to clutch Ainsley's sleeve even tighter. They walked the middle of the room, guided by shadows and the outline of iron that led them past a cell where a grouping of men slept huddled for warmth in the dank underground holding.

At the next cell Ainsley felt Margaret pull away but he himself could not stop. He stepped forward at the first sight of Jonas, who was standing in the middle of a large cell with his back to them. He had his face upturned to the slit of a window that cascaded blue moonlight down onto the floor about his feet.

"Jonas?"

Keeping his hands in his pockets, he turned in place. When his eyes fell on Ainsley, Jonas's expression of sorrow morphed into inconsolable shame. From his place outside the cell, Ainsley could see Jonas's downturned mouth moving as if readying to speak and then thinking better of it. At last Jonas turned his head to the side, and his gaze fell to the floor.

"I had no wish to summon you," he said softly.

"But here I am." Ainsley stepped up to the bars and peered into the cell, where about ten others sat huddled against the wall trying to sleep. One dishevelled man with a week's worth of grime on his face and a month's worth of facial hair sported a relatively new jacket that match Jonas's trousers perfectly.

Jonas followed Ainsley's gaze. "He was colder than I."

When Jonas turned back Ainsley saw the crimson stain at his friend's stomach, hardened now and caked into the fibres of the dress shirt. It matched the blotch Ainsley had seen the evening before when they had returned home from the theatre. He tried not to think of how his mind had known such a detail and instead focused on the precarious predicament of his friend.

"I cannot—" Jonas stopped suddenly when his eyes lifted to see beyond Ainsley's shoulder.

When Ainsley turned he saw that Margaret had stepped into the light of their lantern but she did not come forth to the bars as Ainsley had.

Suddenly, all of Jonas's will to speak was gone. The sight of Ainsley, his good school chum, had made him sorrowful, but the sight of Margaret had rendered him dumbstruck. Even in the dim light, Ainsley could see Margaret willing herself to look forward, ignoring the conditions of the prison—the damp, the smell, the desperation. She licked her lips as she looked over Jonas.

"Are you injured?" she asked hesitantly.

Jonas looked down to the crusted blood on his white shirt, and shook his head. "Nothing of any consequence."

Ainsley swallowed hard after Jonas's black eye caught the light. "Your face?" he said softly, before he could stop himself.

Jonas's hand went to his jaw. "Courtesy of the Edinburgh Police, I'm afraid."

Margaret looked to Ainsley, a fearful plea in her eyes for

him to carry the conversation she could not bring herself to have.

"How did you know to come?" Jonas asked.

Ainsley gave a sideways glance to Margaret. How does one explain the image that found them the night before? "I don't know," Ainsley said. "I just knew we had to come. No one sent for us. We saw the evening edition at the Waverley station and came straightaway."

Jonas nodded and looked away. "It's in the papers already, is it?"

"What happened?" Ainsley asked at last. "The papers said murder."

"Say it isn't so," Margaret said, suddenly pressing herself into the iron bars that separated them. "You aren't capable of such a thing. I know—"

"You know very little about me, Lady Margaret," Jonas said, interrupting her, "or what I am capable of."

Even with her body pressed up to the bars, her gloved hands curled around the iron bars, he stood back, just out of reach and a few inches more. His eye contact with her was broken, focusing on the cement floor in front of him or the darkness just beyond her shoulder.

"I know you are not capable of murder," she said suddenly, her words giving away to a slight growl.

"We are all capable of murder," Jonas said, stealing a glance to Ainsley. "The three of us know that more than anyone."

Abashed, Ainsley knew his friend alluded to his own demons and a split-second decision that had almost landed him on the other side of the iron partition. Had it not been for Jonas, Ainsley would be in a much different place.

"Do not give up hope," Ainsley said, determined to see his friend exonerated. "I can see how much this gloomy place has affected you already."

Jonas shook his head as a slight smile tickled the edges of his lips. "There is nothing for either of you to do. You both should leave this place and never again darken its doors. I know why this has befallen me and neither of you should have anything to do with it." Jonas turned from them slowly and tilted his face to the moonlight that streamed in through the window.

Margaret hesitated as her hands slipped from the bars. Taking a step back, she looked to Ainsley as if pleading for guidance before making up her mind to speak up. "You cannot mean that."

"How can you know what I mean?" For a moment he kept his back to them, his shoulders square and his hands in his pockets.

Even in the dim light, Ainsley saw the determination in his sister's eyes.

"I know—"

"How many weeks has it been since I've heard from either of you?" Jonas snapped, twisting himself around. His face was hardened in anger, his mouth curled into a sneer.

"That isn't entirely fair!" Ainsley could not tell him all that had transpired since Jonas left for Edinburgh. In the very least Jonas was aware that their father, Lord Marshall, had been taken ill and was now bed stricken. Ainsley had written to him to tell him as much. That alone should have excused any faults as a friend, for a short while, at least.

"Jonas, I don't understand what you are tell—"

"I am telling you to leave me. Both of you! Leave me to the fate of my own creation. Leave me and be done with it. It should save me the heartache the next time you disappear from my life." He waved his hand, dismissing them from his sight as he turned his back to them. "You were clearly done with me and now I am done with you."

Margaret stepped forward, her face contorted in anger and frustration. "You are the most sorrowful excuse for a man I have ever met!" she yelled, loud enough for everyone in the entire prison to hear. A few of the sleeping men turned their heads to look at her. "We came here to help you and you turn us away like ... like mangy dogs?"

"Margaret." Ainsley tried to pull her away but she jerked her arm out of his grasp.

"You may not appreciate my presence, or even the lengths it took me to get here, but I am here now and I am not leaving Edinburgh, Jonas Davies, not until I see you permanently on the other side of these bars."

Margaret watched him determinedly for a long while, but he did not turn. He merely bowed his head and shoved his hands deeper into his trouser pockets. She looked to

Ainsley, a cascade of tears filling her lower eyelids. She looked weak and tired, still unable to grasp their friend's refusal to accept help.

"That's it?" she asked, her face twisting into a scowl. "I'm thrown to the dogs, then? After everything?" Her voice cracked as she spoke but the rising tension was not enough to entreat Jonas to turn around. Her hardened face turned to Ainsley and back to Jonas. "Forgive me, Peter. I suddenly haven't the stomach for this place."

Without a lantern, she strode for the stairs with even steps and all the grace instilled in her since she was a child. Ainsley knew her heart was broken despite her great effort to conceal it. Seeing his sister's current state made Ainsley so angry he couldn't speak.

The iron door at the top of the stairs groaned as Margaret passed. Only then did Jonas turn his gaze toward her.

"Jonas Davies, what the hell has—?"

Ainsley's admonishment was cut short by Jonas's quick movement toward him.

"Get her out of Edinburgh," he said sharply. "Take her to London, or The Briar, I don't care. You must get her as far away from here as possible." His words were laced with panic, a state Ainsley had never witnessed in his friend. "I don't want her name slandered alongside mine."

"What is happening?" Ainsley could not hide his confusion.

Jonas began to pace, running his hands through his hair, but remained close to the iron bars of his cell. "Something is terribly wrong."

"I can help you. Tell me what happened—"

"I don't remember anything!" Jonas's words were punctuated by the anguish of his current state. "I don't remember any of it. If I'd killed someone, you'd think I'd remember bits and pieces at least." Jonas covered his mouth with a trembling hand. "I woke up like this in Frobisher's office. I don't remember going there, or why." Jonas closed his eyes. "All of Edinburgh believes I killed him. I have nothing to refute such a claim. I'm as good as dead, Peter."

"No." Ainsley reached between the bars and grabbed Jonas's shoulder, forcing him to look him in the eye.

"You're not. We will prove your innocence."

The lantern light that shone on Jonas's face revealed sudden tears. "I am a surgeon," he said. "The son of a housemaid. I haven't enough money to influence anyone who could help me."

Ainsley grabbed the back of Jonas's neck and together they leaned into the bars that separated them. "I will help you," he said without hesitation, "as you have done for me on countless occasions."

Jonas nodded.

"You are as a brother to me," Ainsley said after a moment when neither of them spoke.

"As you are to me."

"Tell me, friend, what can I do?"

Chapter 4

Margaret charged out the front doors and down the few steps of the jail. Giles, who had been waiting for them just beyond the door, turned suddenly when she appeared. He reached out a hand to her to assist her down the steps but she batted it away.

"Do not coddle me," she barked. A chill nipped at her as soon as she passed through the stone arch and wooden doors but Margaret was still hot with anger, and perhaps embarrassment.

"Forgive me," Giles said, pulling his hand back. "My only intent was to help."

Margaret turned in place at the bottom of the steps, huffing slightly from her determined march from the basement. "Something is not right," she said. She pointed back to the building from whence she came with jagged and punctuated movements. "That man is not the Jonas who my brother and I have come to know and ..." Her face contorted. "And ..." She closed her eyes against an unmentionable pain.

Giles stood awkwardly a few steps above the pavement, one hand on the rail. "Forgive me," he said, "I had not realized you two were ... connected in such a way."

Margaret suddenly realized her mistake. Nothing of their relationship had been made official. As a matter of fact, their entire involvement had been kept secret not only to save Margaret from having to tell her disapproving father but also, perhaps, to allow Jonas time to contemplate whether he truly wanted to end his life as a bachelor.

"We aren't," she said. "I was only speaking for my brother. Jonas and he have been very close for a number of years." A sniffle escaped her before she could silence it.

Giles nodded. "Yes, it has been a number of years, hasn't it?" He smiled and licked his lips. "Those two are always getting into trouble alongside one another. Our anatomy class once came into the theatre to see our male cadaver

33

dressed in a lace bonnet, apron, and rouge. The look on our professor's face, all red and bloated in rage, was one for the history books!" A laugh escaped him as he remembered the sight. "It was another hour before it was determined Peter and Jonas were the ones who had done it."

Margaret listened somewhat unwillingly, unsure she wanted to hear any more about the great relationship shared by her brother and Jonas Davies. It made her feel as if her relationship with him had all been a figment of her imagination. While it was true her commitment to her father and his ailing health had kept her from running away to Scotland with him, she had still held hope that Jonas's feelings for her had not diminished and that sometime in the future they could begin again where they had left off. Less than ten minutes in Calton Jail had proven those dreams to be a mere folly.

"Jonas and Peter were the ones to beat," Giles continued, not noticing or choosing to ignore her discomfort. "Everyone hated them." A moment of silence passed before he forced a laugh. "I speak in jest, of course."

The front door to the jail opened and Ainsley appeared at the top step. Holding the iron railing, he rushed down and went straight for Margaret.

"That man certainly knows how to vex a woman," she said, anger rushing over her once more.

"He is not himself," Ainsley said.

"That's a poor excuse for such a meeting," Margaret said, turning from Ainsley's intended embrace. "I have never been treated in such a manner." Her eyes darted to Giles. She must choose her words carefully.

"We must remain calm," Ainsley said. "There is nothing we can do standing on the steps. We will make our way to the hotel and speak about it over breakfast."

Margaret could feel herself harden at the suggestion of leaving. Jonas could not leave. Why should they be free to move about at will while he languished in such a place?

"Margaret, please. It will all be much clearer in the morning." Ainsley placed a hand on Margaret's back.

He was right. She could do nothing and that was the real root of her anger. This feeling of helplessness was eating away at her very soul. "Yes, of course," Margaret said, fighting back a new round of tears. "There is nothing left for us to do here." She looked to Ainsley, the weight of her predicament borne on her features. "He doesn't want us here."

Ainsley's shoulders sank as she spoke. "I'm not so sure about that."

Chapter 5

The morning sun had hardly a chance to make an appearance in the sky when Ainsley decided he couldn't feign sleep any longer. Before he had extinguished his lantern light the night before he had read the newspaper article nearly fifty times. Each word, and their order, was now ingrained in his mind, but that did not prevent him from lifting up the newspaper once again from his bedside table.

Something just wasn't quite right. There were many details that the so-called journalist had left unaccounted for. The article did a stellar job of outlining Professor Frobisher's history as a pillar of the community, starkly contrasting it against the details of Jonas's fatherless upbringing. There was no mention of Jonas's surgical success in London and why exactly the university had sought him out to join the faculty. Jonas had been right about one thing; he possessed very little influence in Edinburgh. The newspapers, it seemed, had already chosen a side.

Ainsley dressed rather quickly. He splashed his face with water from the basin and raked his hand through his hair. He found Elmira at the end of the hall near the servant's stairs, one of Margaret's blouses draped over her arm.

The old woman stopped suddenly when she saw him and bowed her head. "Mr. Marshall."

"Is Cutter about?" Ainsley asked, peering down the winding stairs, half expecting him to be just a few steps down.

"Yes, sir. He is having breakfast in the servant's dining room." The woman looked abashed and avoided Ainsley's gaze. "We did not expect you or Lady Margaret to wake so early given our late arrival."

"It's perfectly all right," Ainsley said. "I had trouble sleeping, that is all." Ainsley glanced behind him to Margaret's door, her room directly across from his own. He licked his lips as he turned his attention back to Edith. "Shall we go find Cutter? There is a task that I shall need both of you to complete."

Elmira gave a hesitant smile, a smile of obligation rather than pleasure. "Yes, sir."

Ainsley invited them both to join him in one of the parlours, an invitation that did not sit well with Elmira, who was not used to such informal dealings with her employers. The woman sat on the very edge of the sofa, her wrinkly hands folded delicately in her lap as Ainsley took a seat opposite her. A small, glossy table had been positioned between them. It was just large enough to hold their tea tray as well as a small bowl of fruit Ainsley had ordered for himself. Cutter, who was seated next to Elmira, looked less appalled at the informal parley. He had grown accustomed to Ainsley's displeasure toward formality and had learned to merely do as Mr. Marshall bid.

Over the course of half an hour and a full pot of tea, the threesome hatched their plan.

"I shall see that four tickets are purchased, sir," Cutter said with a nod. "Have no worry, sir."

"And see that my trunk is packed as I have instructed you," Ainsley said.

Cutter nodded.

Elmira looked from Cutter to Ainsley, a shadow of doubt overtaking her expression. "But, sir, forgive my impertinence, but a return to London so soon after our arrival? I daresay Lady Margaret needs time to recover from the travel we endured yesterday."

Ainsley nodded. The maid's concerns were not unwarranted but he could see no way around it. Jonas had asked him to get Margaret out of the city before anyone heard that they had arrived. Leaving that on the morning train was the only way to ensure her safety in all this.

"I do not make this decision lightly," he said. "And I am aware of the strain this has placed upon you ... especially given your age."

Elmira clicked her tongue. "Watch your tongue, Mister Marshall. I may not be young in years, but I've got plenty of energy left."

Ainsley wasn't so sure about that. The more he saw of the woman the more he realized she was the absolute worst choice to be Margaret's lady's maid.

"It's important that you tell her exactly what I have told you," Ainsley said. "Once on the train she will understand."

Cutter and Elmira nodded.

"Good." Ainsley slapped his knees as he stood up. "I'll leave you both to it then."

"We shall see you in a short while then, sir?" Cutter asked, standing up and reaching out to shake his employer's hand.

Ainsley returned his strong grasp. "That you will, Cutter. I just have a few things to see to. That is all."

As Ainsley turned to leave he heard Elmira muttering under her breath. "Never have I been asked to participate in such goings-on," she said, keeping her voice low and probably hoping only Cutter could hear.

"You shall become accustomed to it soon enough," Cutter said matter-of-factly. "I can say one thing for certain, this won't be the last time."

Ainsley could not help but smile as he walked the length of the hotel hall, buttoning his jacket and adjusting his cuffs on his wrists. Elmira would do best to accept the absurdity of his family's requests. The Marshalls were not your typical noble family.

❧ ❦

The streets of Edinburgh had changed little since he had last been there. The old city stretched out before him, a grid of tightly formed buildings each molded into each other yet with distinctively different facades. The streets were not as crowded as London's, which allowed Ainsley more room to walk and search the building fronts for the name he remembered well.

At last he saw it, further down the Royal Mile than he had remembered but at least he had found it; the offices of Humphry and Humphry, solicitors of law.

Ainsley was thankful for the break from the wind as he pushed through the right side of the wooden double doors. As he removed his hat, Ainsley's feet fell onto soft, green carpet. His eyes quickly adjusted to the gas light sconces that illuminated the hall. A single desk was positioned to the side where a young man of perhaps sixteen looked up from papers in front of him. A clerk's typewriter was on a separate table, set adjacent to the desk and creating an L-shaped space where the young man performed his work.

"May I help you, sir?" the young man asked, standing up as Ainsley stepped forward.

"Yes, I'm searching for Samuel Humphry," Ainsley said. He could not keep himself from looking about. The offices had changed considerably since his last call. Gone were the tattered and stained chairs and traffic-worn rugs. The room had been completely refurbished with newly refreshed furnishings and refinished trim. "Last I knew him, he was apprenticing below his father, Alexander Humphry. He must be a solicitor in his own right by now."

The young clerk plucked a small stack of papers from his desk. "Yes, well ... I shall take you to him."

Up two flights of stairs they went, passing a number of offices, each with a different name engraved on brass plates fastened to their closed doors. At the end of the hall on the second floor the clerk stopped and gave a light rap with his knuckle. Ainsley noticed that this door did not have a nameplate and the door was slightly ajar. Inside, Ainsley could see floor-to-ceiling bookshelves, each in various stages of disarray. Through the sliver of an opening he could see papers and files threatening to tumble to the floor were it not for the heavy volumes placed in such a way propping the stacks up.

"Enter."

The clerk pushed open the door to reveal Samuel seated in a wooden chair surrounded completely by errant files and misshapen piles of paperwork. Samuel looked over the top rim of his gold spectacles. "What is it?" he asked, gruffly.

"These arrived in the post," the clerk said, plopping the pages down right in front of Samuel. "And there is a visitor for you."

Only when the clerk moved out of the way, stepping back into the hall, did Samuel recognize Ainsley. His face gave a flash of happiness before it faded and he looked about the room. He could not hide the embarrassment that washed over him. "Peter," he breathed, "I do apologize."

Samuel was quick to his feet and scurried from the room, returning a moment later with another chair. There was so little floor space for such an addition that Ainsley was surprised when his friend managed to fit it in the room.

"Please, come sit." Samuel gestured for the chair and held the inside doorknob as Ainsley entered. He closed the door tightly before returning to his desk, sidestepping a heap of books and paperwork lumped on the floor.

Ainsley stepped over a pile of his own, careful not to send anything into disorder, and took a seat in the cramped space. "My, my, Samuel, making partner hasn't changed you at all."

Leaning into his desk, Samuel licked his lips. "Father never named me partner," he said.

"But the sign," Ainsley said, raising a finger as if to point to the front of the building. "It says Humphry and Humphry."

Samuel sneered slightly. "It's my uncle."

"Your uncle? But last time we spoke you were assured he intended to give you the partnership. A bigger stake, that's what you said."

"Father only brought me on, reluctantly I might add, shortly after my wedding." His eyes scanned the top of his desk. He was nervous and apologetic. "I have a mind to believe he never would have given me any position if it weren't for my lovely wife and son."

"Son?" Ainsley laughed at his own disbelief. If Samuel knew of his own intentions to marry he'd no doubt have the same reaction.

Ainsley's friend searched amongst the wreckage of his desktop to find a small pewter picture frame with a photograph placed inside. He handed it to Ainsley. The photograph was of a very young woman, no more than sixteen or seventeen, holding a baby in a long, white christening gown.

"Well then, wonders never cease." Ainsley handed the photograph back over the desk.

Samuel gazed at it and smiled. "She's a lovely woman, Iris," he said. "And James is a good sleeper, so we are told, though we have no other to compare him to."

"Your father gave you a position out of a sense of duty for your wife and child?" Ainsley asked.

"Begrudgingly, I'm afraid. Were my first child a girl, I doubt he would have been so accommodating." Samuel eyed him from across the desk, hesitant to reveal any more.

Ainsley shook his head in disbelief. Samuel had been a brilliant student with top marks and a bright future. Everyone had been assured of his success in the legal field.

Samuel placed the frame onto the highest stack of files on his desk. Ainsley had no doubt that in a week's time it would find its way beneath the papers and folders once again.

"What brings you to Edinburgh?"

Ainsley's cheerful demeanour changed. "Haven't you read the papers?"

Samuel shook his head and scanned his desk with an unsure look. "I'm much too occupied with work, behind even."

Ainsley reached into his inside breast pocket and pulled out the article about Jonas which he had ripped from the newspaper that morning. Samuel read it solemnly without facial expression or response until finally, when he had reached the end, he let the jagged edged paper fall from his hand. He leaned all the way back in his chair and raised a hand over his mouth.

"Never could I have dreamed of such a day," he said, at last.

"We must help him."

"Yes, yes, of course. It's just ... well ... Frobisher is a man of note in Edinburgh, has been for a few years now."

"How do you mean? Regarding his contributions to science?"

"In part, yes, but it's his wife's family who we should be concerned with. Very influential. They will be able to sway the courts to a much higher degree." Samuel pulled in a deep breath and moved about searching in the mess of papers in front of him. "Who is the procurator fiscal they've assigned? Do you know?"

"I have yet to meet him. We know Inspector Hearst is the investigating officer."

Samuel stopped suddenly.

"We became acquainted last evening at Calton." Ainsley slid to the edge of his seat. "I believe the man was drunk or at least that he had been drinking heavily while in the company of the prison governor. Have we any recourse for that?"

"Bertram is his own breed entirely. Untouchable in many respects." Samuel licked his lips. "We should speak with my uncle," he said at last. "He had Bertram charged once for assaulting a client of ours."

"Truly?"

"Well ... Nearly. Charges were dropped due to lack of evidence. But we were very close."

Chapter 6

Margaret opened her eyes and knew instantly that Peter wasn't in the building. The light that slipped past the edge of the drapes told her it was nearing midmorning and that she had slept the early hours away. The night before she hadn't been sure she could sleep at all. After seeing Jonas in such a state, how could she retreat to such comfortable lodgings? She had spent a good hour crying and replaying her conversation with Jonas over in her head. Now her eyelids felt sore and her cheeks flush even after a few hours of sleep.

She sniffled as she sat up in the hotel bed and brushed her wavy, brown hair from her face.

The door opened and Elmira slipped through. "Oh, good morning, Lady Margaret," she said, in her usual even tone. "Mister Marshall has arranged for our return to London. We leave in an hour—"

"Leaving? We cannot leave."

Elmira started, pulling her hands back from the bedding she was trying to lay flat. "I only do what I am told, my lady." She turned from the bed and began pulling back the drapes to let more light through. "I have already seen to your things and Mr. Cutter has asked the kitchen staff to prepare some food that we can eat on the train."

"You are mistaken, Elmira," Margaret said sliding from the bed and crossing the room. "I am not leaving."

"But the tickets, ma'am, they have already been arranged," she said.

Angered, Margaret snatched her brush from the small bureau and began running it through her hair roughly. She couldn't leave Edinburgh, even if Jonas had dismissed her concern. She couldn't abandon him at such a time. Her strokes with the brush grew faster and faster, yanking and pulling at the ends.

Seeing this, Elmira rushed over and quickly took the brush from Margaret's hand. "Allow me, Lady Margaret."

Without being ordered to do so, she guided Margaret to a chair set in front of a toilette table and began brushing.

"I want to speak to my brother," Margaret said, looking at Elmira through the mirrored reflection.

"Mister Marshall decided to visit a friend while you were sleeping," Elmira explained without concern. "He said we are to meet him at the train station."

A few moments passed while Margaret stewed. She could feel her hair being pulled and pinned but cared little for it. Why on earth would Peter arrange for them to leave so soon, when Jonas had not been proven innocent? Surely he was just as convinced as she that Jonas wasn't guilty. He may have been a gambler and a bit of a Casanova, but a murderer he was not.

Margaret's shoulders sank at the thought that he had grown bored of her, like he had of the other women he once wooed. Perhaps he had met someone new in the last months while they were apart and that is why he was so put off by her visit to the prison. Could he be so fickle? Talking of love and vowing marriage one moment, then pledging indifference and resentment the next?

Their courtship had been kept secret for the most part, mostly for the benefit of Margaret, who feared the wrath of her father should their connection be found out. Jonas was a surgeon, a tradesman who worked with the bodies of both the living and the dead. Peter had only been allowed to practice the trade if he took their mother's maiden name and left the Marshall clan untarnished. A second son leading a double life as a surgeon was one thing, but an only daughter pledging her love to one was entirely unacceptable.

So much had happened during their secret courtship but it all served to solidify their connection and did little to tear them apart. Margaret had promised to go to him, to be wed in secret shortly after he accepted his position with the Edinburgh Medical School and the Royal Infirmary of Edinburgh. To prove her commitment, and perhaps erase any doubt in her own mind, she invited him into her room and they shared one night, one very sweet night, before he went away. That night there was no doubt they would be wed and for a short time she was the happiest of women.

But in the end she couldn't leave Father, not after the attack that left him an invalid. Not when he had needed her most. She had feared Jonas wouldn't understand. That her absence and subsequent silence had somehow signalled to him that she had second thoughts. Perhaps he had heard of Blair Thornton's persistent suit of her. She had not meant to encourage him, but how could she deny visits with a man who had saved her life?

She had to explain all this to Jonas, to get it out in the open so he could understand and perhaps not think so harshly of her. She had been so tired and overwrought the night before she was surprised she could say anything while seeing him behind bars and covered in blood.

Margaret pressed on her stomach, which had suddenly started twisting and turning, and took a deep breath to steady her heartbeat. No, she told herself decidedly. She would not leave him. Not now. She must speak with Peter.

∽ ∽

The train station was even busier than it had been the night before. Margaret felt herself being swept along deeper into the crowd, by passing vendors selling their wares and porters manoeuvring mounded carts through the throng. The locomotive engine purred in the background as Margaret followed Elmira and Cutter to the platform.

"I don't see Peter," Margaret said, lifting herself up on her toes so she could see above the crowd. In her mind she wasn't getting on that train. She only needed to speak with her brother.

"He said he would meet us here, Lady Margaret," Elmira said, her voice signalling her exasperation with the heiress. "Cutter, see to the luggage," she ordered before plucking Margaret's valise from the top of their baggage cart.

Cutter nodded and disappeared into the crowd, pushing the small cart with both Ainsley's and Margaret's trunks.

Margaret turned about in place, ignoring the first whistle of the train. Above them on a hill, not too far from Waverly Station, she could see the sand-coloured ramparts of the prison, a Union Jack flapping majestically on the prison's tallest tower. The building resembled a castle with its thick exterior walls and stone construction, easily mistaken for a symbolic relic of Scotland's past rather than a modern place of sorrow and desperation.

Margaret could not shake the image of what she had seen the night before—Jonas, bloodied and broken, behind those rusted iron bars. Had he been given anything to eat, or at least water to drink? Would the other prisoners take advantage of his kind nature? Would the governor see fit to discipline him? Surely the Scottish judicial system would bring to light his innocence. An innocent man could not be found guilty for crimes he didn't commit, not in this enlightened age of police forces and forensic evidence. He would be free again, before long.

Margaret winced at the memory of Detective Inspector Hearst's hardened face. He was not a man easily swayed from his quarry. He would push for the death penalty, would he not? He'd see it as his duty if he believed Jonas guilty.

"Lady Margaret, come." Elmira had already climbed the steps of the rail car and was standing next to one of the uniformed rail workers who waited at the door. She waved her hand frantically, beckoning Margaret to come forward, while her other boney hand clutched the railing with an unsteady grasp.

Margaret could hear the train's engines building in anticipation and then she realized the platform had thinned to only a handful of souls who waved their farewells to loved ones already aboard. She had been so deep in thought she hadn't heard the whistles.

"What about Peter?" Margaret asked in desperation.

"Perhaps he is already on board, my lady," Elmira said. "Come quick or you shall be left in Edinburgh alone."

Margaret turned her face to smile at the lovely thought.

"Come, miss." The rail worker stepped past Elmira and stood with one foot on the platform and one foot on the steps. "You must board the train now."

With a shaky hand, Margaret accepted his help and climbed aboard. The train car vibrated beneath their feet as Margaret followed Elmira down the centre aisle to find a pair of empty seats.

"Here you are," Elmira said, her voice betraying her

relief.

Margaret spied the two empty seats, near identical to ones she and Peter had sat in on their journey north. Peter was nowhere to be seen.

Before taking her seat, she glanced out to see if perhaps he was running across the station yard. There was no sign of him. She began to wonder if he was coming at all.

"Sit, Lady Margaret, the train is about to leave."

All of a sudden, Margaret's stomach began to churn, sending waves of nausea and dizziness in its wake. Even after all she had been through, after everything that proved herself capable, she felt weak and helpless. She could not let him die, not after all this. Even if he no longer cared for her and had changed his mind, she could not abandon him. She'd never forgive herself.

"Forgive me, Elmira," Margaret said suddenly, pulling her valise from the woman's weak grasp. "There is something I must do before I return to London."

Without giving the maid a chance to reply, Margaret turned and retraced her steps down the length of the car. When she reached the back door the train worker was just latching it into place and the locomotive lurched into action.

"Ma'am—"

Margaret pushed by him and unlatched the door. "Excuse me."

"You can't. We are in motion."

The rail worker followed her out the door and onto the iron steps of the car.

Margaret dropped her valise onto the platform and watched as it began to slip away. The train was moving slow, pulling away from the station.

"Lady Margaret! Come back! You'll injure yourself."

Margaret could hear Elmira's commands resonating in her ears even as she stepped off from the lowest step. It took a moment for her to get her balance but thankfully she did not fall.

"Margaret!"

The cries were closer now and when Margaret looked she saw Elmira, old and feeble as she was, clutching her hat and holding onto the iron rail of the first class car. As the train pulled further from the station, gaining speed as it went, Margaret felt an unbelievable rush of liberation. She was free from her lady's maid, her brother Daniel's spy, as Margaret called her. She was free from Marshall House and the call of London. She was free from everyone who conspired to tell her what to do and how to do it.

With an air of triumph, Margaret turned, walked purposefully back to her valise, and plucked it from the platform. Perhaps Peter was on the train and had only been in another car. Perhaps the morning's events had only been a plot of his devising to somehow get her out of Edinburgh. Perhaps she had made a grievous error and would find herself regretting it all by that same time the next day. Margaret chuckled to herself, and stole a glance down the now-empty track.

None of it mattered. Jonas was here. In this city. And he needed her help.

Chapter 7

With his pocket watch in his hand, Ainsley glanced out the window. He could not hear the whistle of the ten o'clock train but he imagined it all the same. Jonas would be pleased to know that Margaret was safely out of the city. She'd be vexed with them both, he was sure, but he could handle a heated argument better than seeing her in harm's way once again.

He smiled as he slipped the watch back into his inside pocket.

"Are you late for an appointment?" Samuel asked, as he approached him with a file tucked under his arm.

"No," Ainsley answered. "Just thinking of a friend."

Samuel cocked his head to the side, coaxing Ainsley to follow him down the hall. "My uncle will see us now," he said, before turning and leading the way.

Mr. Humphry's office was strikingly bigger and better appointed when compared to Samuel's overstuffed closet. The contrast was not lost on Samuel, who bowed his head slightly as Ainsley walked through the threshold. He exhaled and forced a smile. "Father is away in Glasgow at the moment," he said.

Ainsley nodded and then surveyed the room. Papered in a deep green, the walls stretched fifteen feet high with tall, curved windows to match the height. The expanse included two distinct areas, one for Thomas Humphry's large desk, some shelving, and a small tea table set next to the window. The second area was set up near the door with four comfortable gold-upholstered chairs set about a circular table. A small vase of roses was placed on a red square cloth at the centre.

Thomas was standing near the window overlooking an expansive view of Edinburgh with a teacup and saucer in his hand. The man was extraordinarily tall, with a receding hairline and long, bushy mutton chops. He seemed friendly enough when he eventually turned to Ainsley and his nephew, Samuel.

"This is about the murder of the professor, then?" he asked, placing his teacup and saucer on the small table near the window.

"Yes, sir," Samuel said, somewhat hesitantly. "This is Peter Ainsley, the friend from the university I was telling you about."

Thomas approached with an outstretched hand.

"Your profession?" Thomas asked quickly.

"Surgeon," Ainsley answered.

"Where is your practice?"

"London. I am attached to St. Thomas, sir."

Thomas nodded. "And how are you related to the accused?"

"We trained together at the university," Ainsley said, "And have stayed close since."

Thomas eyed him, most likely trying to decide if Ainsley was to be trusted. "I have read the accounts in the papers," he said, before turning to Samuel. "The evidence is very damning, I'm afraid. You insist the accused is innocent."

Samuel stepped forward. "Yes sir, we both feel the same way. Jonas—"

"Is in a whole heap of trouble, that's what." Thomas took on a contemplative air and began stroking at his facial hair.

"He is incapable of doing what they say he has done," Ainsley insisted.

"How so?" Thomas turned to his nephew in particular so that he alone would answer his question.

Samuel hesitated, taken aback by his uncle's line of questioning. "He has the most scruples of all of us, sir," Samuel said. "I remember it from school." He glanced to Ainsley. "We all had our fair share of troubles but not Jonas. He's as straight as they come."

Thomas smirked. "I am well aware of your misdeeds, Sam."

Suddenly, the mood in the room changed and Samuel drew back. Thomas would not accept their appeals regarding Jonas's character, not while he still saw his nephew as a child to be disciplined.

Thomas turned to Ainsley. "As I understand it, Dr. Davies was found in the presence of the body, covered in the victim's blood. How does your friend account for that?"

"He remembers none of it, sir, or so he told me last night," Ainsley said. "He was under the influence of something, something he did not willingly ingest."

"What is his last memory then?"

Ainsley shook his head. "Of that I am not aware."

Thomas waved his hand and turned, clearly disappointed.

"Our meeting was brief and we were able to examine so few details," Ainsley injected quickly. "At this moment in time he is locked in the basement cell at Calton surrounded by thieves and murders—"

"Who all profess their innocence," Thomas answered from his desk. "I cannot help them all."

"But Jonas must be helped," Samuel said, coming to Ainsley's aid.

Thomas slammed a fist onto the desktop, rattling it. "Look around you, boy," he said, regarding Samuel squarely. "We are on the very edge, the very edge." He stood tall and pulled down his vest beneath his jacket. "We have no room for capital murder cases. There is no money in it, not for a surgeon, one who only has surgeon friends. I'm sorry, boy, but if you expect to make partner you'd do better to choose the cases that you bring to my office more carefully."

Samuel opened his mouth to speak but closed it again when he saw his uncle taking his seat at his desk and picking up his pen. He turned to Ainsley, who still stood at the table. "Come then, Peter," Samuel said, "I'll help you find someone else."

Even as Samuel began for the door Ainsley found himself rooted in place. He had a strong suspicion that Thomas Humphry was the lawyer they needed, the only one in Edinburgh who could plead Jonas's case and have him exonerated of all charges. Ainsley could not see himself leaving that room without knowing he had secured someone to represent Jonas in court.

"What if I wasn't a surgeon?" Ainsley asked, keeping his eyes trained on Thomas.

The lawyer raised his head slowly.

"Peter, what are you doing?" Samuel asked.

"Answer my question," Ainsley charged as Thomas sat silently at his desk.

The senior lawyer shrugged. "There would be more money in it then, wouldn't there? More clout when we head to court." Thomas sighed, as if realizing he had made a mistake by being so direct earlier. "I'm sorry if my words offended you. You have chosen a noble profession, a noble profession, but I'm afraid the court will not see it the same as ... others."

Ainsley licked his lips and ignored Samuel's tugs on his arm. "You are in luck, sir," Ainsley said. "My name is Peter Marshall, second son and heir to Lord Abraham Marshall, third earl of Montcliff."

"Peter, this is ill-advised—"

"I speak the truth," Ainsley said, shaking his sleeve from Samuel's grasp. "I attended the medical school under my mother's maiden name, the Ainsleys. I work as Peter Ainsley. No one knows of my birthright."

Thomas laughed but stopped short. Ainsley watched as he and Samuel locked eyes, each man evaluating his claim for plausibility. "You had no idea of this then, Sam?" Thomas asked, tossing his pen to his desktop before leaning back in his chair.

"No, sir." He bowed his head and avoided Ainsley's gaze.

The side of Thomas's lips curled into an amused smile. "You have money, I presume."

"Yes, sir," Ainsley said. "And I can access more of it should we need it for Jonas's defence."

Thomas nodded. "All right. And you'd be willing to sit in court as a character witness? Your secret would be out, a matter of public record."

Ainsley knew this would mean the end of his secret, though he could see no way around it. He'd do anything to secure Jonas's freedom. And the prospect of freeing himself of the burden he'd held all these years was something else he was very much looking forward to.

"I am aware of what this entails, sir," Ainsley said, "My only worry is with my employer. I am unsure how this will affect my place."

"Bah"—Thomas waved his hand—"a pittance. I doubt it will provide much difference to your comfort."

Ainsley nearly corrected him. It wasn't about the income, and never had been. The ability to study the science of death and all its secrets had been enough to keep him moving forward following tragedy after tragedy. His mother's death. The loss of innocent lives. Even the forfeit of his own soul. Medicine and his contribution to it meant more to him than some inherited title or all the money in the empire. Ainsley knew enough not to argue, though; pity was not the sort of thing offered to the upper tiers of society.

"What time is it, then?" Thomas asked, breaking Ainsley's reverie.

"'Tis nearly eleven o'clock, sir," Samuel said, somewhat sheepishly. Ainsley looked to him but Samuel quickly averted his gaze.

"Very well," Thomas said. He stood up and made his way toward Ainsley. "Please secure as much money as you can, both for our fees and Dr. Davies's freedom. I will meet you both at Calton promptly at one and see what we can do to have him released to our care. Is this agreeable to you, Mister Marshall?"

Ainsley started when the lawyer used his real name. "Highly agreeable, yes," he said, still somewhat stymied by the change in the tone of their meeting.

Thomas looked past Ainsley to his nephew. "See that you draw up the contract so Mister Marshall and our accused may sign it this afternoon."

Samuel nodded.

They walked to the door. "I want to thank you for coming to see me today," he said. "We will do our best for your friend, yes?"

Ainsley nodded as he reached the hall. "Thank you, sir."

"We can chat more about the case once the accused can help fill in the details." Thomas shook his head in disbelief as he pulled the door closed, most likely his mind still coming to terms with what had just been revealed to him. "A gentleman masquerading as a tradesman … never heard of such a thing." His voice trailed off in amusement as the door closed.

When Ainsley turned to Samuel, he was reminded of how his friend's demeanour had changed. "I'm sorry for not telling you. It was—"

"Does Jonas know?" Samuel asked sharply.

"He found out early on. I couldn't keep it from him."

Samuel grimaced. "That settles it then."

"Settles what?"

"A number of us had an ongoing bet regarding who was your benefactor." Samuel smiled. "You weren't fooling anyone, Peter. We all knew you weren't like the rest of us. And now we know why. Jonas never said anything to any one of us. He's loyal, I'll give him that."

Despite these remembrances Ainsley feared awkwardness would wedge itself between them. It could change their easy dynamic.

"Nothing changes," Ainsley reminded him. "The title means nothing to me."

"Good," Samuel said, gesturing for Ainsley to follow him down the hall. "Because there's no way in hell I'm going to start addressing you as Your Lordship."

Chapter 8

The valise in Margaret's hand grew heavy with each step she took down Dundas Street in New Town. She had so little money with her that she feared taking a hansom from the train station would empty her purse, but the walk was longer than she anticipated, especially with her bag to lug along beside her. Jonas's house couldn't be far, she reasoned, but each time she thought she drew near a passerby directed her further and further down the street.

Everything had looked different the night before and Margaret had been so tired that she paid little heed to where Giles called home. She regretted her lapse exceedingly now. Had she realized how far the house was from the station she would have taken a hansom straightaway, to hell with the expense.

Fortune was in her favour, however, when the paper saw need to publish Jonas's home address, an offering to the citizens who relished the macabre details of any murder or grisly misdeed perpetrated in the city. It was unfortunate for his housemates, who'd suffer the stigma of association. She imagined Jonas would have no rest for many years to come. Even if he is exonerated—*when*, she corrected herself—when he is exonerated, she knew many would still look at him with suspicion.

The thought made her steps heavy and her resolve waned slightly before she finally saw the terraced house Jonas shared with a handful of others from the university. The front walk was filled with people who had been drawn to the doorstep of the unassuming three-storey house in the middle of the block. Two uniformed officers stood at either side of the steps, and a police carriage sat at the kerb. Their presence did little to dampen the anger of the crowd, who hurled obscenities and tossed rotten food at the exterior stone of the building. As Margaret drew nearer she could see a considerable pile of splattered produce had accumulated on the front step and in the surrounding crevices.

"He should be hanged for what he done!" one woman yelled as she raised her fist in the air. A man, most likely her husband, pulled her away from the crowd and guided her down the street toward Margaret, who hung back with considerable apprehension.

"To think we live ten houses from such a murderous man," she said as they walked nearer Margaret.

"We could have been murdered in the night," the man proclaimed, stealing an uneasy glance over his shoulder. "If there is any justice in the world he will be hanged publicly for all in Edinburgh to see."

Margaret shivered to hear them speak and pushed back tears that threatened to overwhelm her. Jonas's name had been tarnished, perhaps beyond repair. Some would always view him as a murderer even though she knew he was no such thing and hoped she could clear his name quickly. Stepping slowly, she neared the edge of the crowd and looked up to the windows of the second and third floor. She could see the drapes had been drawn in all rooms except one, where a man stood looking down at the scene. She recognized him right away as Inspector Bertram Hearst and reasoned that that room must be Jonas's room.

The hum from the crowd grew louder and more frantic all of a sudden and when Margaret looked she saw Giles pushing his way through. He held a satchel in one hand and moved slowly between the tightly spaced bodies that crowded the stoop.

"Out of my way," he growled against the renewed fervour of those gathered. "Can't a man get to his own front door?"

Someone grabbed his satchel and pulled him back just as he reached the highest step.

"Let me be!" he yelled, yanking it back. His eyes met Margaret's then as she stood nearer the back of the crowd. "Miss Margaret?"

Margaret's heart leapt.

"What are you doing here?" He surveyed the mob and looked back at her.

A moment later, Giles was pushing his way through the crowd toward her. "Come quick," he said, beckoning her with his hand, "Inside."

He provided a barrier for her through the crowd. Even still, her dress and valise were tugged by unseen hands and when they finally reached the top of the stairs she felt something hard hit her on her shoulder. She couldn't help crying out in pain.

"Animals!" Giles yelled into the crowd before quickly closing the front door behind them. "Forgive me, Miss Margaret. Their behaviour is abhorrent."

"Man finds no greater accelerant to his anger than when he is with like company," Margaret said, still trying to catch her breath.

Giles's face betrayed his surprise at her observation. "How very astute." He reached for her bag, which she was much relieved to be free of, and placed it next to the hall stand by the door. "What brings you to New Town"—he pointed to her valise—"with luggage, no less?"

"I haven't any proof, but I believe Peter may have tried to trick me into leaving Edinburgh." Margaret was somewhat embarrassed to admit her morning's misadventure, but Giles had been so friendly with her since the moment they met at the train station in York the day before. When she saw the look of concern on his face she decided to try for a more lighthearted approach. She smiled. "He wishes to have all the glory to himself when Jonas is set free," she said with a laugh.

"That certainly is Peter's way. He told me last night before we parted that he was going to try to have Jonas released pending his trial. He said he would stop in to see me whether his plan met with success or not." Giles glanced down the hall. "I think you should stay here until he—"

An army of feet marched down the stairwell, eliciting all manner of creaks and groans from the aged wood. One by one, six uniformed officers passed them in the halls, each carrying a crate filled with random things, most likely taken from Jonas's room. At the end of the line sauntered the detective Margaret had seen peering down at her from the window.

Her throat went dry at the sight of him and for some reason she wished Giles was not separated from her on the other side of the hall. She could tell immediately that she did not trust this man. His angular face was so stern and his eyes were cold and dark. She knew he had already made up his mind about the case and had no doubt Jonas was their murderer.

"You are a fair distance from home, Lady Margaret," Inspector Hearst said.

Margaret recoiled at the use of her proper name. She looked to Giles, who seemed thoroughly confused.

"I took a precursory look into your and your brother's histories," the detective explained. "You've led a charmed life, it seems, until recently."

"How did you know—?"

"You brother signed the logbook last night using his proper name, his legal name, which I admit, was very wise." Hearst stole a glance to Giles. "Tell me, Lady Margaret, is anyone else aware of your brother's duplicity?"

Margaret chose not to answer.

"Is the university aware?" Hearst didn't bother to wait for an answer. "Is his medical licence even legal given that a Mr. Peter Ainsley doesn't actually exist?"

Margaret swallowed down her panic. She held no answers for the detective's pointed questions.

"How long do you and your brother intend to stay in Edinburgh?"

"As long as it takes to see our friend, Dr. Davies, exonerated," Margaret said, finding her voice.

The detective raised his chin at the mention of his accused. "How unfortunate of you," he said. He took a step closer to her. "As it is a fool's errand."

Margaret could tell he was laughing at her, amused by the thought that she, a woman, could affect anything in their man's world of murderers, deviants, and thieves.

"Not as foolish as blindly believing a man guilty without proper evidence."

Hearst raised an eyebrow and crossed his arms over his chest.

"Our friend is happy for our assistance," she lied.

"What sort of assistance are you and your brother expecting to provide, exactly?" Hearst asked.

"We expect to prove his innocence," she answered coolly. Internally, she shook. She had already lied once, by telling him Jonas was happy for her help. She knew Jonas was not going to be pleased when he found out Peter had not been successful in getting her out of the city. And she had no idea if her presence was going to be a help or a hindrance, but she was determined not to show this man any of her apprehension.

When the detective looked to Giles, she squared her shoulders and raised her chin slightly. She was not going to be intimidated.

"Innocence." He repeated her word with an air of amusement. "Of course."

He was still laughing as he walked out onto the steps and Giles closed the door after him.

"He arrived here early this morning before I left," Giles said, almost apologetically. "He was intent on searching for evidence." He twisted his mouth into a frown as he said the last three words. "He wished to interview everyone. Thank goodness I was spared such a fate." He smiled. "I had a meeting at the university to discuss how to handle this tragedy." He glanced out the window alongside the door as if to take one last look at the inspector. "Not sure how I would have stood up against a man such as that."

"He looks quite severe," Margaret said, finally allowing herself to relax. "I shall not rest knowing he is so determined to prove Jonas's guilt."

A moment of uneasy silence blanketed them. Margaret saw Giles's expression falter before he suddenly clapped his hands and forced a smile. "I was going to offer you some tea before we were interrupted." He made a sweeping gesture with his hand to invite her down the hall. "Shall we?"

"Yes, of course."

She followed him, stealing quick glances through the open doors they passed. There were two sitting rooms and a sizeable dining room complete with a table large enough for ten people to sit about. The furnishings looked worn but not overly so. Everything seemed well in place, without even a book lying around unclaimed. The main floor was quiet with most of the noise emanating from the kitchen at the back.

It seemed, Margaret observed, that whomever they had contracted to take care of them was doing a commendable job of it, judging by the state of the place.

Giles pushed open the door to the kitchen, giving a gentle wrap of his knuckle as he entered.

Margaret entered the room and saw a woman standing over the sink, while two men sat at a small table set in the middle of the room. A fire in the stove burned, keeping the kettle and another large pot steaming. One of the men held a damp handkerchief in his hand, twisted and pulled in his hands, which were set on the tabletop. All the murmurs Margaret had heard prior stopped suddenly when they entered.

"Mrs. Crane, we have a visitor," Giles said.

Mrs. Crane turned toward the door and both men stood quickly when they realized a woman had entered.

Margaret started at the sight of her. "Mrs. Crane?"

She placed a hand on her stomach, as if to supress the shock. Mrs. Crane had been the housekeeper for Dr. Bennett, a physician who had contacted Peter after a series of deaths in the town of Picklow. At the time, Mrs. Crane was aghast at Margaret's lack of domestic skills. She offered some quick lessons and encouraged her to continue practising which, Margaret was ashamed to say, she had not.

"Gracious Providence!" Mrs. Crane pushed back some curls from her forehead. "Margaret, my dear. Never did I expect to see you again." She stepped forward and took up Margaret's hand in a very soothing manner.

Margaret smiled broadly, glad to be seeing a familiar face. She could feel a heavy weight being lifted from her shoulders, which almost sent her into a fit of tears.

"You have heard then," Mrs. Crane said, sniffling. She glanced to the two men at the table. "You have heard of our agony."

Margaret could tell Mrs. Crane had been crying. She did not doubt she was glad to see her, but their reunion was tempered by Jonas's arrest.

Searching for the words, Margaret nodded. "Yes. I have heard. I saw him last night at Calton—"

"You went there?" one of the men asked suddenly.

Margaret could see he was a studious man, with gold-rimmed spectacles and a whisker-free chin. The man who sat beside him could have been a sibling, matching the first man in every way, clothing and hairstyle, save for the spectacles.

"Yes," Margaret answered matter-of-factly, before turning her attention back to Mrs. Crane. "He is shaken, but well." She decided to not confess his outburst toward her. She could not say if it truly were his feelings or if his words were born out of his heinous predicament. "Peter and I are going—"

"Peter is here?" the other man asked.

"Yes, we travelled here yesterday from London by train." Margaret hesitated. "Sorry … who are you?"

The men exchanged glances.

"Forgive me." Giles stepped forward and went to the men, gesturing to the first man with spectacles. "Miss Margaret, may I introduce Ezra Pefferlaw and John Gilbert. They work jointly as professors of biology at the university, sharing the position, if you will."

Both men reached out a hand in greeting and gave Margaret the lightest of handshakes.

"Yes, well, we wouldn't have to share if we could pry him away from his laboratory," Ezra said of John.

"If you did pry me from my research, I imagine you'd be out a job," John teased.

Margaret smiled at the jest, but wasn't so sure their jabs at each other's egos were so innocent.

"Plenty of time for making acquaintances later," Mrs. Crane interjected. "Peter and you have come … for Jonas then?"

"Yes, of course. We mean to see that he is given a fair trial and freed, as he ought to be."

Ezra scoffed, running a hand through his hair as he turned to the window behind him. "Such optimism."

Margaret felt herself grow angry. She grew tired of everyone disbelieving her resolve or, worse, believing Jonas capable. "What other emotion shall I employ?" she demanded sternly. "Despair?" She raised her eyebrows to emphasis her point.

The two men stared at her. Out of the corner of her eye she could see Mrs. Crane smile and raise her head slightly.

"I agree with Miss Margaret, wholeheartedly," she said

jubilantly. "It's about time we stop doubting our Dr. Davies and afford him more credit of character."

Margaret surveyed the room, wondering who it was who had thought Jonas guilty of such a crime as murder. Ezra and John must have noticed her condemnation, as both looked away.

"I, for one, think it's wonderful that Jonas should have such a formidable force in his corner," Giles said, giving Margaret a wink. "Mrs. Crane, may we have some tea so that we may sit in the sitting room to generate our strategy?"

Mrs. Crane nearly bounced at the request. "Yes, of course. I'd make a thousand teas for those who will see our beloved Dr. Davies on the right side of that awful place." She turned to Margaret and nipped her chin. "I am so glad you have come, my dear." She turned to the counter to ready the tea service. "Once all this is behind us, you can show me how much better you are in the kitchen. If memory serves, the last time I saw you there was still much you needed to learn."

Chapter 9

As they walked to the main door, Ainsley stole a glance to the fortified stone building towering above them. The shadow of the structure engulfed them when they reached the steps and began their scamper up to the top.

His confidence was boosted now that he had both Samuel and his uncle willing to speak and file motions on Jonas's behalf. The convoluted structure of Scots Law and all its particulars were like a foreign language to Ainsley. He knew one thing, however—money and status made all the difference. While attending the bank to procure more funds, "enough to nudge the governor in our favour" as Samuel so eloquently put it, he pondered the quick turnabout of Jonas's situation since he had confessed his heritage. What do the others do? he wondered. How could anyone in the lower classes expect fair and equal treatment if money and clout were the only currency recognized by prison personnel? Ainsley tried not to let this revelation anger him, not then. For the time being, getting Jonas on the right side of these walls was all that mattered.

There was a different guard at the desk this time who directed them down a corridor to a row of chairs placed along the wall. They were not forced to sit and wait. Instead, the guard announced their presence, making sure the prison governor, John Smith, was aware that a Mr. Peter Ainsley, son of Abraham Marshall, Earl of Montcliff, accompanied the lawyers.

After the standard pleasantries, Thomas wasted no time proclaiming the reason for their visit. "You have a gentleman in your prison who is wrongly accused of the murder of Professor Frobisher. It is our intent to have him released to our care so that we may begin to formulate our defence."

"I would gladly release Dr. Davies to your charge"—the governor smiled broadly from behind his desk—"but we have protocols, you see." His fingers were knitted together but his thumbs danced circles around each other. He turned his gaze directly to Ainsley. "We need a guarantee, an offering if you will, that he will not leave the city and that he will cooperate with the investigation. And, naturally, his appearance in court is of the utmost importance."

"Naturally." Already, Ainsley could not stand the man. He appeared old, though not feeble, and quite comfortable in his position of authority. "I will take personal responsibility and see that he stands trial, if it comes to that."

Smith raised an eyebrow. "You question our legal process?"

"No, sir," Ainsley said. "I only wish to prove his innocence."

The governor laughed piteously. "He was found—"

"With the body, I am aware. But to be found guilty of murder one has to perpetrate that murder, yes?"

Smith glanced about the room but did not answer Ainsley's question.

"Let us not bore you with the particulars of the case," Thomas interjected quickly. "We have come to see Dr. Davies free until trial." Thomas moved his hand in front of Ainsley with his palm up.

Ainsley pulled the envelope of money from his inside breast pocket and placed it in Thomas's hand.

"We have procured the standard fee for capital murder cases." Thomas placed the envelope gently on the governor's desktop and slid it across the surface. He did not remove his fingers, however, and let them linger for another moment more. "We have also included a small sum as a gesture of our appreciation for your swift action."

Once he was finished speaking, Thomas pulled his hand away and Smith lifted the envelope from the table. He stole a peek inside and suppressed a giddy smile. "I must apologize, Mr. Marshall. Had I known our good doctor had such friends I would have installed him in much finer accommodations."

Ainsley's jaw tightened as the governor spoke, sickened by his willingness to be bought.

"*Swift action*," Thomas repeated.

"Of course, kind sirs." He slipped the monies into his own pocket and stood. "It will only take a few moments to draw up the paperwork."

❧　☙

Ainsley waited in the lobby with the others for what felt like ages, when actually it was only half an hour. He had signed some papers, reading each line carefully to ensure nothing had been slipped into the contract that he could not guarantee.

"You are very wise, Mr. Marshall," Thomas said, when he finally did pick up the pen. Samuel said nothing during their entire time at the prison until Jonas was finally spotted at the end of the hall.

"Goddamn," he said at the sight of him, shirt bloodied and trousers torn.

Ainsley turned in place to watch as Jonas made his way toward them slowly. Jonas squinted against the light somewhat as he neared the doors at the front of the building.

"Thank you, Peter," Jonas said softly, when they were finally standing opposite each other. "You sent her back to London then?"

Ainsley nodded and stole a glance over Jonas's shoulders to the guards who flanked him. "As promised."

Jonas smiled and turned to Samuel and Thomas, shaking their hands in turn.

"Hello, Dr. Davies, I am Thomas Humphry. You know my nephew, Sam. We shall be your lawyers in this case. We will be fighting on your behalf."

"Thank you, sir." He glanced to Ainsley. "I imagine my friend went to great lengths to secure my release."

Thomas looked uneasy and shifted his weight. "Well, yes, but that is merely the beginning of our battle, I'm afraid. You must tell me everything, with great honesty, and we shall see what can be done—but not here." He gestured for the door. "Let us get as much distance between us and this God-awful place."

❧　☙

Once everyone was installed in their carriage seats the

door was closed, latched, and they were on their way. Thomas wasted no time and quickly opened his Gladstone bag to retrieve his notebook. With one ankle crossed over his opposite knee, he rested the notebook on his knee and gipped his pen. Ainsley could tell already that Samuel's uncle was the sort of man they needed, stern yet likeable, focused and unwavering.

"Now," he said, keeping his focus firmly on Jonas. "What can you tell us about ... the event? Leave nothing out," he cautioned. "Every detail is of vital importance."

Jonas's Adam's apple bobbed as he prepared to speak. With an exhale he shook his head and gave the slightest of shrugs. "I can't say really."

Thomas's expression soured.

"I told Peter I don't remember how I got to Professor Frobisher's office."

"But that is where you were found," Thomas said, not bothering to raise his chin. He quickly scribbled something down on his papers.

Samuel leaned forward. "What do you remember about that night?"

"I accepted an invite to have drinks with friends—"

"Which friends?" Thomas interjected.

"My flatmates." Jonas stopped and looked to each of their faces. "We were celebrating a breakthrough John had with one of his experiments. He's studying the limb regeneration of starfish. It's tedious work."

"So one of them is named John." Thomas continued to scribble away. "The others?"

"Ezra, he works alongside John, but isn't as interested in the hands-on experiments John has in the attic."

"Who else?"

Jonas shrugged.

"Giles Grant lives with you as well," Samuel said, "Was he there?"

"Yes, I mean, no." Jonas closed his eyes. "I'm sorry, but everything is all distorted." Jonas appeared angry at himself. He balled a hand into a fist and used the other one to rub his eyes.

"Giles was visiting his sister in London," Ainsley said, saving his friend from having to explain.

"I don't see why they need to be named," Jonas cut in.

"I must speak with them all." Thomas looked at Jonas over the rim of his glasses. "I'm sure the authorities have already questioned them thoroughly."

Jonas took a breath and ran a hand through his hair.

"Whose idea was it to celebrate?" Samuel asked, anticipating his uncle's next question.

Ainsley could tell recalling the details was difficult. Jonas had always had a stellar memory, with the ability to see his own school notes exactly as they were written while performing a practical exam. It was a skill that served him well while obtaining his medical degree.

After a moment of thought Jonas spoke. "I don't know really. I came home and I was promptly ushered out the door again."

"Where did you go?" Ainsley asked.

"Some pub. I can't ... I can't recall the name." Jonas closed his eyes before shaking his head. "The sign had a picture of a dog on it, I think."

"It's all right," Ainsley said, wanting to put his friend's mind at ease.

Thomas gave him a look from the other side of the carriage. "I cannot help either of you if you are not truthful with me."

"This *is* the truth!" Jonas rolled his hands into fists before looking away and relaxing them. "I spent every second in that cell trying to recall what happened and I draw a blank every time. We had a few drinks. There was a girl. She fancied Ezra ... I think. I don't remember her name or even what the barkeep looked like." Jonas looked distressed enough to cry, but he didn't. "Everything comes up blank. I woke up covered in my colleague's blood. I—I— was dizzy and incredibly tired. When I saw the knife near my hand my first thought was that I had fainted during surgery, but I quickly realized that wasn't it."

"What did you do when you saw the body?" Thomas asked.

"I froze." Jonas's gaze grew distant. "And then I realized what I was covered in and I dropped the knife."

"Then what happened?"

"The door burst open. Someone was pulling me from the

floor."

"Someone?"

"An officer. They came in like a swarm of bees, circling me, ready to subdue me instantly if I so much as blinked."

"Did you say anything to them?"

"I told them I didn't do it, but I knew it was fruitless. Professor Frobisher's blood was all over me. Who else could it have been?"

Thomas sighed and removed his spectacles. "Mister Marshall here led me to believe you are not capable of such a crime."

"We are all capable, given the proper circumstances."

"Someone has gone to great lengths to make it appear as if you perpetrated this crime," Ainsley said.

"To what end?" Samuel asked.

"Blackmail. Revenge. Entertainment."

"Who would be entertained by such a thing?" Samuel asked, a slight laugh escaping his lips.

"Take me to any murder scene in any of Britain's cities and I'll show you dozens who would gather for hours to gawk at the carnage."

A gloom set over the carriage. Ainsley's words rang true with each of the men, who in their own way had been witness to such morbid excitement. A salacious trial. A grotesque murder scene. A theatrical showcase of medical dissection. These were all examples of the Victorian public and their insatiable appetite for sordid affairs.

Samuel was first to break the reverie. "Supposing someone has positioned against Jonas, wanting him blamed for the murder of Professor Frobisher—what possible motive could they have?"

All eyes went to Jonas.

"Your guess is as good as mine," he offered. "I have angered no one, save perhaps Frobisher himself."

Ainsley shifted uncomfortably in his seat.

"It will all come out in the trial so it's best not to surprise me," Thomas cautioned.

Jonas let out a quick breath before responding. "In recent weeks it became apparent that we disagreed on a fundamental matter regarding the future of our institution. There has been some discussion amongst the faculty about whether we are prepared to admit women to some of our lectures and courses. Not grant them degrees"—Jonas looked to Ainsley before shaking his head at the absurdity—"that would be too much, apparently."

"The Medical School of Edinburgh will be admitting women?" Thomas asked, an eyebrow raised.

"Yes, that is our hope. It's my belief that women are able to provide a unique perspective on the care of their sex. Women have been treating women for some time, in such things as childbirth and the like, but Peter and I know how little time is spent studying female anatomy and ailments."

Ainsley nodded. "No major studies have been done on female health and there is much that remains a mystery," he explained for the benefit of Thomas and Samuel.

"And Frobisher disagreed with your stance?" Thomas asked.

"He more than disagreed with it. He forbade it. On more than one occasion he threatened me, and others, with disciplinary action if we persisted in supporting such a change to our policy. I refused to back down," Jonas said, pulling a frown. "He may have been my superior but he would not act as my conscience."

"That hardly seems enough to formulate motive for murder," Samuel said with a laugh. "No prosecutor could win by bringing that forward in trial."

"Except, it went deeper than that. It wasn't just about our change in policy. Frobisher wanted us to reverse decisions that had already been made regarding the role of women at the infirmary and throughout the school." Jonas looked about the carriage. "About ten days ago I found him with one of our female clerks." He paused briefly before continuing. "He had her by the collar, about to strike her. I had no doubt he would have had I not intervened."

Everyone in the carriage gave a look of discomfort at the details.

Thomas wrote furiously on his book. "What was his reasoning for the violence?" he asked, taking his time to choose his words carefully.

Jonas sneered at the memory. "I hadn't a mind to ask. I was so incensed by what I saw it was enough for me to stop the violence."

"What is the girl's name?"

"Rebecca Stewart. She's an assistant for Dr. Waters mostly."

"Let's hope she can corroborate your version of events," Thomas said, jotting down notes at a furious pace.

"I'm not telling falsehoods," Jonas said sharply.

"I am aware, Dr. Davies," Thomas said. "It would be remiss of me to not perform due diligence."

Jonas cast a sideways look at Ainsley and settled back into his seat.

"Had any of Professor Frobisher's arguments with you taken place in front of third parties?" Thomas asked.

"Many of them. His difficulty as a colleague is well known. I daresay there won't be many with kind things to say about him. My blood boils every time I think of the terrified look on that young woman's face. What he did was inexcusable."

Ainsley could see the frustration in Jonas's face as he explained their quarrel. Opportunities to further the medical establishment's understanding should not be wasted so.

"This is concerning, Dr. Davies," Thomas finally said, nearly tsk-tsking as he spoke. "A proven track record of discord may only serve to hinder our case."

"I did nothing wrong. It is Frobisher who should answer for his actions, not me."

"But Professor Frobisher is not here!" Thomas's voice reverberated through the carriage and no doubt beyond. "If you speak of Professor Frobisher again in such a way, to anyone, the prosecutor will have enough to see you are hanged."

Jonas quickly turned to Ainsley, who was equally alarmed. "I only speak the truth," Jonas said.

"We know," Ainsley said quickly, taking care not to alarm Jonas further.

"Truth or not," Thomas said, folding up his book, "a judge will most likely see a motive amongst your confession. Pray that the prosecution does not sniff out your animosity. A single witness who testifies to a quarrel is enough to rip our defence to shreds."

"There needs to be more evidence than that to convict a

man," Ainsley said, slipping to the end of the bench.

"You forget how our esteemed doctor was found," Thomas said. "The evidence is already damning enough. If you expect to free your friend, Mr. Marshall, you'd better collect enough evidence to prove that Dr. Davies did not use that knife, or any other tool, to snuff the life out of Professor Frobisher."

Chapter 10

Margaret smiled as she watched Mrs. Crane fuss over the care and feeding of John, Ezra, and Giles. The housekeeper clearly relished her role of caretaker and enjoyed her new position with the professors. The men, for their part, did not abuse her doting nature. They all showed their eagerness to assist, making multiple trips to the adjoining room with cups and saucers, trays of baked goods, as well as the sugar and creamer.

Once everything was set, John pulled out Mrs. Crane's chair while Giles pushed past Ezra to hold Margaret's for her. "Brute," Ezra muttered softly against the sounds of teacups and chairs. If Giles heard, he made no note of it and promptly took a seat next to Margaret.

"So, Miss Margaret, you have met our wondrous Mrs. Crane before?" Giles asked.

"She was the housekeeper for Dr. Bennett at the time."

"Lord rest his soul." Mrs. Crane's eyes lifted to the heavens before passing Margaret a filled teacup and saucer.

"Mrs. Crane has told us bits and pieces over the past month, since Jonas first told us about you," John confessed.

"And then Jonas filled us in on the rest," Ezra added, nearly laughing when he saw the look of shock on Mrs. Crane's face.

"'Tisn't a time one wishes to remember," Mrs. Crane said disapprovingly. "Were it not for Miss Margaret, Dr. Davies, and Dr. Ainsley I don't think I would have managed the ordeal so well. One does not expect their employer to wake up dead."

Giles and Margaret exchanged amused glances at Mrs. Crane's choice of words.

"Tell me, Mrs. Crane, how anyone wakes up dead?" Giles teased.

Mrs. Crane waved a dismissive hand at him. "Oh for Pete's sake, Dr. Grant, you know of what I mean." The housekeeper began spreading the jam on her biscuit more pronouncedly than previously. Margaret wondered if this dynamic was typical for the household. She imagined it was hard for a woman, even an older one, to live amongst four learned men.

"Well, I for one, am glad to see Mrs. Crane so well cared for this past year," Margaret interjected, flashing a smile to Mrs. Crane. "She looks so happy and well. It is a credit to you all."

The doorbell rang, which broke the tension much better that Margaret's words. John was first to his feet. "Do not trouble yourself," he said to Mrs. Crane, coaxing her back into her chair. "I know it is for me. I'm expecting a parcel."

With John gone, Mrs. Crane reached over to Margaret and clasped her hand tightly. "It warms my heart to see you too, deary."

A few moments of silence passed before Margaret realized Ezra and Giles were leaned together and speaking in hushed tones across the table. They both looked to her abashed.

"Ezra has something to ask you," Giles said, clearing his throat.

"Giles!"

Margaret looked at Ezra expectantly.

"Jonas told us it was you who performed the dissection on Dr. Bennett."

Mrs. Crane dropped her knife on her plate. "Merciful heavens!" She stood up. "I shall see if we have some more hot water." She went for the door only to turn back for the teapot.

"Don't mind her," Giles said, after Mrs. Crane closed the door behind her. "She always does that when we wish to speak of university matters."

Margaret eyed the closed door to the kitchen.

"So, is it true?" Ezra asked.

Margaret nodded. "Yes. I was eager to learn."

Ezra smiled broadly while an irritated look flashed over Giles. A second later Ezra was holding out his hand, palm up, and Giles was sliding a folded bank note into it.

"Giles thought Jonas had made the entire story up. He said a woman wouldn't have the stomach for such a thing.

Whereas I had heard so much about the *Formidable Margaret* from Jonas that I knew it must be true." He slipped the bank note into his trouser pocket.

Margaret was amused by the idea of their little wager. "During what possible conversation did this topic come up?" she asked out of curiosity.

"There was a discussion, amongst the faculty," Giles offered reluctantly.

"About what?"

"A woman's suitability for medical school."

A minute later the tea service was cleared away and the dishes brought to the kitchen. Margaret pulled an apron from a peg on the wall and positioned it at her waist.

"No, no," Mrs. Crane yelped. "There will be none of that. I shall see to it, deary, as I always do."

"But how shall I repay your kindness?"

Mrs. Crane stopped and looked down her nose at Margaret. "Your presence here today has lifted my spirits considerably." She placed a loving hand on Margaret's upper arm. Her eyes glistened slightly as she spoke. "You should not believe a word of what's been printed in the papers. Our Dr. Davies is an exemplary man and I do not believe for one moment that he is capable of such a deed. And neither should you," she added.

It had never once occurred to her that Jonas could be guilty of such a thing as murder. Everything was either a misunderstanding or part of something much more nefarious.

"Now away with ye," Mrs. Crane snapped, playfully waving a towel at Margaret to shoo her from the room. Margaret found herself laughing as she allowed herself to be pushed out. "Very well," she said, "very well."

Margaret was easily guided into the hall. Near the front door, John was hunched over an open lid box that was set on the corner of the hall table. The box itself was a wood crate and held another box, this one made of tin. As Margaret approached she could see fine wood shavings were pushed in between the two as a cushion.

When John straightened his stance he pushed his glasses higher on his nose. "My shipment was delayed," he said with concern. "The driver told me he almost turned around when he saw the crowd. I must say, I am rather grateful he didn't."

"Something for your research?" Margaret asked.

John produced a giddy smile. "Would you like to see?"

John's laboratory was housed on the fourth floor, the attic space once reserved for the servants of the families previously living there. Margaret followed behind him as he carried his shipment up the narrow stairs. He placed the box on the top step as he fumbled for his key.

"One can never be too careful," he said, as he slipped the key into the lock and opened the door.

John hurried inside, despite the dark, whereas Margaret went in slowly, using the wall to keep herself steady. After John placed the box on a centre table, he used a match to light a lamp on the table and then the gas lamps that hung overhead.

The room was easily the largest in the house with an expansive floor space and high beams overhead. Mismatched counters were pushed up against the wall in between high shelves. No surface or shelf was left unclaimed. All manner of scientific necessity and apparatus were housed in John's laboratory, as well as a number of oddities like baby crocodile skulls and a dried puffer fish.

Margaret couldn't stop herself from reaching to a dangling string of bones suspended from the ceiling and realized it was a collection of human vertebrae placed in order to resemble the human spine.

John moved the lamp in front of him to reveal a sizeable glass box that took up much of the centre table. As Margaret drew closer she realized the glass box was filled with water nearly to the top edge. Small stones lined the bottom and a few plants resembling ones found by the sea were placed inside.

"It's my aquaria," John said, beaming. "I've been working for years to get the balance and temperature right." He skimmed his hand over the top of the water and then watched closely when he pulled it out as the droplets made ripples in the water's surface.

Margaret came alongside him and smiled as she looked down. Inside was a starfish splayed out over one of the larger rocks. "I saw one of these when I was a child," she said, crouching down to look at it from the side. "Mother took us to the Fish House at the London Zoo when it was first installed. I remember Peter and I were so fascinated by it."

While still crouched down, Margaret reached her hand over the top. The water was soft like the ocean but warm as it was in the Mediterranean, nothing like the waters on the shores of England.

"Is this part of your research?" she asked.

John turned to his shipment and pried open the tin box. Margaret saw that it too was filled with water.

"This *is* my research," John said.

He pulled the tin box as close to the aquaria as he could before reaching in and pulling out a sea creature Margaret had never seen before. The creature looked stunned as John transferred him to the larger box of water. Once it was in the water, Margaret was afforded a better look and realized it was a wide fish of some sort with stumpy legs, each with fingers laid out similar to a human hand. The fish had a long, wide body that slimmed down into a flat tail. Its skin was slick and light pink with a fan of tentacles framing its head. Two tiny black eyes stared back at her through the glass of the aquarium.

"I've never seen one before. What is it?" Margaret asked, unable to take her eyes away.

"Axolotl," John said. He lifted the tin box and gingerly poured the water into the large tank.

Margaret saw a few tiny axolotls fan out into the depths of the aquarium. "Those ones don't have legs," she pointed out.

"Not yet. They're amphibians, like frogs. They start out more like fish and as they mature they grow legs. But these guys"—John crouched down beside Margaret—"they don't ever lose their gills."

"So they can't breathe out of water."

"That's right." John smiled. "I wasn't sure if they were going to survive the trip." John stood and circled the table. "I have a friend in Paris who was willing to send some to me with the understanding that they may not survive the journey."

"They look healthy enough to me."

"They are only found in Mexico." John crouched down on the other side to observe some of the smaller ones. "They are essential to my research. I'm experimenting with limb regeneration. Both star fish and axolotls can grow back entire limbs if they become severed. Certain species of lizard can grow back their tail, if for some reason it gets separated from their body."

Margaret regarded him quizzically as she stood up from her crouching position.

"Say in a predator situation"—John turned and pulled a preserved lizard specimen from the shelf behind him—"a large animal snags an iguana by the tail." John pinched the end of the lizard's tail with his fingers, using them as if they were the mouth of a larger predator. "The iguana has evolved to release its tail, which allows it time to scamper away to safety."

Margaret nodded.

"Nature decided it was better for the iguana to lose its tail than its life. But what I want to know is, how does the iguana grow its tail back? Perhaps if we can figure that out we can help humans grow back a finger that was crushed in the mill, or even a limb that needed to be amputated."

"And the university funds your research?" Margaret asked.

"Oh yes," John said, pushing his glasses back. "Well, begrudgingly. I won't pretend that I am their favourite researcher. Ezra and Giles believe I am wasting my time, but I've made a lot of progress in the last few months."

"How long have you been focusing on this project?"

"Four years, less a few weeks."

Margaret worked hard to hide her surprise. "Oh. You must be very dedicated."

John kept his eyes on Margaret for a few extra seconds before looking away and nodding. "Yes, sometimes too dedicated, I think."

Even in the dim light Margaret could see regret in his eyes. She regarded him for a few moments before he turned and began gathering some books from his desk and stacking them in a single tower.

The doorbell rang and they both froze.

"Do you think that could be Peter?" John asked.

Margaret recoiled slightly at the thought. She was still angry with him for trying to trick her into leaving the city. When she saw him again, she knew their meeting would not be a comfortable one. Margaret gave a closed-mouth smile and hoped John didn't recognize her apprehension.

 ❧   ❧

As Margaret manoeuvred the stairs to the main floor she made some decisions on how she would approach her brother. She couldn't allow him to believe he could shuffle her about at will as if she were some sort of adornment or accessory. She also couldn't allow her anger to boil over. She knew by doing so she wouldn't be taken seriously. In the end, she decided it was best to show her displeasure coolly. He never was capable of withstanding her rejection for long. She would show him she had not been unseated and remind him how much her opinion of him mattered.

And if Jonas is with him? Margaret paused midstep at the thought. She could not trust herself to be so calculated around him. He was the only person who could pull the air from her lungs and the sense from her brain. For the past year she had been fighting the hold he had on her before finally succumbing just a few months ago. Even now she wondered if he was meant for her. Perhaps their promises to each other had all been born from lust and not genuine feeling. He had weakened her, defiled her, and now had no need of her. She winced at the thought.

Giles stood at the door, his back toward the stairs as Margaret came down the last couple steps. Through the closed kitchen door, Mrs. Crane hummed a folk ballad while going about her work.

"Is it Peter?" Margaret asked, hopeful.

Giles turned to face her and stepped away slightly. Beside him, resplendent in a newly fashioned blue taffeta dress with bustle and tilted hat, stood a tall brunette with a beautifully slim neck and oval face. She was a familiar sight, though Margaret couldn't say precisely from where. The pair looked to Margaret expectantly, giving her no choice but to come down the last few steps and approach them.

"And who is this?" the woman asked Giles, as she switched her folded gloves from one hand to the other.

"This is Miss Margaret, Peter's sister," Giles explained.

The woman raised her chin and allowed her lips to form a slight smile. "Ah yes, the *Formidable* Margaret." She slid her hand toward Margaret in greeting.

Margaret could almost feel the woman's gaze burning into her skin, trailing her up and down as one would survey a farm animal for auction.

"I've heard so much about you," the woman remarked, pulling her hand back.

Giles pressed his lips together in an awkward smile. "This is Miss Eloise Locke."

Margaret's throat went dry. The woman, once just a name from Jonas's past, was now staring her down. Eloise had been like a sister to him for many years before their relationship turned sour. Their connection was a convoluted one that began out of desperation before evolving into attachment and then love. There was no love for Eloise but rather her father, who had become as dear to Jonas as his own late mother. After they were abandoned by Jonas's father, his mother began work with the Locke family. Mr. Locke was a chemist who saw to it that Jonas received adequate education and, seeing promise, encouraged his entry into medical school. Eloise was Mr. Locke's daughter but as the years went by it was clear she saw herself as Jonas's future wife.

"How lovely it is to finally meet you," Margaret lied.

"Oh, we've met before," Eloise said, "though perhaps not formally." Her mouth twisted in a knowing smirk.

Margaret tilted her head to the side slightly, confused. "I don't recall." Telling falsehoods did not come easy to Margaret. If she could have stricken their first meeting from memory she would have without regret.

"At St. Thomas." Eloise nearly giggled and turned her attention to Giles. "Margaret here happened upon Jonas and I in a rather compromising position. I was utterly mortified but Jonas did much to settle my fears. He told me Margaret is a benevolent and sweet woman. I see now how right he was in saying so."

The events of the day were not as innocent as Eloise

would like everyone to believe. She had been using her position as the daughter of Jonas's patron to force herself upon him, to strong-arm him into proposing marriage, something which Jonas had no desire to do.

Eloise's smile sent a slight shiver up Margaret's spine. There were hints of challenge in her tone along with an undercurrent of animosity.

"How kind of him to say such things," Margaret said, working hard to conceal her disdain. "He told me he regards you as if you were his own sister."

Eloise laughed. "I dare say, we are a bit more dear to each other than that." She tilted her head up, revealing an amused grin that Margaret recognized from many young ladies she had been forced to speak with over the years. It was the bravado of female youth, one conceived through large fortunes and even larger opinions of themselves.

"Then you must be absolutely beside yourself given our current events," Margaret said, knowing very well her words would only provoke further scorn.

"Naturally. I can't stop weeping." She looked to Giles. "I only came to see if there is anything I can do for his comfort in that ghastly place."

"Peter is arranging for his release," Giles explained, "or he had hoped to, in any case. I'm not sure how successful he shall be given the circumstances."

"You mean Jonas will be cleared of all charges?" Eloise looked genuinely delighted at the idea.

Giles's expression remained doubtful.

"He will still be required to stand trial," Margaret said, "unless the real murderer can be identified."

"Oh, listen to you, Miss Margaret, amateur detective for the Edinburgh Police." Eloise laughed. "All ne're-do-wells should be on the lookout now."

As should any woman who expects to coerce the man she loves into a loveless marriage, Margaret thought.

An uneasy quiet slipped over them, forcing Margaret to think up a response quickly. "Have you visited him?" she asked sharply. "Your presence there will bring him comfort, don't you think?"

For the first time Eloise's confidence waned but she regained her composure quickly. "I do not think they admit women to such a place; visitors, I mean."

"Oh, but they do," Margaret said.

Eloise looked to Giles, who shifted uncomfortably.

"Miss Margaret visited Jonas last evening," he explained, "without incident."

"Very well done," Eloise said. "That settles it then, I shall go tomorrow, should my father allow. He is quite ill, you understand, and cannot be left for long periods of time."

Margaret did, indeed, understand. "Yes, of course."

Eloise took in a deep breath. "If there is anything further you need, Giles, don't hesitate to send word. You as well, Margaret. I am your servant whilst you are in Edinburgh. Whatever you need, you shall have it." She turned to leave, but stopped suddenly. "How long do you plan to stay in the city?"

"I imagine until things have cleared up and Jonas is no longer in prison," Margaret said.

"Lovely. We shall work together then," she said with a pasted smile, "to see what can be done."

Giles closed the door following her departure and turned to Margaret with an apologetic expression.

"What an interesting woman," Margaret said.

"Yes, indeed," Giles answered. "I suppose that's why Jonas is so besotted with her."

Margaret tried to hide her smile. "Did he say as much or is she merely imagining things to be so?" A self-satisfied giggle escaped her before she could stop herself.

Giles gave a look of confusion.

Margaret watched as that confusion morphed into pity.

"Forgive me for saying this, Miss Margaret, but I feel compelled in order to save yourself from further embarrassment."

Margaret's amusement vanished.

"Jonas has already asked for Miss Locke's hand and she has accepted. You would do best to direct your attentions elsewhere."

Chapter 11

Ainsley shielded Jonas as best as he could from the objects pelted at them from the crowd. There wasn't an alternative entrance to Jonas's lodgings and so they were forced to face the fray.

"Murderer!"

"Scoundrel!"

"Lowlife!"

"I shall meet with you both in the morning," Thomas yelled above the raucous insults echoing from the crowd. Ainsley heard the carriage door clasp shut and the horse hooves drumming on the pavement.

"Jonas, over here." Ainsley spotted a break in the crowd and steered his friend there. He resisted the urge to pluck a half bruised apple from the house steps and return it to the crowd with considerable force. Within seconds they were in the safety of the foyer, shaking the potato peels and brown cabbage leaves from their coats. Ainsley used the heel of his palm to remove something wet from his jowl.

"How long do you think that will last?" Jonas asked, looking past his friend to the window along the side of the door.

Ainsley shook his head. He hoped not long.

"Hello, brother."

Ainsley stopped suddenly and turned at the sound of Margaret's voice. She was seated in the parlour, Giles in a chair at her side.

"How—?" Ainsley looked to Jonas, who shared his disbelief. "You are supposed to be heading back to London today."

"And miss all the jubilation when Jonas's good name is restored?" She stood and started making her way to Jonas, her hands knitted in front of her. Ainsley saw how her excitement was tempered and her approach filled with caution.

Jonas exhaled and began rubbing at the back of his

neck. "I wanted you far from here," he said softly so only Margaret and Ainsley could hear. "This was the one time I needed you to do what you are told."

Ainsley winced internally, knowing Margaret would take offence.

"Perhaps if I were told something instead of being tricked I might be more inclined to follow your lead," Margaret said through gritted teeth.

Ainsley turned to Giles. "Can you give me a few minutes to speak to my sister alone?"

Giles bowed slightly before leaving the parlour. Ainsley entered the room and went to the window to ensure the drapes were properly closed. When he turned he saw Margaret and Jonas had come further into the room but now stood on opposite sides.

With her hands on her hips, Margaret's gaze darted between them both. "Whose idea was it then?" She waved them off before giving them a chance to speak. "It doesn't matter. It's clear to me now that both of you would benefit from my prolonged absence."

"Margaret, be reasonable," Ainsley said, stepping into the space between them. "Jonas feared for your safety—"

"Am I not permitted to fear for his?" Margaret looked hurt beyond words. She raised a hand to her forehead and half hid her face. She closed her eyes to stop the tears. She took a moment to compose herself before speaking again. "I'm here now and I refuse to be shut out again."

Jonas turned to her. "Margaret—"

Margaret's gaze did not waver. She met his eyes squarely and without apology. "All day I believed it was Peter's doing. Now I see the truth of it." She rubbed her nose and gave a slight sniffle. "Your fiancée stopped by this afternoon," she said, wiping away some tears from her lower eyelids.

"My what?"

"A Miss Eloise Locke." Margaret let a disheartened smile touch her lips.

"Whatever she told you, don't believe her. We are not engaged."

Ainsley couldn't believe the exchange he was witnessing. Part of him wondered if he should leave the room, but another part of him told him to stay to make sure Margaret was all right. In the end, he took a seat in one of the chairs and raised his hands to his face.

"She wasn't the one who told me," Margaret corrected Jonas. "It was Giles who confirmed it."

"Giles?" Jonas looked startled by the accusation. "Margaret, the woman is—"

The pocket doors to the dining room suddenly slid open on one side. Ezra gave an apologetic look before turning to pull back the second one. Beyond him the dining room table was set, complete with lace tablecloth and lit candles.

"Mrs. Crane wished me to tell you supper is just about ready," Ezra said.

For a second Ainsley thought he had only been hearing things and then Mrs. Crane herself used her backside to push through the door from the kitchen into the dining room. She turned to the table, revealing a large platter in her hands.

"Dr. Davies!" She set down the platter quickly and spread out her arms. "Oh!" She rounded the table and came straight for him with a wide smile. "I thought ye'd never come home!" She embraced him without a hint of hesitation. When she finally released him she turned her attentions to Ainsley, who stood dumbstruck a few paces away.

"And I can say the same for you, Dr. Ainsley."

"Mrs. Crane, you are a ghost from days gone by," Ainsley said with a laugh before wrapping his arms around her.

"Oh, such a merry night we shall have now that ye both 'ave returned." She turned to Jonas then, an erect finger pointed in his direction, "Ye, however, are not to be seated at my table until ye wash and change."

Jonas nodded in agreement, giving Margaret a pleading look before ducking from the room.

Mrs. Crane pushed down the folds of her apron as she took in the others. "And for the rest of us, there shall be no talk of murders, or prisons, or other such things. For once we shall act as if we were bedfellows to decorum herself."

❧　❧

While they waited for Jonas to change his clothes,

Ainsley and Margaret waited in the parlour, gathering their thoughts. Ainsley noticed Margaret's valise set on the floor just outside the room and gestured to it. "You came here straight from the station, I see. Where is Elmira and Cutter?" Ainsley asked, clearing his throat.

Margaret shrugged. "Halfway between here and London, I suspect."

"Margaret—"

"I have just as much desire to see Jonas cleared of any wrongdoing as you. Why shouldn't I take it upon myself to examine all avenues?" She turned from him and went for a chair set in the corner. "It's a shame neither of you see the value of my presence."

"That simply isn't the case," Ainsley said. "Jonas hasn't said much, but I know he genuinely fears for your safety."

"As I fear for his!" Margaret's voice rose in frustration.

Ainsley looked to the kitchen, wondering if anyone else in the house had heard. Margaret licked her lips before speaking again, this time with a more hushed tone. "I could never forgive myself if he went to prison and I did nothing to prevent it."

"Margaret, you don't understand, someone has made it look as if Jonas did this. For some reason they want him to hang."

"You are the one who doesn't understand," she answered harshly, slipping to the edge of her seat. "That man will never see the inside of that prison again, not if I can do something about it."

"Don't you see how whoever is after him could use you?" Ainsley shook his head, trying to banish the thought of his own love in a similar predicament. "His mother has passed. His father is long gone. No brothers or sisters. You are his only weakness."

"I am his strength."

The door of the kitchen opened suddenly and Ezra appeared, a stack of china plates in his grasp. "Everything is settled then," he said as John and Mrs. Crane walked though. They fanned out around the dining room table setting the places. Ainsley counted enough to seat all of them, including himself and Margaret.

"What's settled?" Margaret asked, walking from the

parlour to the dining room.

Jonas appeared at the door to the parlour and looked on as he buttoned his vest.

"You are both to stay here," John said triumphantly. "Since Carl moved to Munich we haven't been able to let his room."

Jonas smiled slightly at the thought.

"It's empty at the moment." Ezra looked to John. "And there is another room we could use ... in the attic."

"Molly stayed there," John cut in, "before ..." He glanced nervously to Ezra and then Jonas.

"Perhaps Peter should take the attic room," Jonas offered.

Ainsley saw Margaret furrow her brow at the suggestion.

"It's fine, Jonas," Margaret said decisively. "I'll take the attic room."

Mrs. Crane looked up from the table. "Are you sure, Miss Margaret?" the housekeeper asked as she pressed out a crease in the tablecloth. "'Tis a mighty cold room at times, hotter than Hades in the summer. I would not like to see someone like yerself in such a room."

Margaret gave an unsteady look to Jonas before a look of determination flashed over her face. "I shall be quite all right. I'm not one to place myself above the hired help," she said somewhat unconvincingly. "If it was good enough for Molly, then it is good enough for me."

Ainsley and Jonas exchanged doubtful glances.

"It's settled then," Mrs. Crane said, her voice faltering slightly. "Dinner will just be another minute, my dears, as I bring everything to the table."

Mrs. Crane left the room first, only to have both Ezra and John follow quickly behind her. Ainsley saw a nudge and a shove as they pushed through the door side by side.

Margaret raised her eyebrows at the sight. "They are both rather ... odd," she said.

Ainsley nodded.

"I believe because there is an eligible young lady in the house," Jonas said.

Ainsley leaned in so only the three of them could hear him. "Since I have known them neither has been very successful in the ways of wooing women. I see very little has changed."

Jonas nodded. "John would have more success if he could bring himself to leave his laboratory once in a while."

"And Ezra?" Margaret asked.

A crash could be heard in the other room, followed by muffled shouts of outrage from Mrs. Crane.

"He's hopeless."

ᘓ   ᘒ

Dinner was a subdued affair. The buzz emanating from the pavement out front grew steadily, though no one looked to see if the size of the crowd grew. Ainsley had little doubt the evening editions of the papers had proclaimed Jonas's release from prison and that many were drawn to their front door in the hopes of seeing the murderous professor, fallen from grace and now reviled by the entirety of the city.

"This lamb is delicious," John said, in an obvious effort to lighten the mood and encourage conversation.

"I'll make sure Mrs. Crane hears of your compliment." Giles reached over his plate and pulled his wine glass to his mouth. He downed what was in his glass before looking around the room.

Ainsley cleared his throat. "So tell me, how was it that you all decided to live together?" he asked.

Jonas didn't bother to lift his attention from the plate in front of him, leaving his flatmates to tell the tale.

John searched the table and readied himself to speak before Giles cut in. "It was Frobisher," he said curtly.

The room fell silent at the mention of the murdered professor's name.

"He gave me the idea last year when this house became available to let." He moved his tongue around the inside of his mouth before Ainsley realized it had formed into a deep scowl. "I asked John, Ezra, and Carl if they were interested in leaving whatever hole in the wall they were letting and come join me here."

"We all jumped at the chance, didn't we, John?" Ezra asked.

John nodded. "Jonas arrived a few months ago and Carl left for Germany shortly after that. It's a wonderful arrangement, if you ask me. Imagine having a laboratory of my own at my age." He smiled broadly before bringing a piece of meat to his mouth.

At the opposite end of the table, Ainsley saw Giles tilting his wine glass to the side while staring at its empty state. A second later, Giles was on his feet and heading for the sideboard, where a new bottle sat waiting. "Would you like another, Miss Margaret?" he asked, walking around the table and pulling the cork.

Margaret shook her head. "No," she said. "Thank you."

Ainsley looked to his own glass, still full and without a single drop taken. It was a matter of will, he reminded himself. He must remain sober for as long as his addiction allowed. He was better sober, more alert and ready. He could think more clearly and respond to situations with better emotional stability. The relief brought by drink was only temporary, an illusion, he told himself; it made none of the hardships disappear.

Ainsley pulled his eyes from his wineglass and saw John looking at him from across the table.

"You should have some, Peter," he said softly. "Fifty-five was a very good year."

Before Ainsley could say anything Giles plunked the nearly full wine bottle down at the other end of the table with a pronounced thud. He didn't sit down. Instead, he raised his glass over them all. "To Jonas," he said, his mouth twisting in a closed-mouth smile, smug and unconvincing. "May your many friends see you through this horrible ordeal."

Suddenly, John stood up and raised his glass over the gathering as well. "May his troubles be but a faint memory before long."

"May he find peace and prosperity," Ezra added, joining the others by standing.

Obliged to join them, Ainsley stood, his glass lowered in front of him at first. He looked from Jonas to Margaret and then to Giles at the head of the table. "May his innocence be proven beyond a shadow of a doubt and may we all join the task of finding Professor Frobisher's true killer."

Giles's smile broadened as he bowed his head toward Ainsley, acknowledging his tribute.

A chorus of cheers rang out, "Hear, hear!" before everyone took a drink from their glass. The liquid was soft on Ainsley's tongue, sending a sensation of titillating memories pulsing to his brain. He allowed the wine to flow down his throat and relished the taste in his mouth that followed. It had been three weeks since his last drink and this toast only served to remind him how much he missed it.

Ainsley's reverie was cut short when Jonas stood up suddenly, pushing his chair back so forcefully the legs reverberated banefully on the wood floorboards. He stood for a moment, head bowed, knuckles curled into the tabletop. Ainsley wondered if he wished to say something, perhaps overcome by his friend's tribute, but now struggled to find the words.

The three men and Margaret waited, looking at Jonas expectantly. He snatched Ainsley's wine glass from his hands, and downed the remaining contents before turning and marching from the room. A look of worry flashed over Margaret's face as she looked up to Ainsley.

"Maybe he is still tired," John offered, slowly lowering himself into his seat.

"That's one way to drink." Giles tilted his head back to down the rest of his wine in a similar fashion before pouring himself another glass. "My apologies, Miss Margaret," he said, without bothering to look at her. "You can appreciate the trying day we have all had."

But Margaret couldn't have cared less if Giles drank all the wine in the empire. Ainsley saw her staring at the door where Jonas had left, as if contemplating whether to follow him. Before she could stand, Ainsley outstretched his hand, pleading for her to stay. "I'll see to him," he said, rounding the table. "Just stay."

At the bottom of the stairs, Ainsley could hear Jonas upstairs, walking the length of the hall before shutting his bedroom door harshly. Ainsley stole a look past the curtain out the foyer window and saw the crowd staring at the house. The look of them reminded Ainsley of a hive of bees, packed together and buzzing about. He heard the hum clearly, every few seconds a loud pronouncement of disgust rising above the din and followed by a thud, which was probably another rotten vegetable making contact with the door.

At the top of the stairs, Ainsley held the bannister and peered down the hallway. A long line of doors on either side stood before him, any one of them belonging to Jonas. One by one, Ainsley knocked, before slowly opening the door. The first two he noticed were empty. At the third, Ainsley slipped open the door and peered around the opening.

He saw Jonas at the window that overlooked the street. He stood with his shoulders slouched and his hands in his pockets. He looked over his shoulder, saw Ainsley, and then returned his attention to the outside.

"It's one of them," he said matter-of-factly.

Ainsley stepped inside the room and made sure the door was closed behind him. "One of your flatmates?"

"Yes, I've run everything over in my head a million times. I don't want to believe it but ..." his voice trailed off as his thoughts ran away from him. "But there it is." He turned, his defeated stance reminding Ainsley of how he had looked in that cell the night before.

"Giles was in London," Ainsley pointed out.

Jonas nodded.

"You feel either John or Ezra are behind this."

Ainsley had a hard time imagining either of them capable. Neither one was particularly strong nor vindictive. For having such high intellects, they were both fairly simple men.

"Or they know who is," Jonas offered, as if reading Ainsley's thoughts. "It's just, how can they smile and offer toasts at a time when I feel my whole life is crumbling? Everything I have worked so hard for is dissolving before my very eyes. My career is over. Any respect I had has vanished. And worst of all, Margaret hates me."

"I don't hate you."

They both turned to see Margaret at the door. She slid in through a narrow opening and pressed the door closed behind her.

"I may not appreciate being left out of things," she said, with a fleeting glance to her brother, "but I could never hate you."

The mood in the room was strained. Ainsley could see it

in the expression on the faces of his sister and friend. Ainsley crossed the room to the doorway and reached for the doorknob behind Margaret. "I shall leave you so you may speak in private."

No one protested and Margaret took one step to the side so Ainsley could leave.

Chapter 12

"You do not listen, Margaret Marshall."

Jonas turned from her, unable to look at her face while her eyes threatened tears. Margaret worked hard to steady herself—her breathing, her movements, her heartbeat.

"Correction," she said forcefully, "I do not obey."

She saw his rueful expression reflected in the mirror above his bureau.

"That is hardly an amiable quality to be found in a wife," he said, keeping his distance physically and emotionally.

"I haven't any interest in being your wife if such requirements are placed on me," Margaret said. She could feel panic itching at her throat. She could hardly believe what she was saying but each word, each syllable, was right to say. If Jonas had wished to marry her merely so he could control her, then she no longer wished to marry him. That was the truth of it.

Jonas was quiet, his gaze focused on something unseen in the mirror.

Margaret could not stand the silence between them. "I can love, trust, and take care of my husband," she paused, "whomever that may be ... but never will I obey him merely because he is the man and I am the woman."

"Good." Jonas turned and looked her in the eyes. "The last few months have not changed you." He smiled. "For the worst, at any rate. You're still as beautiful as ever."

He walked toward her. With each step she wondered if she should turn away and ignore the magnetism she felt for him. She turned her face but kept her eyes on him as he came forward. "Not another step," she said, putting her hand up between them.

He stopped at her words.

"Never have I had a mind to strike you as much as I do now," she growled. She squared her shoulders to him but did not close the distance. "How dare you treat me in such a fashion?"

"I am a fool," he said, his shoulders sinking. "I deserve your admonishments and your scorn."

She waited, confused. She hadn't expected him to be so easily won over.

"You are the only one I wanted at that dinner table," he said. "You and Peter. Everyone else can go to hell."

"Jonas—"

"I mean it. You are my only true friends and always will be." He hunched his shoulders to look at her in the eyes. "I should never have sent you away. I was only meaning to protect you—"

"And then who shall protect you?"

"I realize that now. Sitting there, listening to their toasts to me, it's all meaningless. It made me realize how much you and Peter would fight for me when all everyone else does is wish me well. A token sentiment but not followed by action. You are a woman of action. I've always liked that about you. It's why I love you."

"I was beginning to think you did not love me anymore," she said, her voice cracking with the heartache of it all.

"Never." He took a half step forward, close enough to reach over to her and touch her elbow. Without thinking she laid her forearm on top of his to hold. "I could never stop loving you."

She looked up at him, and was glad to see the kind man, who she had already given herself to in mind and body, reflected in his eyes. With him home and out of the horrible place, he resembled the man she knew him to be, the man she loved. With her other hand she pushed away a tear from her eye and forced a smile when she realized Jonas was still looking at her. "I love you too."

She reached for him and wrapped her hand around the back of his neck as he scooped her up into his arms. Their kiss reflected their long separation, the two months that had passed and the apologies on both sides for the confusion and lack of communication.

"We will help you, Jonas Davies," she said, resting her head on his chest and shoulder. "We will do everything we can and before long you will be free once more."

~ ~

Giles climbed up the servants' stairs ahead of Margaret and Ainsley, gripping the railing tightly and taking each step slowly as he went. The narrow, wooden stairway, with its nonuniform succession and dry, aged wood, creaked and groaned under their weight. It seemed as if every other tread buckled slightly, sending a piteous screech into the evening air before releasing a sigh of relief once it was allowed to pop back into its place. The threesome said nothing as they ascended to the fourth floor. They all knew not a word could be heard above the raucous protest of the stairs.

At the very top, Giles unlocked a door using a thin, black key that he left in the lock before pushing the door into the room. When Margaret was finally able to step inside the tucked-away servants' quarters she gave an internal sigh of relief at the sight. The room was nearly three times larger than any other servants' room she had ever seen, with two large dormer windows along the right wall. A metal bed, rusted slightly at the joints, was placed between the dormers with a tiny table, scarcely big enough to hold a lamp, next to it. On the other side of the room sat a tall bureau, its finish chipped and faded with age, and a sitting area with a floral print armchair and matching green velvet footrest. An offering of fresh linens had been piled at the end of the bed, neatly folded and waiting to be spread out.

Other than this, nothing else filled the space, which gave the vast room an empty, heartless feeling. Giles crossed the floor, heading for a closed door opposite the one they had just entered.

"John's laboratory is just in here." Giles jiggled the handle and turned to Margaret. "He uses the main stairs. Not to worry. This door never opens. There was a key once, but no one knows what became of it."

Margaret nodded as she circled the room, avoiding Ainsley's gaze. He hated the thought of her being placed in such a room but she was in no mood to argue. Sleep would be her refuge after such a trying day.

The lodgings were a far cry from the hotel they had stayed at the night before and resembled nothing of their manor house back in London. In all her twenty-five years Margaret had never stayed in such a sparse and humble place, unlike Ainsley, who had become accustomed to near-empty rooms and unadorned furnishing. As a young surgeon not yet hired at St. Thomas, Ainsley travelled a lot, accepting any spare room that was offered to him by physicians or other community members. He had told her once he enjoyed the break from the oppressiveness of their city home, though she was certain he spoke of the absence of their father and not the absence of amenities.

"The washbasin at the bottom of the stairs, in the hall, is yours," Giles said, crossing the room and grabbing the key out of the lock. "Three flights of stairs is too far for Mrs. Crane for just a pitcher of water," he said apologetically.

Margaret nodded, but could think of nothing to say in response.

"The windows look out over the park," he said, trying to find something chipper to report. He crossed to the windows and peered outside. "Well, partially."

Margaret didn't bother to look out. Any view at this storey would be of chimney stacks and the odd treetop. When Giles turned from the window, he presented her with the key. "You can use this key to lock your door from the inside or the outside. Mrs. Crane's room is just below us. You can see her if you need anything."

Margaret nodded at she took it in her fingers. "Thank you, Dr. Grant."

The young man grew half an inch taller as his face alighted. "Please, Lady Margaret, call me Giles."

"Yes, of course."

Giles gave one last awkward nod before passing by Ainsley and slipping out the door.

"I'll switch rooms with you," Ainsley said before Giles's footsteps made it halfway down the stairwell. "I believe you'll be more comfortable on the third floor."

Margaret looked to him and gave a soft smile. "Nonsense. It's fine, Peter," she said.

Truth be told, the arrangement allowed her to show Jonas that she wasn't averse to such humble living conditions. He had told her once he believed her too accustomed to privilege to be a surgeon's wife. What better way was there to show him she was not put off by creaky floors and sparse furnishings?

"There can't be ballrooms and dining halls in every house in Great Britain," she said truthfully.

"But you are not used it—"

"What better time is there to get used to it?" she asked, sharpness in her tone. "Really, Peter, you treat me as if I were a china doll, so fragile and only suited for adornment." She stepped toward the window and looked out beyond the grey glass. "In the morning, you and I shall go to the Royal Infirmary to find out as much as we can about Professor Frobisher's death."

"There is no need for you to accompany me."

Margaret raised an eyebrow. "Isn't there? I believe there is all the reason in the world." She made sure she gave him a determined look, one in which she displayed no room to be knocked down. "After the day you and Jonas put me through, you have to make things up to me somehow."

❧ ❧

An hour later, Margaret changed into the nightdress Mrs. Crane had offered her and took a seat on the edge of the bed. The shift was balloon-like and much too big for the shorter, less plump Margaret, but she couldn't turn it away. She had so little now that her trunk had made its way back to London. It was bad enough she would be wearing the same undergarments and petticoats as the day before. At the end of the day she was just glad to be rid of the stays that often left bruises on her ribs.

The attic room was surprisingly quiet given the house's location on the edge of Old Town and the location of her room directly above five grown men who had yet to settle for the night as they said they would. Exhausted, Margaret slipped between the covers, adjusting the fabric of her nightdress that twisted about her legs as she moved. The metal of the bed groaned somewhat at her movement and continued to send out pangs into the night even after she settled. The mattresses, one made of horsehair and another of feathers, were uneven and hard in places. The ropes that kept them from hitting the floor were loose and in need of a good tightening.

Margaret pushed all these things from her mind, resolved to rid herself of her spoiled upbringing.

Before long Margaret was carried away in a restless sleep. Her body was exhausted from the events of the last two days while her mind was busy replaying them. She kept seeing Jonas locked in that frigid, dark cell, his shirt stained with blood, his spirit broken. Margaret shook her head on her pillow, trying to rid the image from her mind.

She took a deep breath and pushed all thoughts from her mind, which only paved the way for invasive images of the train tracks moving beneath her feet, the ground moving farther and farther away as the train she was riding lifted into the air. Then she realized she wasn't on a train but was actually floating. The thought sent a jolt of fear through her and felt real enough to shake her in the bed.

Chasing sleep was hopeless. She knew she would only be jerked from one unsettling image to the next, but she could not move. She was simply too tired to pull her head from the pillow.

Open your eyes, Margaret.

It took a moment for Margaret to realize the voice was not her own. She felt the soft tickle of breath on her cheek as it spoke again.

Open your eyes. Now.

Margaret snapped her eyes open and saw a black shadow on the other side of the room. It had the outline of a person, a man tall and slender, but she could not make out any more.

"Giles?"

There was no answer.

"John?"

She could hear the faint sound of breathing but wasn't sure it came from the corner where the figure stood.

"Get out of here," she heard herself saying. "Leave me!" Her voice cracked with fear. "Leave me alone!"

She closed her eyes, unsure if she was still dreaming or if there really was someone in her room. She visualized the door only three steps from the bed, the key to open it on the small bedside table. Could she make it to the door and unlock the iron latch before whatever it was descended upon her?

She looked back to the corner of the room. It was gone. Margaret kept her gaze on the empty space where the shadow had stood and allowed her eyes to adjust to the darkness. Once again, she was alone.

Chapter 13

Mrs. Frobisher had every right to deny Ainsley and Margaret admittance but surprisingly, with the brother and sister standing on her front step, she nodded, and stepped aside so the pair could walk in. Ainsley nodded his gratitude and allowed Margaret to walk ahead. They were two blocks from the edge of Old Town, in a development similar to where Jonas called home and within easy travelling distance of the university.

A wall of flowers greeted them in the foyer. Arrangements in varying sizes were displayed on tabletops and along the floor beginning at the door and stretching on further into the depths of the house. Margaret's tiny offering, a nosegay of chrysanthemums and daisies, seemed superfluous next to the showcased blooms of roses and lilies.

From the shadows of the hall a young servant girl stepped forward. She bowed her head and took the arrangement from Margaret's hand before disappearing somewhere at the back of the house.

"I've run out of vases, I'm afraid," Mrs. Frobisher said without any hint of regret in her tone. "Nonnie will have to find a jar or glass or … something." She walked between two French doors, propped open by an iron doorstop on each side, and made her way into the parlour.

Next to one of the doors sat a small table with a lace doily placed in its centre and a pile of condolence cards with handwritten notes spilling out in a misshapen pile. Mrs. Frobisher gestured absently to the table.

"You may leave your card there," she said, walking by without even glancing back to see if Ainsley or Margaret obeyed her. Giving a sideways glance to Ainsley, Margaret pulled a prepared card from her reticule and laid it on top of all the forgotten others.

"Come," Mrs. Frobisher said sharply. "Sit."

Ainsley and Margaret promptly did as instructed, seating themselves directly opposite their host.

The Frobishers's withdrawing room had no such flower displays as the entrance hall had. Instead, Mrs. Frobisher used every inch of available space to house her expansive collection of live song birds. The cages, some suspended from the ceiling, others secured to their own ornate stands, were filled with two or more birds each and all of them flitted about in their tiny confines singing hapless songs.

Ainsley saw how Margaret's eyes were drawn to the tiny, trapped creatures, her expression revealing the sympathy she felt for them.

"You must have pity," Mrs. Frobisher said, unaware of her guest's discomfort at seeing so many live creatures held against their natural will. "I have been forced to endure tea with a number of guests such as yourselves and I cannot stomach the thought of another sip. Forgive me if I don't offer you any."

"Of course," Margaret said sweetly, pulling her gaze from the sights all around them. "We are merely pleased you agreed to speak with us."

Mrs. Frobisher nodded, assured of her own thoughtfulness. "Which department of the university did you say you were from?" she asked, turning her attention to Ainsley.

"I was a student not too long ago."

"A student of Charles's?"

"Yes. He taught me chemistry and he was present for most of my examinations."

Mrs. Frobisher's face turned sour. "Did you know that Davies monster was also a student of my husband's? You look about his age ... Do you remember anything peculiar about him?"

Ainsley grimaced and lowered his head. "No, ma'am, not Dr. Davies. I cannot believe him capable."

She scoffed. "I bet there is any number of murderers with similar statements said about them." Her expression remained stern and unflinching as her gaze went between Ainsley and Margaret. "I do not mourn the loss of my husband, only the manner in which he was taken." She raised her hand to her forehead and pushed back on the curly mound of hair as if checking to ensure everything was in its place. She heaved a great sigh and settled into her seat.

"Were you and Professor Frobisher not close?" Margaret asked carefully.

Mrs. Frobisher looked as if she was completely bored with the matter. "How close can one be in a marriage?" she asked. She turned to the nearest bird cage then, and opened the small gate. A tiny yellow bird popped out onto her outstretched finger. She made clicking noise with her tongue and stroked the bird's breast with her free hand. "Do not fear," Mrs. Frobisher said, seeing her guests' eyes widen. "Their wings are clipped. They cannot fly the coop even if they had a mind to." She pursed her lips as if to kiss the bird's small head. "Charles spent so much time away that my beauties became my comfort." She smiled when the bird let out a contented whistle.

Ainsley gave an uncertain glance to Margaret at his side while Mrs. Frobisher replaced the bird to its cage.

"I understand that some women know when their spouses die. They can feel it somewhere inside, like a piece is missing," she said. "My mother knew the instant Father died. We had all been sitting around the table eating an early dinner and expecting him home at any moment." A smile played on her lips. "Mother, who had been smiling moments before, suddenly stopped and looked to the door. My sisters and I knew something was wrong just by the look on her face." Her gaze focused on her guests once again. "He had suffered an attack of the heart on the train," she explained. "Charles was absent two days before the officer showed up at my door yesterday around noon. They said he had died in the night." This was the closest Mrs. Frobisher had come to crying since the start of their visit, but still no tears fell. "I had no idea. I felt nothing. Even now I feel nothing. Is that horrid of me?"

Margaret shook her head, but neither of them could think of any words to offer in consolation.

Suddenly, Mrs. Frobisher's features hardened. "That Davies man—I won't call him doctor because a true doctor would never behave in such a way—he lured my husband away, drugged him, and completed his ghastly deed without the inconvenience of a struggle."

"Is that what the police have said, that the professor was

influenced by something?" Margaret asked suddenly.

Mrs. Frobisher looked surprised by such a direct question. "It would make sense, wouldn't it? My husband was not a weak man. He could have easily defended himself." Mrs. Frobisher shook her head, dismissing an alternative possibility outright. She looked to Ainsley. "The apple doesn't fall far from the tree, so I hear. Mr. Davies is fatherless and his mother was a mere washerwoman. Why the university ever agreed to admit such a man is a mystery to me, further still why they would offer him a professorship." She scrunched up her nose as if a foul smell suddenly permeated the air.

Ainsley shifted uncomfortably and glanced to Margaret. He noticed her hands were balled into fists at her side and she pinched her lips together determinedly. Slowly, he reached over and placed his hand over hers before speaking.

"Mrs. Frobisher, do you know if the professor had any recent arguments with anyone, perhaps in a professional capacity?"

She thought for a moment, as a deep frown set into her features. "If he did he would never say anything to me. We never spoke of such things." She closed her eyes with an air of disinterest and used her smallest finger to smooth out her eyebrow. "Our marriage was one in which we both operated under certain parameters. He kept to his duties and I kept to mine." A muscle at her neck flexed. "Yet it vexes me greatly to think Charles had come to such an end by the hand of such a man."

Ainsley saw a tear slip from the corner of her eye and trail down the outer curve of her cheek.

"Forgive me," she said stoically. "I must take leave of you." She stood stiffly and turned from them. She left with her back straight and her head held high.

Margaret and Ainsley exchanged glances as they rose and began making their way to the foyer. "She's in shock," Ainsley said quietly. "She needs to lay blame and Jonas is her chosen target."

"Jonas is the only target they have offered her," Margaret said. "He bears the brunt of her anger while her husband's true killer remains unknown."

Ainsley paused at the front door, his hand resting on the brass knob. "The atmosphere of their marriage seems strange, don't you think?" he asked.

"Nothing any stranger than our own parents'."

"He had been stepping out on her." The voice of Nonnie, the maid, startled them. They both turned and saw her a few steps from the bottom of the stairs, her arms laden with folded linens.

"Mrs. Frobisher knew about it too." She reached the bottom of the steps but did not lower her voice. It was clear she hadn't any concern whether or not her employer overheard them talking. "They cared very little for each other. I heard Mrs. Frobisher say once to her sister that she wished they hadn't sold their cottage in the Cotswolds because she would have liked to live separately from him there. Now she doesn't have to worry about such things."

Ainsley and Margaret were too shocked to say anything straightaway. The maid turned and began to walk down the hall.

"Nonnie, is it?" Ainsley called out, stepping toward her to prevent her from leaving.

The maid looked to them.

"Is it true what Mrs. Frobisher said, that the professor had been gone for two days?"

The maid nodded. "Aye, 'tisn't unusual."

"Where does he sleep when he's not here? At his office?"

The maid shrugged. "I told you. He had other interests."

❧   ❧

Margaret and Ainsley left the Frobisher residence with all they had learned pressing on their minds. They climbed into their waiting hansom and sat silently for the first few minutes of their ride to the university.

"Do you think Mrs. Frobisher is capable of arranging her husband's murder?" Margaret asked, finally breaking the silence. "I mean, she wanted to be rid of him. That much is clear."

"Wanting to be rid of him and doing the deed are two very different things," Ainsley said. "The newspapers described the attack as *passionately done*. Mrs. Frobisher is indifferent. If there was any passion it disappeared long ago."

"And you believe what's written in the papers?"

"I believe in my own instinct, which is telling me, in this case at least, that Mrs. Frobisher was content in their arrangement. Whether he was having an affair ..." A sign hanging over the neighbouring pavement caught his attention.

"Peter, what is it?"

"Stop the carriage!" Ainsley pounded the ceiling with his fist. "Stop the carriage!" He did not wait for the carriage to stop completely before he leapt from the carriage door. Margaret leaned forward in her seat just as Ainsley reached a shadowed doorway.

"Peter! Where are you going?"

Ainsley paused long enough to point to the wood sign hanging on a chain above the door, *The White Wolf,* and then disappeared inside.

Chapter 14

The drapes in Jonas's room were parted just enough to allow Jonas a look outside to the front of the house. The crowd along the pavement had thinned somewhat, but the fervour remained unchanged. Mrs. Crane had already gone out once, under John and Ezra's protection, to sweep away the rotten filth that had been hurled at the front door throughout the night. Her efforts proved fruitless, however. It did little good as the city folk awoke and began their commute through the city, making sure to pass the house of the now famous *Professor of Murder*, dubbed so by local papers.

From his hiding place, Jonas spotted refuse scattered along the pavement. Bits of paper, wilted cabbage leaves, and a broken vegetable crate. The curious and fearful had brought bruised apples and rotten carrots just to delight in throwing them at the house. The act temporarily bolstered their courage and allowed them to believe they were the righteous ones in a society riddled with sin.

Their fury was misdirected. Jonas knew this. He no longer thought himself capable. No memory of the killing existed in him. He did not possess enough anger or rage to propel him to such a deed as murder. It simply was not possible. He knew this now. But the details were sketchy, the night a near haze of bits and pieces.

Jonas eyed the crowd, scanning each face and wondering if any of them could have been behind the accusations against him. He recognized no one and, despite their antagonism, he doubted any of them were capable of something so manufactured. The evening had been preplanned, of that Jonas was sure. Someone intended to catch him unaware, perhaps forecasting his drunkenness or even enabling it and using it to gain his compliance.

The worst thoughts had come to him the night before when he was seated at the dinner table. Was one of his own housemates to blame? They had enticed him to pub, hadn't they? None of them made sure he returned home and not one of them had come forward with an explanation. Was it one of them or perhaps all of them?

A rotten tomato hit the window pane near his hiding place with a pronounced thud. He stepped back from the window and snapped the opening in the drapes closed. How long, he thought, how long would he be a prisoner for something he did not do? He could scarcely imagine ever being free again.

He went to the top drawer of his bureau and pulled out a small, blue velvet box he had hidden in the back of the top drawer. He had performed this ritual at least once a day since he had bought it home from the jeweller months ago. With the cover off he pulled the dainty ring from its cushion and slipped it to the first joint of his finger, only so far as the gold band would fit. He had hoped to see it on Margaret's finger long before this day.

Months ago she had agreed to follow him to Edinburgh even without the blessing of her family. Until he had heard her promise to him he never dared to dream it could be possible. She was a highborn lady who had been pursued by a number of suitors, men in greater positions of wealth and power than he could ever imagine. He was a surgeon, a tradesman in the eyes of good society, those who got their hands dirty.

He had been content to love her from afar, no matter how maddening it was. While he had been driven mad with longing so had she. The future was very clear; either they both suffered alone or gave in to their desires. Good society be damned.

He loved her. And she loved him. At one point that was all that mattered.

Jonas struggled to stave off tears before returning the ring to its box and placing it at the back of the bureau. He used the stability of the bureau to hold himself upright and bowed his head.

Her father became ill, and he waited. He was content to wait and would have waited until the end times knowing she had promised herself to him. She would come. Eventually. Of that he was certain.

Jonas closed his eyes and brushed away the tears that

slid onto his cheeks. Look at him, weak at the thought of her and the promise of what was to be. Of what could no longer be. All but convicted of murder, a crime he no more committed than Mrs. Crane in the kitchen downstairs. How could he ask Margaret to wed him now with such a stain on his character?

"Sad times, this."

Jonas snapped the bureau drawer shut and turned to John, who stood at the door.

"Didn't mean to startle you," he said, pushing open the door a few inches more.

There was an awkward silence between them. Jonas found himself distrustful of everyone he had once called friend, save Peter.

"Are you feeling all right? You look ... pale." John studied him with a slight tilt of the head before pushing his spectacles back to the bridge of his nose.

"How could you do it?" Jonas asked.

"Do what?"

"Leave me there! Not ensure I get home safe. How can any of you call me friend when you left me in such a state?"

"You were drunk—"

"I had two drinks! That is all."

"Well, it was enough to make you forget your beloved Margaret, that is for certain." John looked down the hall and lowered his voice. "I did not tell her, if that is what you are concerned about."

Jonas started. "What are you on about?"

"We didn't leave you there. You left of your own accord with a woman. There was no stopping you."

"Which woman?"

"The woman who had been seated next to us the entire night. Ezra and I were very surprised at how forward you were with her, especially given your professed longing for Miss Margaret."

Jonas shook his head and closed his eyes. If someone was determined to hurt him Margaret would be a surefire way to destroy him. "I should never have told you about her."

"I'm sure you aren't the only man who looks for diversion in the arms of others, but don't blame your friends when you finally give in to your carnal desires."

"I don't remember a woman!" Jonas nearly growled, more angry with himself than with John. How could he have allowed himself to get so incapacitated? He pounded the top of the bureau with a closed hand and rubbed his face with his other. "I don't remember anything," he said, his tone softer.

John looked on with puzzlement and uncertainty. "I know you didn't do it," he said at last. "It's just not possible. They're saying you did it because of Frobisher's complaint against you, but I know—"

"What did you say?"

"I know it's not possible. You wouldn't—"

"No, the other thing. Frobisher filed a complaint against me?"

John blanched. "I thought you knew. He filed it the day before yesterday. Unfortunate timing, if you ask me."

"Oh, God." Jonas ran both his hands through his hair and turned from the door in anguish. "I didn't know anything about it."

"Well, then that proves it. You didn't know. There'd be no reason for you to ... do what they say you did."

Jonas turned to him and shook his head. "They would have to take my word for it and no one is going to believe the son of a washerwoman." A silence fell over them as the implications became clear. The reasoning was flimsy, but it would be enough to convince a judge that Jonas, a man of humble birth and low rank, had planned the attack against his superior, a man of impeccable character if only believed so by his elevated position in society, the knighthood bestowed upon him and his accumulation of wealth. These facts, the juxtaposition of their respective places in society, would surely be enough to see Jonas hang.

Chapter 15

Margaret pushed open the heavy wooden door to the pub and paused momentarily as her eyes adjusted to the dim light. Ainsley had already moved ahead to the counter. A barkeep, rotund and unkempt, turned at the sound of the door and gave them a wary look.

"What'll ye be needing, eh?" He looked Margaret over from head to toe with a fat, red tongue pushing at the side of his mouth.

Margaret crossed her arms over her chest and tried to ignore the man's inappropriate staring.

"We're looking for some information," Ainsley started.

"We ain't got information. We got drink." The barkeep gave a long, deep snort and rubbed beneath his nose with the full length of his forearm.

Ainsley nodded slowly. "All right then, we'll have two pints and some answers to a few questions." He glanced to Margaret, who was slow to come to the counter.

"She don't look like she wants any *pints*." He had his hands spread out to the sides and was using his grip on the counter to keep him upright.

As Margaret neared she caught a whiff of him, a mixture of stale alcohol and the lack of a bath.

She gave a half smile at his comment. "It's not like I expect you to have a chardonnay," she said with challenge in her voice.

The barkeep chuckled and turned back to Ainsley. "Well now, the way I sees it, ye can ask your questions for two pints but ye won't get no answers for anything less than four." He plunked four glasses, two in each hand, onto the bar top with such force they clinked together solidly. He filled them one by one with what looked like watered-down urine, much of it spilling over the side.

"Peter." Margaret reached forward to prevent him from touching one of the drinks.

Ainsley turned his head so only she could see and gave

her a wink. Then he pulled a fistful of coins from his pocket and slapped then on the counter.

"Two evenings ago there was a man here with some friends—"

"Yes, of course! That one!" The barkeep erupted in a fit of laughter, entertained by his own wit.

"Peter, let's go."

"Wait a minute now, even genies allow more questions than that." The barkeep still chuckled slightly as he spoke.

"You mean wishes, you halfwit," she said, glaring at him with her arms crossed over her chest.

The barkeep's attention snapped to Margaret. "What'd you call me?"

Margaret unfolded her arms and stepped into the empty space between them. "I don't have time for this!" she yelled, meeting the man's gaze squarely. "The man I love is facing execution and you're making a mockery of it! Now either you recall the events of two nights ago or you don't."

Amidst her speech Ainsley began pulling on her arm and hissed her name.

Margaret jerked her arm from his grasp. "I am not leaving until I get an answer."

She found herself short of breath and faint but pressed on.

"Yeah," the man said after a moment of hesitation, "I remember." He glanced to Ainsley with uncertainty. "Is this about that murdering professor? He who killed his superior?"

"Do you remember him?" Ainsley asked. "I was told he came here with some friends."

The barkeep nodded. "I remember him. Good-looking fella with black hair and good teeth. He were here. Sat at that table." He pointed to a circular table next to the door with four chairs placed around it. "Had two friends with 'im too. They ordered drinks, food, the whole lot. It were like they was celebrating something. I never asked, though." He turned to Margaret with a gentler expression. "Not my place."

"Can you describe the men with him?" Ainsley asked.

The barkeep went on to describe John and Ezra in turn.

"Was there an older gentleman, fifty years or older?"

Ainsley asked.

"The professor?" The barkeep shook his head. "No, sir. I remember him, though, from the evening before. I remember thinking to myself 'now there's a fella who needs more than a pint.' Carried the weight of the world. Thought maybe he'd lost a patient or something."

"You knew he was a professor?"

"Of course. They all come here on account of us being so close to the school, I'd wager."

Margaret watched as Ainsley's shoulders slumped. She knew there was a reason for his line of questioning. Margaret herself wasn't exactly sure what he was aiming for, but clearly he missed his mark.

"Thank you, sir," Margaret said as Ainsley turned from the counter dejected.

"Don't you want to hear about the woman?" the barkeep asked.

"What woman?"

"The woman who were here with them. She sat at the table beside them for most of the night before moving to sit beside the murderer ... I mean, the doctor. They both left together. He was having trouble walking and she was holding him. He hadn't drank much, though. Not that I recall."

Ainsley and Margaret exchanged glances.

"Can you describe the woman?" Ainsley asked, examining the positioning of the two tables and their respective chairs.

"Well ... she looked like her." The barkeep pointed to Margaret.

"Me?"

"Yeah." He squinted one eye, outstretched a hand, and made a curving motion with it. "Only more slender-like."

"What did you say?" Margaret's voice rose in a shriek.

"Thank you, sir. You've been very helpful." Ainsley moved quickly toward his sister and ushered her outside to the hansom, which had dutifully waited for them.

"Did he just call me fat?"

Chapter 16

The police presence at the university building next to the Royal Infirmary was unmistakable. Even the plainclothed officers who leaned against the bricks along the front of the building stood out. Lectures for the rest of that week had been cancelled and only a few administrators were left to assist the investigating officers. Margaret and Ainsley were keenly aware of the many pairs of eyes that followed them as they alighted from their carriage and made their way up the steps to the university's front doors.

"Peter, we need to take care," Margaret cautioned, twisting her gloved fingers together in front of her as she glanced about. "We don't want to make things more difficult for Jonas. Inspector Hearst is far less approachable than our Inspector Simms."

"I imagine it makes their job much easier when the assailant is caught alongside the victim," Ainsley said. "It prevents them from having to exhaust other avenues."

The front doors opened up into a wide hall with a staircase located at the midpoint of the building. Numerous doors, all closed, faced out onto the hall, even those on the second floor that could be seen past the landing. A single soul, a uniformed officer, stood on guard outside one of the rooms on the second floor. Ainsley and Margaret couldn't help but meet the officer's gaze.

"Is that the professor's office?" Margaret asked in a hushed tone.

"Yes." Ainsley guided her to the stairs.

"How are we going to get in?"

"I haven't figured that out yet."

Just before they reached the first step Samuel appeared from further down the hall. He looked up at the sight of them but then his face grew stern.

"What on earth are you doing here?" His words came out in a hiss, angry but desperate to remain quiet. "You are not doing Jonas any favours," he said as he guided them away from the stairs. He gave an apologetic look to Margaret.

"This is my sister, Margaret."

"My apologies, ma'am. The courts don't look kindly to meddling. If they see either of you here it will most assuredly look bad."

"We do not trust them to investigate fairly," Margaret said, stealing a glance to her brother.

Samuel went for a closed door at the side and waved them in. Once inside, he scanned the hall before closing the door. He had led them to a small clerk's office, a very narrow room with a large window at the far end.

"Can you get us inside Frobisher's office?" Ainsley asked.

Samuel shook his head. "Never. They have had a guard outside that door since Jonas was arrested. The only reason that they keep the building open is so that some of the clerks can continue to work. Lectures resume tomorrow but that office will still be off-limits."

"We have to find out what we can," Ainsley pressed.

"I know. I know. I am in agreeance on that." Samuel opened a file in his hand. "I was just heading out to New Town to conduct a few interviews of my own. I've been here most of the morning." He pulled out a paper and laid it on top of the dossier in his arm. "Did Jonas tell either of you he had a formal complaint filed against him?"

Ainsley and Margaret leaned in to look over the paper, which was embossed with university insignia in the top left-hand corner. Samuel pointed to a signature at the bottom.

"This was filed by Professor Frobisher himself," he said.

"When did he file it?" Ainsley took the paper for a closer look.

"Three days ago, less than twelve hours before Frobisher was found dead."

Margaret slipped the paper from Ainsley's hand to study it herself. "Insubordination during surgery. It says he was antagonistic, preventing the acting surgeon from carrying out his duties, which nearly resulted in the patient's death. That doesn't sound like Jonas at all."

Samuel pointed to the paper. "This is all they need to prove motive. Well, and the fact that Jonas himself confessed to animosity with Frobisher."

"Regarding what exactly?" Margaret asked. She looked to

Ainsley.

"Jonas is one of a handful of faculty members who are championing a policy change to allow the admittance of women," he explained.

A look of elation and pride swept over her face. "Truly?"

"He said so himself," Samuel said. "Such a move would make Edinburgh one of the first facilities in the world to make such a ruling, but it doesn't come without a fair bit of controversy."

"Frobisher was opposed then?" Margaret asked. "Could that be the true motive behind this complaint?"

"Perhaps, but in truth I haven't a clue what the school plans to do with this complaint. The original complainant is no longer alive. And, given Frobisher's new notoriety within the school and amongst the general public, I believe it will look very bad if we try to slander his memory in any way."

"We have to try." Margaret's tone sounded desperate.

"Absolutely. I am trying my best, ma'am ... er ... Miss— Lady!" Samuel closed his eyes and shook his head at his misstep. "My apologies. I'm still getting used to the idea of my school chum being the son of an earl."

Margaret looked to Ainsley with disbelief.

"It was the only way to get Jonas out of Calton," he said. He saw the look on her face. "I don't regret it," Ainsley admitted. "Not in the slightest."

"But Father and Daniel ..." Her voice trailed off at the thought of the repercussions.

"Oh, to hell with it all, Margaret," Ainsley said sharply. "Our lives need not be dictated by the wishes of our father and brother." He stole a glance to Samuel and licked his lips. "Our happiness is better served when we endeavour to follow our own hearts and minds. You and I have learned as much in recent months."

Margaret looked abashed. Out of everyone working to set Jonas free, she cared for him the most. She had defied her father when she entered into a relationship with him. She defied society by just contemplating a life alongside him. Yet somehow she clung to the notion that everyone might be appeased by her peacemaker mentality.

"Lady Margaret, your brother coming forward ... all I can say is it adds a tremendous amount of weight to our defence."

Margaret nodded and lifted her eyes to look at Ainsley. "I am glad of it," she said, determination in her eyes. "We must do away with fear." She looked to Samuel. "We discovered something about the professor that may dampen the public's elevated opinion of him. Frobisher was having an extramarital affair."

Samuel raised an eyebrow.

"We haven't been able to verify the claim," Ainsley said. "But I imagine it to be very likely given the state of his marriage and the indifference of his wife."

Samuel nodded but didn't say anything straightaway. "Mrs. Frobisher's family, the Belmots, are a lesser noble family. My father represented them once regarding a land dispute. It's possible Frobisher married into the family to access her wealth, which if I understand correctly, would have been considerable for a man of his aspirations."

"This would explain why they suffered a loveless marriage," Ainsley said, turning to the window and running a hand through his hair.

"A childless one as well," Margaret offered. She turned her attention to Samuel. "Mrs. Frobisher told us her husband had been gone two nights before his body was found here."

Samuel regarded her warily. "I'm not sure I like the idea of you both questioning witnesses before they can be brought in to give official statements," he said. "You will be accused of interfering."

Ainsley turned. "What are we supposed to do? Sit in that house, with the crowds gawking at us, and wait? That's what circumstance is forcing Jonas to do and he's nearly jumping out of his skin." He stepped away from the window. "We need to find the connections that the investigating officers are not willing to entertain. We know Jonas didn't murder Frobisher, but that means *someone else* did."

"Please, Mr. Humphry, let Peter and I do this. We promise to be as discreet as we can. We will inform you of any information we glean, whether we feel it will help Jonas's case or hinder it."

Ainsley marvelled at Margaret's ability to win over

anyone. Samuel didn't respond immediately, most likely considering the probable outcomes.

"No," he said sternly. "You mustn't tell me anything else, not until you have proof." He gave a small exhale, no doubt second-guessing his decision to allow them to proceed on their own. He looked to Ainsley. "I either need proof, beyond a doubt, that Jonas is innocent or that someone else committed this crime." He turned his attention back to Margaret. "Anything else is of little help to us. Do you understand?"

Margaret nodded.

"All right then." Samuel pulled at the bottom of his jacket and straightened his tie. "We are going to leave this room together and you both are going to follow me." He gave Ainsley a pointed finger. "Do not stray."

Margaret chuckled. "I see you two are well acquainted."

"Oh yes, ma'am," Samuel said. "We are indeed." A stern look flashed over him before he waved his hand, beckoning them to follow him. "Come then."

He opened the door and stepped aside to allow Margaret to walk through first. In the hall, Samuel made mundane remarks to the weather as he led them to the back of the building and down a set of cement stairs. Once in the basement, he relaxed. "Peter, you'll recall Jonas telling us about a female clerk who Frobisher assaulted."

"Miss Rebecca Stewart," Ainsley said.

"Yes. I've already spoken with her, and she is still fairly shaken up. She didn't want to talk to me until I mentioned she would be helping Dr. Davies's case."

"Is she willing to corroborate the events?"

Samuel nodded. "And she's offered to help us in any way she can." He gestured for a door. "It's just through here," he said, more so for Margaret's sake. Ainsley already knew where they were headed.

They walked down a narrow passage with low ceilings before the room opened up, revealing a large, heavily used mortuary. The ceiling was held up by four large columns and gaslights dangled from the rafters of the ceiling. A man in a white smock was hunched over a body at the far end of the room. A woman, who wore an identical smock, entered the room from a doorway to the left. She looked up from the papers in her hand and pulled off her glasses. "Mr. Humphry, I was just going to make copies of the notes you requested."

"It's all right. I can wait until tomorrow. I am just bringing a colleague of mine down so he can see the body for himself." Samuel turned to Margaret and Ainsley. "This is Miss Rebecca Stewart. She's a recent addition to the university staff."

The young woman nodded in their direction as she skirted them, heading for a small desk set against the wall next to where Margaret stood.

"They keep me down here mostly," Rebecca said. "Wouldn't want to embarrass any of the men in the upper offices." She flashed a grim smile. She shot an unsure glance over her shoulder to the man who showed little interest in acknowledging their presence. "And I spend seventy percent of my time fetching tea."

"Cecil," Samuel called out.

The man jolted upright as the mention of his name. He wore a long white coat and a pair of leather gloves. His half-moon spectacles looked as if any moment they would slide from the beak of his nose. Ainsley did not recognize him even though during his medical training he had spent many hours in that very room.

"These are my friends, Peter and Margaret," Samuel explained.

"Yes." Cecil did not move from his place amongst the dead nor did her raise his eyes as he spoke.

"Would one of you be willing to show them what we were discussing earlier?" Samuel asked, looking from Cecil to Rebecca and back again. "They both have a keen interest in the case at hand."

Cecil stood stoic for a moment. "Can the little lady hold the contents of her stomach?" he asked, his tone betraying his cynicism.

Ainsley snorted. "As well as any man. Sometimes better."

Rebecca smiled and looked to Margaret. "Excellent. You have the perfect disposition to fetch tea as well."

❧ ❦

Cecil was a man of peculiarities. His speech was stunted, his height as well, and all the while Ainsley and Margaret were in the mortuary, he refused to make eye contact with either of them. He pointed to one table to the side. "It's here."

When he pulled back the white sheet a body with a gaping chest cavity greeted them. Ainsley drew as close to the body as the table would allow and saw Margaret do the same beside him in his peripheral vision.

"What was determined to be the cause of death?" Ainsley asked.

"Don't you read the papers?" Cecil asked, looking over the top of his spectacles.

"I'm not interested in what the papers have to say. Give me your expert opinion."

Cecil seemed overly preoccupied and ill at ease.

Rebecca walked toward them and rounded the examination table so she could face both Margaret and Ainsley. "He was stabbed ten times," she said before turning to pull a file from a table behind her.

Ainsley saw a handful of puncture wounds in the skin, superficial and scarcely an inch in width. "Where exactly?"

Heaving a sigh of annoyance, Cecil snatched the papers from Rebecca's hands and opened the file. Leaning over the body toward Ainsley, he pointed to a rough sketch, an outline of a human body. On it was marked where each wound was located, all of them on the torso. The measurements of each were listed along a column next to the sketch.

"They all measure an inch, or less," Ainsley said.

Cecil nodded.

Ainsley glanced up at Rebecca, who was making her way to the cache of tools. She returned to the group with a long, thin blade in her hands.

"Is this the murder weapon?" Margaret asked.

"Yes, but—"

"Perhaps there is some filing work you need to attend to," Cecil interjected, darting a hardened stare in Rebecca's direction. "I specifically recall Dr. Waters telling you not to keep him waiting for you again."

With a hardened stare, Rebecca was quick to gather her

paperwork, hugging it to her chest. She left the room the same way Margaret and Ainsley had entered it and never gave them a backward glance.

"The actual knife Dr. Davies used is being kept as evidence but this is the type of blade he would have had available to him as a surgeon."

Ainsley took the surgical knife in hand and looked it over carefully. He remembered the tool well. During his studies, they were taught to use it during amputations to cut away the skin and severe the arteries before tying them off. A different knife, which resembled a saw more than anything else, was used to cut through the bone.

"These are standard in all medical kits," Ainsley said for Margaret's sake. "Any number of students and doctors would have access to them."

"That narrows down the suspects," she answered, taking the knife in her hand.

"How deep are the punctures?" Ainsley asked, leaning in closer. He pushed his finger into one of the openings and felt around.

"Some as long as the blade itself," Cecil replied. He leaned onto the edge of the table and kept his gaze on the corpse in front of him.

"You measured them?"

"Naturally." Cecil seemed to bristle at Ainsley's line of questioning. "I'm not sure what second-rate country hospital you are used to working for but this is the University of Edinburgh and we take pride—"

"St. Thomas."

"Excuse me?"

"I work for St. Thomas in London. Hardly second-rate."

A muscle in Cecil's cheek began to twitch. Ainsley ignored him and reached for the paperwork Cecil had left lying across Frobisher's legs. "Says approximate time of death is estimated to be ten to twelve hours before the body was discovered." Ainsley pointed his finger at the sentence before looking up.

"How is that possible?" Margaret asked, leaning in to look for herself.

"It must have been written in error," Cecil explained.

"But this is the University of Edinburgh," Ainsley said,

"not a second-rate country hospital."

"Minor details." Cecil shrugged and feigned disinterest. "Hardly matters."

"It matters because another man's life is at stake."

"A man who was found alongside the body."

"Ten hours after Frobisher is believed to have expired."

"He had the knife in his hand!"

"A knife that could have easily been placed there! Good God, man, when will you stop searching for evidence that fits the narrative and look at what's actually in front of you?" Ainsley flicked the file at Cecil in disgust. "It says an estimated pint of blood was found at the scene. A pint! The man had ten wounds to his abdomen but his body only secreted a pint of blood out of a possible nine?"

"Peter." Margaret tried to calm him by touching his arm but Ainsley shook her off.

Cecil began to stammer under Ainsley's direct questioning. "I ... I believe—"

"Don't tell me what you believe. Tell me what you know! This is science!" Ainsley rounded the table that separated them and before he realized it he had Cecil by the collar. "My friend's life depends on this."

Forced to look him in the eye, the man faltered. "I'm only a porter," he yelled out in desperation.

"What?" He could feel the man shaking in his grasp. "Why would they let a porter complete a dissection of such importance?"

"I didn't complete it, sir."

Confused, Ainsley lowered him and eyed him suspiciously.

"But we saw you standing over a body when we entered," Margaret said.

"I was cleaning it," Cecil answered honestly. "I wouldn't know what to do with a body beyond that." He pushed his spectacles up the bridge of his nose. "Sometimes, when no one else is here, I like to pretend I'm a surgeon. You'd be surprised to learn how people who don't know any better treat you. It's only for a bit of fun. I'd never ... well, hurt anyone."

Ainsley snorted in disgust and finally turned from him. The man made a mockery of his profession and toyed with

Jonas's life.

"Where is the real doctor?" Ainsley asked.

"He's not here, sir. He won't return until after the funeral."

"When's the funeral?"

"Tomorrow morning. I have to see that the body is stitched up and cleaned before six this evening. That's when the mortician comes to take him away."

Ainsley nodded. "Finally, something I can work with." He unbuttoned the front of his jacket. "Margaret, time to roll up our sleeves."

Chapter 17

Margaret stood at the enamel trough sink and washed her hands carefully, ensuring all of Professor Frobisher's blood was removed from the tiny creases of her skin. There was a time, not so long ago, when she had hoped to be a doctor herself. She had spent a good portion of the last few years watching Ainsley as he pursued his medical career. She started off begging to visit him in the morgue when she visited Edinburgh and eventually she began borrowing some of his medical texts without his knowledge. If Father discovered her interest she had no doubt he'd send her away to live with some of their country relatives until such a time as he could marry her off to some noble's son. She was lucky that Ainsley tried their patriarch's patience to such a point that she looked like an angel by comparison. Lord Marshall never suspected anything and if he discovered it now ... well, there was very little he could say.

Lord Marshall's condition had deteriorated considerably since his head injury. He had lost all his verbal abilities. Even his earlier grunts and moans had been lost in recent weeks despite Margaret sitting daily with him, completing exercises as their doctors suggested. She wondered how Aunt Louisa was managing with him while she and Ainsley were gone. She wondered if her father even noticed their absence.

"Margaret?"

She shook her head free of her thoughts and twisted the faucet closed.

"We need to speak with Dr. Waters," Ainsley said, looking over the paperwork for Professor Frobisher. "He completed the initial examination. I need to speak with him about the lack of blood at the crime scene." He squinted and raised the paper closer to his face. "Perhaps he meant to write seven, instead of one."

Margaret pulled a coarse towel from a nearby hook. "It's late. Can we speak with him tomorrow?" She glanced to a small sliver of a window. The dark sky of twilight confirmed her suspicion.

Ainsley ignored her suggestion and continued to study the papers. Cecil had left an hour before and they hadn't seen Rebecca since Cecil's harsh words to her. As far as Margaret could tell they were the only ones left in that section of the building.

"I'm tired," she said, putting the towel back on its hook. "I didn't sleep well last night." She thought about the vivid dreams and fits of uneasiness that had plagued her the night before. Now the nausea was taking hold of her insides again. "Peter?"

Again, he said nothing.

"Peter!"

He looked up with a start.

"I must get back to the house. I'm afraid I'll crumble if I stand here much longer."

His features betrayed his disappointment, but he relented. "Yes, of course. My apologies."

❧ ❧

The main hall of the department was dark but not entirely devoid of life. A seated, uniformed constable stood guard outside Frobisher's office. Further along, a light emanated from a room on the opposite side of the hall. As Margaret and Ainsley passed they both looked in. A man with a crate of bottles and tins in his hands slipped past them through the doorway. When the way was clear Margaret recognized Eloise instantly and her heart sank.

"Miss Margaret!" Eloise turned from the counter and greeted them with a smile. "Hello, Peter."

Their well-mannered upbringing forced them to step inside the room. A clerk stood behind a tall counter, a ledger in front of him on the desk and a vast array of bottles and jars displayed behind him. The room, which looked more like a storage closet, went much further back than the gaslight above them could reach.

"Good evening, Miss Locke," Ainsley said, his tone mirroring Margaret's feelings of disdain. "Seems rather late for you to be here."

"I'm just picking up a few things for Father," she said. "With all the excitement yesterday I couldn't make it past the front doors. And Father's arthritis was making him very sour today, so I couldn't make it here earlier."

Margaret ventured to look beyond the clerk to see what exactly lay in the shadows. It looked like mostly chemicals and compounds, bell jars and bottles.

"Father's a chemist, Miss Margaret," she said.

"I am aware," Margaret answered, a little more harshly than she intended. "Jonas told me."

"Oh. I hadn't realized you two were so ... informal together." Before Margaret could formulate a curt reply, Eloise turned to Ainsley. "Would you be a dear, Peter, and help me shuttle this to the carriage?" She gestured to the front of the building. "It's just waiting outside."

Ainsley nodded and pulled the crate from the counter. He walked quickly to the carriage, leaving Margaret to walk alongside Eloise.

"It's so nice to have a capable young man around, isn't it?" Eloise asked as they walked the length of the hall slowly. A downcast look overcame her seconds later. "I don't know how I shall bear not having Jonas at my side if he ... if he ..."

Her distress looked truly genuine to Margaret, who struggled to find the correct manner with which to respond. Eloise seemed so convinced that Jonas was meant for the gallows and didn't allow herself the chance to believe that he could be innocent. Eloise's lack of loyalty was sickening. It took a great deal of effort for Margaret to shield her frustration.

"Peter and I are determined," she said, unable to bring herself to look in Eloise's direction, "it shall never come to that. Jonas will be exonerated." She stole a glance to Eloise in time to see a look of elation wash over her.

"Do you mean it?" she asked.

The last thing Margaret wished to spend her energy on was allaying Eloise's fears. She'd prefer to watch the woman stew in her own anxiety, especially after the way she was patronized the day before. But in the end, Margaret was not the vindictive sort and before she knew it she was offering words of comfort. "I believe, before long, this will all be but a faint memory," she said, keeping her gaze straight. If Margaret were truthful she'd admit to having complete faith in Jonas while possessing nothing but contempt for the inconsistency of the Scottish legal system.

"Well now, Miss Margaret, you have just summed up the philosophy by which I live my life." Her walking pace slowed as she slipped her arm under Margaret's and held her hand as if they were dear friends. "The dark days never last long, do they?"

Margaret preferred not to answer. Her dark days had been many and the only thing that kept her heading forward was the promise of a new day and new possibilities. In the end, even the darkest days would be but a small dot on the expanse of her life.

The dark days of which Eloise spoke of, however, seemed to be of a different sort altogether. Despite her uppity demeanour and laissez-faire bearing, Margaret got the impression that Eloise was anything but forgiving. She had a perfectionist quality about her, a ruthlessness which demanded absolute adherence and a promise of brutal retaliation if her expectations were not met.

"You are so clever," Eloise said, squeezing Margaret's arm and drawing even closer. "I shall like to have you come visit us regularly once Jonas and I are married." Eloise stopped, and placed her other hand over her mouth. "I'm so sorry, dear." She twisted slightly to face her, a look of delight masquerading as regret on her face. "I had forgotten that he asked me not to tell you just yet."

The woman was either trying desperately to alarm Margaret, or the delusion ran deep. Margaret tried hard to keep her expression steady so as not to give Eloise any indication either way. She offered an indifferent shrug. "Seems a happy enough announcement. Why would you ever wish to keep it a secret?"

Eloise faltered. Her bait had been avoided. "You truly feel that way?" Eloise looked at her with an air of pity.

"Of course." Margaret flashed a contrived smile and started walking toward the front of the building again, desperate to be within earshot of Ainsley. "Your happiness is of greater importance than any discomfort I may feel."

Eloise hesitated. "Forgive me. I was under the impression

you had your heart set on him."

"Certainly not," Margaret lied. "I'm only glad to hear any infatuation he may have had for me is now relegated to the past."

A relieved smile touched Eloise's lips. "I'm very glad to hear you say that, Miss Margaret."

They reached the front doors where the cool October air greeted them, nipping at their exposed skin and sending a breeze into the curls of their hair. Ainsley stood alongside the carriage. The crate he had been carrying had been stashed with all the others.

"Everything's here," Ainsley said as the women made their way down the front steps. He unlatched the carriage door and offered a hand to Eloise as she climbed inside.

"Thank you very much, Peter," she said through the carriage window. Her attention turned once again to Margaret, who stood next to him on the pavement. "If you ever tire of only men in the house, Margaret, do come visit me. There is much I'd like to talk about. We can have tea."

Margaret said nothing. She only nodded and gave a small wave as the carriage began to roll down the laneway.

"And that is exactly why I wish we had left an hour ago," Margaret said bluntly. With the carriage slipping into the fog at the end of the lane, she turned and headed down the pavement in the opposite direction toward their hansom.

Begrudgingly, Margaret allowed her brother to help her up into the rickety conveyance. Ainsley gave orders to the driver to take them home before joining Margaret inside. Seconds later the carriage jerked into motion.

"The nerve of that woman," Margaret said, before she could stop herself. The conversation had done much to vex her, sending her nerves into a tizzy where even slow, calculated breaths could not calm her down effectively. "As if anyone would believe Jonas is capable of loving such an insecure creature."

"What exactly did she say to you?" Ainsley asked.

"Only that she'd like me to visit once she and Jonas are married."

Ainsley waved a dismissive hand. "Jonas himself has decried her claims as false."

"I am aware," Margaret said. "I know he speaks the truth

about her. I can be gullible at times but not so gullible to believe more than half of what that woman says."

"She is simply trying to unseat you," Ainsley said, leaning back in the carriage bench. "And it appears to me she had succeeded as well."

Margaret bristled at the suggestion. "You would be unnerved as well if such a situation existed between you and J— Cassandra." She turned her attention outside the carriage, where light rain gathered on the small window. "I've been forced into two separate conversations with the woman and each time it feels as if she is rearing up to eat me alive. It's the manner in which she looks at me." A shiver slipped down Margaret's spine, forcing her to pull her shawl tighter around her arms. "My only hope is that my protestations regarding Jonas's connection to me have done the trick. I mean to convince her that Jonas and I have no feelings for each other in the hopes that she will let us be."

"How long can you keep up such a charade?" Ainsley asked, lowering his head to the back of the carriage bench, suddenly exhausted.

"Long enough to prove his innocence in the eyes of the courts," she answered. "I must concentrate on one thing at a time and this case is of greater importan—" Margaret stopped suddenly and her expression soured. "Does Eloise look like me?"

Ainsley closed his eyes in exasperation. "Margaret, you are much prettier."

"But if it's dark and you'd been drinking," she suggested. "Is there a chance she could look like me?"

Ainsley's eyes popped open and he turned his head to look at her. "The barkeep."

Margaret nodded and flashed a delighted smile.

Chapter 18

Margaret was quiet most of the journey home, which Ainsley was grateful for. Their breakthrough was significant, but there was little they could do for it then with night falling fast. The examination of Professor Frobisher had been difficult, made especially so since a dissection had already been undertaken. In the end Ainsley couldn't determine why so little blood had been found at the scene. Judging by the state of rigor mortis, the time of death was accurate within a span of a few hours. But what the autopsy couldn't reveal was why Jonas would have killed Frobisher at night and then waited until morning to make his getaway. Any man with an intention to kill, even a highly intoxicated one, would have known to leave the scene.

By the time they stepped out onto the kerb in front of Jonas's house, the crowds had dispersed once and for all, leaving only garbage and litter in their place. Ainsley used his shoe to push aside a mound of cabbage leaves from the front step so Margaret could get to the door.

"At least it's quieter," she remarked as they walked inside.

The voice of Mrs. Crane bellowed from behind the kitchen door. "'Tisn't proper! I cannot have her sleeping in that attic. Not another night!" There came a loud bang as if something sturdy had hit the table or counter. "They must be taken to a hotel."

"Mrs. Crane, calm yourself."

Ainsley recognized Giles's voice coming from the other side of the door.

Margaret had to round two large trunks left in the hallway in order to make her way to the kitchen. There was an off-white envelope balanced on the curved top of the one closest to Ainsley. Ainsley realized the name scrolled on the outside of the envelope was his.

"Calm myself? Calm myself? If they stay here another

night, I will quit. I cannot have this on my conscience too!" Mrs. Crane sounded completely irate and inconsolable.

The door to the kitchen opened and John slipped out while the argument between Mrs. Crane and Giles continued. Even in the dim light Ainsley could see John was forcing back tears. When he saw Ainsley and Margaret in the hall, his face went slack with the shock before morphing into concern. "I would not go in there, Lady Margaret, if I were you," he said, placing himself between the door and Margaret.

Margaret looked over her shoulder to Ainsley, who flashed the envelope.

"It's from Cutter," he said.

When it looked as if Margaret would obey him, John moved from the door and headed straight for the stairs. Ainsley watched as John circled the bannister, keeping his head low, and jogged for the next floor. The commotion in the kitchen continued even as Margaret came back to her brother in the foyer, a look of utter confusion on her face.

"What has gotten into everyone?" she asked.

Ainsley shook his head and rubbed the back of his neck with his free hand. "Cutter sent our trunks back once they reached York."

"Oh, thank heavens."

"And Elmira has taken leave of us," he added. "It would seem our unorthodox manner is too much for her sensibilities."

Margaret chuckled and pulled the letter from her brother's hands. "I can't say I am distraught at the notion. I feel liberated actually," she said. "She was a good-intentioned woman, even if a bit old-fashioned for our tastes. We should tell Cutter that we'd be happy to provide her with a reference."

Before Ainsley could nod in agreement, the kitchen door opened and Giles escaped as the voice of Mrs. Crane followed him out into the hall.

"I won't be quiet, Dr. Grant, not this time!"

When he saw Margaret and Ainsley in the hall he contemplated a return to the kitchen for a quick second before deciding against it.

"That woman has worked herself into hysterics," he said,

quickly finding his composure. He marched toward them. "You've discovered your belongings, I see. Peter and Jonas will have to help you take them to your room, Miss Margaret. I have an appointment with the dean of medicine and I mustn't be late."

"Of course ..."

Giles was quick to head for the stairs.

"But Giles ..."

He stopped and looked down at her.

"Would it be better if Peter and I went to a hotel?" Margaret glanced to the kitchen door. "Perhaps Mrs. Crane would be happier with such an arrangement."

"Nonsense," Giles said, somewhat unconvincingly. "You both are perfectly welcome to remain here."

He passed Jonas on his way up the stairs, but didn't bother giving the man a sideways glance.

"What's the ruckus?" Jonas asked, coming down the stairs. He paused at the midway point and looked over his shoulder as Giles charged ahead before coming all the way down. "I've never known him to argue with Mrs. Crane before."

"It's about us, I'm afraid," Margaret said. "Peter, I think we have outworn our welcome. We should return to the hotel."

Ainsley eyed the trunks between them.

"I wouldn't hear of it," Jonas said. He reached over and took Margaret's hand, sandwiching it between both of his. "Your presence here has been a better help to me than I realized." Margaret's chin elevated a notch, and an endearing smile came to her lips. She did not say she had been justified to defy them or anything so self-righteous, and that was a credit to her character. Instead, she regarded him squarely and squeezed his hand.

"Very well," she said, struggling to hide her pleasure at such an invite. "I believe we can manage to stay. Perhaps we can find a way to make it up to Mrs. Crane somehow."

Ainsley nodded but wasn't exactly sure how that could be accomplished.

∿ ∽

Ainsley and Jonas removed Margaret's trunk to her room first before taking Ainsley's less burdensome trunk to his room next. They placed the trunk at the foot of Ainsley's assigned bed and together breathed a sigh of relief.

"Thank you, my friend," Ainsley said, giving Jonas a pat on the shoulder as they rose to their full height.

Ainsley's room was similar to Jonas's with a single wooden bed, a nightstand, a bureau of drawers, and a decent-sized desk with a leather swivel chair. His window faced north, however, with a view of the New Town neighbourhood and villages beyond. The room was only steps away from the stairs that would take him to Margaret's attic room.

"You two were gone for most of the day," Jonas said, when Margaret entered. With a lamp in her hand, she crossed the room and set it on Ainsley's windowsill.

"We made some headway," Ainsley said. He took a seat on the lid of his trunk and gestured to the desk chair for Jonas. "And we have a question to ask."

Margaret kept her eyes trained outside, as if not entirely interested in Jonas's answer.

"Would you happen to have a picture of Eloise?" Ainsley asked.

Jonas bristled in his seat. "Why in God's name would I have something like that?"

"It's perfectly all right, if you do," Margaret said, turning to face them both. "I am not offended. She is the daughter of a very special person in your life. He was your adoptive father in many respects."

Jonas looked uneasy at the suggestion. His face contorted in discomfort as he rubbed his hands over his thighs.

"Margaret and I formed a theory today and it involves Eloise," Ainsley explained reassuringly. "We can confirm it with the barkeep at the pub if we had a picture to show him."

Jonas stood suddenly and began pacing the room. "I try to keep my contact with that woman as minimal as possible. My only interest in her is to visit her father. Which, to my greatest pain, isn't often because she always seems to cling to me relentlessly when I do call." He turned

131

to Margaret as if suddenly remembering something. "And I never asked her to marry me. I don't care what she says."

"She's quite convincing," Margaret said. "I'll give her that."

Jonas looked disgusted at the thought of Eloise convincing anyone they were intended for each other. "That woman." He growled. "If she wasn't bound and determined to marry me, I'd say she is behind all this." With shaky hands, he pulled out a case from his breast pocket and offered Ainsley a cigarette. "But it doesn't make sense for her to drag her name in the mud alongside mine," Jonas said, the cigarette pressed gently between his lips. He struck a match and lit both his and Ainsley's cigarette with it.

"No, and that's why I'm confused." Ainsley pulled away his cigarette and licked his lips. "I need a photograph. She may be in on it in a way we least expect."

"I don't have anything we can use. Mr. Locke's wife was an avid photographer. I know such a photograph exists. They have many of them. I've seen them, but they would all be at the house."

"I'll get it."

They both turned at the sound of Margaret's unwavering voice.

"I'll go to her house. You say they have many. They'll not miss one small one."

Jonas shook his head with determination. "No."

"Why not? You can't be seen in public. If Peter goes she'll know something is amiss." She smiled before the next words left her lips. "I, however, have a standing invitation for tea."

"Margaret, this woman is not known for level-headed thinking," Ainsley said. "You were just speaking about her in the carriage. She can't be trusted."

"And now, neither can I." Margaret smiled. "I am aware of her calculated manner, but I won't stand idly by while Jonas is wrongfully accused of murder. If this woman had something to do with any of this then I want to be the one to expose her."

Jonas looked weary. "I'm not sure I approve this plan."

Margaret scoffed. "I'm not looking for your approval."

"I can send a note to her father asking for one," Jonas said, turning to Ainsley. "He might be willing to do as I ask."

"A letter from you will only encourage her." Margaret stepped forward, her tone forceful. "You want this woman to stop following you, don't you? To leave you alone?"

"I want peace. Yes."

"Then this is the only way. Peter, tell him I am right."

Ainsley rubbed the back of his neck. He hated the idea, but how else could he have the barkeep identify her? "How likely is she to lash out at Margaret?"

"I'd say it's fairly likely." Jonas gave them an uneasy look before taking a long pull from his cigarette. "In grade school she overheard me tell one of the other boys that I liked Moira's hair. She was a girl one year lower and she had the most beautiful auburn braid that almost reached her waist." Jonas smiled at the memory but his reverie was short-lived. "The next day in the yard, Eloise cut the braid off at the base of the neck and threw it in a pile of horse dung in the gutter."

"Oh, dear God. That poor girl." Margaret raised a hand to her mouth.

"Moira was mortified. When I confronted Eloise about it she laughed and said she could never live knowing I was meant for someone else. She said I belonged to her." Jonas closed his eyes. "I quickly learned to never like anyone or anything because she would always find a way to destroy it. I never wanted her to have that kind of control over me again. I've tried to limit my contact with her over the years but her father ... well, he's the reason I am who I am. I owe so much to him. Margaret, you have to understand—"

"I do. I don't begrudge your contact with him."

"I never discouraged her either, that fault is mine. I was afraid any rift between us would cause her father to end his funding of my education. I couldn't risk losing my only means of support, not with my mother so recently passed. But I swear, never in my life did I make any promises to her. Everything she has told you about us marrying is a complete fabrication, a delusion of her own making all these years." Jonas took another drag from his cigarette, his hand shaking slightly in frustration.

"Is she capable of murder?"

Margaret's question was greeted with silence. No one wants to believe someone they know is capable of such a heinous crime as murder.

Jonas licked his lips and looked her hard in the eyes. "I don't know, but I imagine it's possible."

Chapter 19

Margaret tried not to think about what she planned to do the next day as she readied herself for bed. If she was honest with herself she'd acknowledge her own apprehensions about going to Eloise Locke's home, the lion's den in many respects. There was no telling who might be present the next day when Margaret paid her a visit, but she secretly prayed she wouldn't be expected to be alone with the woman, especially after learning what she had done to Jonas and that poor girl with the long auburn braid.

She felt a chill rip right through her as the October winds rattled the small panes of glass that made up her windows. There was no place to light a fire, so before she undressed Margaret searched the room for extra bedding, anything she could throw over her bedclothes to keep her warm through what she expected would be another cold, restless night. She couldn't bring herself to ask Peter to exchange rooms, not when she had been so adamant that she would be fine in the maid's quarters.

Inside the chest at the foot of her bed she found two folded blankets of white, one felted and one knitted. Already her chin had begun to quiver against the cold. Hastily, she pulled the blankets from their place in the chest and threw them over the footrail of the metal bed.

PING!

Margaret stopped at the sound and realized it was something attached to the knitted blanket. A gemmed ring! Realizing the claws securing the gems in place were wrapped in the fibres of the blanket, she gently twisted the ring left and right until the piece of jewellery was free. She brought it to the light of her bedside lamp and saw that it was an emerald ring, with three tiny gems clustered together on a thin band of gold, a small trinket to some or a glorious collection of precious stones to others.

Margaret moved it around in the light but saw no

engravings or markings to indicate who the ring might belong to. It was definitely a woman's ring that could slide down all of Margaret's fingers except one. Could it belong to Molly, Mrs. Crane's kitchen maid? Margaret doubted the girl could afford such a piece. A gift, perhaps. Or pickpocketing spoils?

Margaret closed her eyes against such a negative thought. The events of the last year had made her distrustful and quick to assume the worst. Leaving the ring on her finger, Margaret searched the chest and looked for anything else that could help identify the owner. She found nothing but a piece of braided string. Now that she thought of it, Margaret hadn't happened upon anything in that room that belonged to the maid. If she didn't already know Mrs. Crane to be an honest woman, she'd doubt that a maid named Molly even existed.

The girl had likely just gotten married or decided to live out. She decided she would ask Mrs. Crane about it in the morning. With these thoughts on her mind, Margaret locked her door using the iron key, readied herself for bed, and hurriedly ducked beneath the covers. She turned out her lamp before pulling the blankets right up to her chin to stave out the cold. Slumber seduced her quickly and had nearly taken a solid hold when she heard the floorboards next to her bed creak. The sound was unmistakable, and recognizable as the very same cracks and groans that rang out as she went about the room.

Things are merely settling back into place, she told herself. Old houses always made their personalities known.

Another moan escaped the flooring, this time just next to her.

Margaret's eyes shot open. She could see nothing. Her attention immediately went to the corner of the room where the shadow had lurked the night before. She could make out nothing. Only able to rely on her sense of hearing, Margaret listened to the blackness of the room.

Another groan.

Something was walking straight toward her but she could see nothing. Her throat went dry, preventing her from calling out. She listened instead to the deafening silence and felt her own thumping heartbeat drumming rapidly in her head. After a time, she heard nothing. No new sounds rang out and nothing stirred in the darkness.

You're a fool, Margaret, she told herself.

She turned over in the bed and rested on her side, using her arms to cradle her head as it lay on the thin pillow. She felt the small, emerald ring press into her cheek and moved her hand slightly to ease the discomfort.

A hand grasped her shoulder.

Margaret let out a gasp and moved quickly to light her lamp. By the time the flame of her lamp was lit the room was empty and there was nothing to see. Everything was as it was when she first closed her eyes. The key to her room was on her bedside table just where she had left it.

❧ ❦

By morning Margaret had decided that Molly must have returned late at night and had been just as startled as she to find someone sleeping in her bed. Margaret expected to see someone with Mrs. Crane that morning but was surprised when she entered the kitchen and found the housekeeper alone.

"Good morning, Miss Margaret," Mrs. Crane said as she bent over a large pad of bread dough. "I trust you slept well." She did not look Margaret in the eye as she spoke and instead huffed and puffed over the great mound of flour, water, and yeast.

"Well enough," Margaret lied. In truth she hadn't slept much at all and kept waking at the slightest sounds and even went so far as to light her lamp numerous times to allay her fears when she believed someone was in the room with her.

Margaret inched toward the table where Mrs. Crane worked.

"Is Molly coming to help you today? I think I should like to meet her finally."

Margaret saw Mrs. Crane peek at her from behind a tuft of flour-laced curls that trailed down over her forehead. "I shouldn't say so ... no," Mrs. Crane answered hesitantly. "Is there something the matter with yer room?"

Margaret shook her head and was about to deny any

problems but stopped herself. She turned the ring around on her finger and felt the thin metal press into her skin. "Why would there be anything the matter with my room?"

Margaret saw Mrs. Crane shrug but the housekeeper still hadn't looked up from her task. The woman looked ill at ease and trembled slightly. "Mrs. Crane, is everything all right?"

With a great heave and exhale of breath, Mrs. Crane folded over the dough and began pressing it into itself with accelerating punches, each one more pronounced than the last.

"I told those boys not to invite ye to stay," she said with an sigh. "I told them we di'not have the room. The attic room is not suitable for either of ye but they were so insistent. The least I could hope for was for Dr. Ainsley to take the room, then I wouldn't have laid awake so long these last two nights worrying about ye."

"Worrying about us?"

"Aye." Mrs. Crane stopped suddenly and used the back of her floured hand to push away the curls that clung to her forehead.

Margaret spied tears pooling in the housekeeper's eyes. "Mrs. Crane?" She rounded the table and laid a hand on Mrs. Crane's arm. "My brother and I are very thankful for your hospitality. And I know Jonas appreciates our presence as well. The room is of little consequence to me—"

"It's Molly, my dear," Mrs. Crane said, breaking Margaret off suddenly. "She took her life in that very room not one month ago."

"Merciful heavens!" Margaret couldn't hide her surprise. She closed her eyes against the images that sprang to mind.

"Oh, it was awful," Mrs. Crane said, weeping into a handkerchief she pulled from her sleeve. "Just awful. You see, my dear, you cannot stay here. Ye and the doctor should go to yer hotel, as I said before." A new round of piteous cries escaped Mrs. Crane.

This explained much to Margaret. It's not that Mrs. Crane didn't want them as guests. She felt guilty for holding such a secret and felt that Margaret would be angry for being placed in a room with such a dark past.

Margaret took a breath. "Mrs. Crane, it breaks my heart to think that a young woman would feel so desperate about her situation as to take her own life, but I'm not afraid of sleeping in a room where such an event occurred. I cannot profess to be superstitious in any way. And, if it's all the same to you, I'd like to remain here for Jonas's sake so that I may ... what I mean to say is, so that *we* may provide him comfort and assistance at this time."

Mrs. Crane's fearful expression turned to awe as Margaret spoke. "Of course, you may stay, my dear, but ... Miss Margaret, are you sure?"

"Completely positive. Nothing you have said to me is frightening in the least." The new revelations had quite the opposite effect as now Margaret understood more about who the ring belonged to and why it may have been inadvertently left behind.

Margaret turned to leave but just before she reached the door she asked, "Mrs. Crane, does Molly have any living relatives here in Edinburgh?"

Mrs. Crane paused for a moment. "She has a sister, who's married down in Glasgow. I can fetch her address for ye." Mrs. Crane looked down to her dough-covered hands. The flour stretched nearly up to her elbows.

"It's all right," Margaret said. "I can collect it from you another time."

Mrs. Crane nodded in thanks and returned to her task.

As Margaret left the kitchen to seek out Peter, she told herself she would find the owner of the ring just as soon as she knew Jonas was no longer in danger of the noose.

Chapter 20

A hardened stare was the only thing needed to scare away the last lingering spectators who strolled down Heriot Row to have a look at the Professor of Murder's house. It was a show of strength Ainsley was more than willing to provide as he used a broom, metal dust pan, and a sack tucked over the sides of a crate to collect the last remaining bits of debris that littered the street in front of the house. Mrs. Crane had already said she would hire a boy from down the way to wash the windows of the grime. She tried to shoo Ainsley from his task but he would not budge.

Since before dawn he had had a nervous energy that kept him jittery and looking for something to do to ease his racing mind. The work had done wonders for his mental state. As the remnants of those hectic first days were cleared away he felt a sense of control over the situation even while other parts of him felt constrained by circumstance.

His spirits fell when Margaret slipped out the front door, tightening her shawl around her shoulders as the cold winds greeted her.

"I had hoped you wouldn't have to see this," he said, using the dustpan to scoop up the last bit of cabbage leaves. The smell was at least manageable thanks to the colder temperatures.

"Did you expect I would believe it was all just a bad dream?" she asked, standing at the top of the steps.

Ainsley shrugged. "Something like that."

He dumped the contents of the dustpan into the crate and then pulled the crate to the side of the steps along the railing.

"I think you should go to Professor Frobisher's funeral without me," Margaret said, bracing against a sudden gust of wind. "I want to get this business with Eloise over with so we can approach the barkeep this evening. We only have so much time before the trial."

"Are you sure you don't want me to come with you?"

Margaret shook her head. "If you go with me she will know something is amiss. She specifically said I should visit her when I bore of all the male company in this house. Your presence would definitely tear apart my pretenses."

The door opened and Jonas slipped out. "Margaret, you should get out of this cold."

Margaret dismissed his concern with a wave of her hand.

With the broom and dust pan in hand, Ainsley made his way back up the steps, taking in the image of his sister. She looked tired and out of sorts, not the least bit like her usual, glowing self. "Are you all right, Margaret? You don't look well."

"I'm experiencing a touch of nausea this morning, which is probably because I didn't sleep well last night," she said, looking him square in the eyes. "Perhaps if someone had told me a certain maid committed suicide in the very room offered to me I may have been prepared for her ghost to come for a visit."

"Slow down, what did you just say?" Ainsley reached out to her but she pushed his hand away. Ainsley turned to Jonas. "Did you know about this?"

"I tried to tell you both to switch rooms," Jonas said. "Perhaps then Peter could befriend the spectre and find out why she chose to end her life."

"I don't speak to them," Ainsley said incredulously. He squared his shoulders. "And it can't be helped if they speak to me."

"Did Peter tell you that's how we knew to come to Edinburgh?" Margaret asked Jonas.

Jonas shook his head.

"He saw you in front of our house." Margaret turned to Ainsley, who wished she hadn't brought it up.

"I thought that only happens with the dead?" Jonas asked.

"Apparently not."

Just the thought of what he had seen made him uncomfortable. The spectres themselves could not be controlled, nor could Ainsley control what his mind chose to see. He had only recently come to terms with the idea of witnessing the souls of the dead. He was not prepared to see the souls of the tormented as well.

Margaret used her hand to brush away something from Ainsley's sleeve. "You've less than an hour before the funeral and you smell like the pile of scraps in The Briar's kitchen garden. Go wash up." She touched the side of his face, drawing attention to the emerging whiskers. He felt something cold and metallic touch his skin. He grabbed her hand gently and pulled it away so he could see it. On her ring finger was a tiny gold band with three green gemstones clustered on the top.

"What's this?" He looked to Jonas, who shrugged.

Margaret pulled her hand away. "I found it in my room." She looked to Jonas. "I think it belonged to Molly. Mrs. Crane is helping me track down her sister so I can return it." She eyed the gems. "Right now I have more pressing concerns that need my attention." She raised her blues eyes to meet Jonas's.

Ainsley could think of a hundred reasons why Margaret should not call at Eloise's house but any protest from him would only serve to spur Margaret on all the more. She was tenacious, he'd give her that. He only hoped that her tenacity and strength of spirit was enough to see her through any repercussions that came their way because of it.

❧ ❦

The cemetery where Professor Frobisher was to be buried was west of Dean Village, not far from the neighbourhood where both Frobisher and Jonas lived. Ainsley had the carriage driver deposit him at the entrance gate, which allowed him a slow walk through the cemetery grounds before meeting up with the gathered mourners near the west wall. Mrs. Frobisher, in her hastily acquired widow's weeds, was surrounded by friends and family, who all doted upon her as if she were a child incapable of doing anything on her own. The widow herself seemed more interested in the birds that fluttered about in the trees hanging over her husband's grave than she was about the body of the man being committed to the earth.

Ainsley recognized a number of faculty members from

the university, many of whom nodded toward him as they passed.

"Dr. Ainsley."

"Dr. Ainsley."

Only one stopped when they saw him. "Good to see you, Dr. Ainsley." Dr. Fellowes extended a meaty, weathered hand at Ainsley and patted the side of his upper arm as they greeted each other. He took a place along Ainsley that offered the best advantage over the gathering. "It's unfortunate that we are to be reacquainted under such sad circumstances," Fellowes said, leaning in toward Ainsley's ear so no one would hear their conversation.

Across the crowd Ainsley spotted Giles, but the man pretended not to see Ainsley at all. Ainsley watched as Giles greeted other men from the faculty. He donned a sullen expression, shook hands, and spoke a few words with each of them. There was something in his manner, a willingness to set aside the tragedy before them so that he could profit from the newly vacated position. Ainsley's heart sank at the thought, wondering if Giles were capable of such manoeuvering. Could he be already vying for Frobisher's position?

"Had you worked with Professor Frobisher since graduation?" Fellowes asked, stealing Ainsley from his train of thought.

Ainsley shook his head. "I am employed in London for the most part."

Fellowes raised an eyebrow. "London, is it? My, my. Congratulations, young fellow. The man who did Frobisher in was from London, did you know?"

Ainsley shifted his stance and raised his chin reactively so that Fellowes would not see his discomfort.

"David ... Davis ... Davies!" The word came out in a determined whispered. Fellowes lowered his voice even further. "That's it. Dr. Davies. He had only been recently hired on by the college as well." He clicked his tongue. "Imagine being one of those devils on the hiring committee. Wouldn't want that decision on my conscience—"

"Can you point me to the doctor currently in charge of the morgue? Dr. Waters?"

Fellowes looked put out for a moment before regaining

his thoughts. "Yeah, he's that man down on the other side." Fellowes trailed off as he searched his memory. "Weren't you good friends with a man named Davies? You two were always playing each other for top marks. Imagine having the same last name as ..." Fellowes stopped.

Ainsley could almost see the grey matter behind the doctor's eyes making the connection between Ainsley's school chum and the man accused of murdering his colleague.

"If you'll excuse me, Dr. Ainsley." Fellowes made no attempt to explain his sudden departure.

Ainsley watched as he passed between a number of people before taking a stance on the opposite side of the gathering. It was then that Ainsley realized how all the other mourners kept a distance, preferring to stand further along the back than rub shoulders with him. As a known friend of the accused he was a pariah, allowed a wide berth for fear that murder and violence would spread like a disease.

The funeral was a long drawn-out affair. For an hour Ainsley and the others stood in the autumn cold as eulogy after eulogy was delivered. By the end Ainsley decided the man was as near a saint as anyone could expect, or at least that was how people chose to see him now that he had met such a grisly end. Ainsley doubted he was even half as good a doctor, friend, and neighbour as they all claimed. Ainsley knew he wasn't much of a husband. Mrs. Frobisher's indifference and his extramarital affair were proof enough of that.

Finally, the words of praise came to an end and the priest offered his final prayer. "Blessed be the God and Father of our Lord Jesus Christ, who has blessed us all with the gift of this earthly life."

The crowd thinned quickly at the end as mourners sought refuge from the biting winds. Ainsley went directly for Dr. Waters and was thankful to reach him before he could climb into his carriage.

"Dr. Waters, sir?"

The older gentleman turned. "Yes?" He sneered slightly when he saw it was Ainsley who commanded his attention.

"I was wondering if I may have a word."

"It's doubtful you can say all you wish to say in one word, young man."

Ainsley cringed at the pandering tone often received from teachers who viewed themselves better than nearly everyone else in existence.

"Yes, sir. What I mean to say is, May I have a few moments of your time?"

"Hop in, young man," Waters said, turning to pull himself into his carriage. "I haven't much more time than the carriage ride to the university will afford me."

Ainsley promptly did what he was told, thankful to gain Dr. Waters's undivided attention. "My name is Dr. Ainsley. I was a pupil at the college of which you now travel to."

"Yes." Waters leaned on his cane set in front of him and used both gloved hands to lean into it.

"I took the liberty of reviewing Professor Frobisher's body—"

"You did what, young man?" A vein pulsed on Waters's forehead as he lurched forward. "When was this? How dare you? Out of this carriage this instant." He tapped the inside of the door with the end of his cane.

"Allow me to explain. I am a morgue surgeon myself with a practice out of St. Thomas Hospital in London."

Waters tempered his outrage for a moment longer but eyed Ainsley with suspicion.

"My good friend stands as the accused in Professor Frobisher's murder."

"So you are friends with the ingrate too, eh. Take my advice, son, and distance yourself. Word will make its way south faster than the train that brings you home and once it does there won't be one door left open to you." He pulled on the door handle and popped open the carriage door.

"Sir, my friend is innocent."

"Professor Frobisher was brutally attacked!"

"Yes, I agree. It was a most heinous crime, but I seek to find the hand that did it, as I truly believe my friend, Dr. Davies, is innocent of all charges against him." Ainsley glanced to the open door and saw that the carriage was slowing down its pace and pulling up to the kerb. "Please, sir, I have no mind to convince you. I would just like a moment to discuss your findings further so that justice can be dealt swiftly yet truthfully."

The carriage stopped, but Dr. Waters remained silent for another moment as he regarded Ainsley.

The young doctor thought to plead his case further, but doing so could also jeopardize his chances of an agreeable outcome. In the end, Ainsley sat quietly, hoping the old doctor would see the sincerity in his features and allow him the meeting he sought.

"Very well." Waters snapped the carriage door shut. "I will speak only of what I know as a doctor, not of what I know as a colleague."

"That is all I require, sir."

Waters tapped his cane on the ceiling of the carriage. "Drive on." Only when the carriage moved forward, pulling away from the kerb, did Ainsley give himself permission to breathe.

Chapter 21

Passing through the shadows of Tron Kirk, Margaret made her way down High Street in Old Town. She told herself not to look at the piece of paper in her hand again, the one on which Jonas had written Eloise Locke's address. The words on the paper had been etched into her memory following the last twenty times she looked down at it. She knew the exact location by heart by then but only continued to look to the paper to allay her nerves.

She had not believed it when Jonas first wrote the words Blair Street. It was as if fate were taunting her with the memory of her would-be beau. She had told herself she had no interest in the man, not in any way beyond friendship, not even after he saved her life, but still he had continued to show up at her house in London, encouraged by her somewhat meddlesome Aunt Louisa. Thankfully, Jonas said nothing about the duke's son and Margaret's previous connections to him. When she left Jonas's house that morning he kissed her briefly on the forehead and wished her luck, something she insisted she would not need.

During her time in Edinburgh she had almost forgotten that such a complication to her life existed. She had been relatively happy in Jonas's company, despite his present circumstances. And now, standing below the street sign bearing the name of the man her family would wish her to marry, his face came to mind and she dared not smile. She knew that if Jonas were found guilty of the charges against him she would never recover. Now that Ainsley had aligned the Marshall family with that of an accused murder their last few society connections would dry up, along with any prospective marriage proposals as well. They'd be shunned. Not that Margaret would ever entertain the idea of marrying if Jonas went to the gallows. How could she tarnish his memory like that? How could she betray the love he had offered her? It would be one thing if he had denied their attachment and broken her heart. Under those circumstances there was a chance she could move on, but not now. She was locked in by her love and there was no escaping it. A judgement against Jonas was a judgement against her as well.

The pharmaceutical storefront where Jonas's adoptive father lived and worked occupied a corner storefront on Blair and South Bridge. The windows that faced out onto both streets displayed an assortment of large glass bottles and tin boxes. A balance scale was displayed prominently with dried herbs and a mortar and pestle on one side and a small placard with the words "Your body" scrolled on it on the other side. A young man of maybe fourteen was busy inside the window case, pouring bright green liquid into a glass jar that was nearly the same size as him.

When Margaret walked in, the tiny bell above the door signalling her arrival, she was surprised to find a number of patrons. The young man continued his work at the window while another, an older fellow nearly Margaret's age, stood behind the waist-high counter conversing with a female customer.

The room itself displayed countless jars and concoctions, all lined up and on display behind the counter. The counter had a flat surface but also served as a display case for items such as shaving kits, and household items like lye and carbolic soaps. The woman at the counter nodded her thanks to the clerk and moved toward the door.

"Can I help you, miss?" the gentleman behind the counter asked, turning his attention to Margaret.

Wondering if she was indeed next in line, Margaret glanced to the other patrons, who seemed happy to browse about, looking at scalp powders and brushes for the teeth.

"Are you ill? Something for sleep perhaps?"

Margaret was taken aback by his line of questioning. Was her restless night so very evident on her face?

She shook her head. "No, sir. I am looking for Miss Locke. She said I should call upon her during my visit to Edinburgh."

The man nodded, though he looked rather disappointed. "One moment, miss," he said, moving toward a door that led to the back of the shop. "I shall ring for her." He pressed a finger into a tiny knob in the wall at chest level. Margaret heard the faint sound of a bell ringing on the upper floors and instinctively looked to the ceiling.

"She will be down in a moment, miss."

Margaret nodded a thank you and then decided to take a turn about the shop while she waited.

"Do not fret, miss," the young boy said, jumping down from his window ledge in front of her. "Miss Locke will set you to rights. She always does."

Margaret stammered. "Oh, I'm not out of rights," she said with a tiny laugh. "I'm just visiting ... as a friend." The words had been hard to choke out but she had done it, rather successfully too, she was forced to admit.

The young boy and the man exchanged peculiar glances. "But your scar. Surely you'll be wanting to treat it so it's not so ... bold."

Margaret's hand went to her neck and collar and found that her silk scarf, one she had worn religiously and checked almost constantly, had been dislodged, most likely by the wind as she walked over.

"I could make a few suggestions to make it more inconspicuous, if you like," said the man behind the counter. "An ointment ought to return the skin to its natural ivory."

He surveyed the display case as Margaret drew near and then smiled when he found what he was looking for. "This ought to do it." He pulled a round, blue tin from a collection of others and presented it to Margaret with a flat palm.

"Belmare's Beauty Ointment," Margaret read.

"Uses your skin's natural pigment to conceal unsightly blemishes," he said, rhyming off the wording exactly as it was printed on the box.

The man rounded the end of the counter and proceeded to twist off the top of the tin. He placed a small amount on his middle finger. "May I?" he asked, nodding to Margaret.

Margaret gave a half-hearted nod and turned her head to the side. The cream was cold and greasy but the clerk was gentle as he applied the ointment. After a moment he stood back and smiled. He presented her with a mirror on a stand.

The ointment, which lightened the colour of the scar, did nothing to diminish the elongated bump in her skin, or the tinier bumps where the stitches had been placed.

"A few more applications and you won't remember it existed," the clerk said.

Margaret was doubtful but pulled a few coins from her reticule anyway, if only to appease the two eager salesmen. The man and the boy beamed with pride as she paid for her purchase and slid it into her bag.

A moment later footsteps could be heard marching down a set of stairs behind the storefront. In the doorway to the backroom appeared Detective Inspector Hearst with his bowler hat in his hands. He turned when he reached the storefront and then Margaret saw Eloise behind him.

"Thank you, Miss Locke. You've been very helpful with your fiancé's case." He replaced his hat and touched the brim as he passed Margaret. "Ma'am."

She didn't think he recognized her.

"Margaret!" Eloise flew across the room. "I'm so glad you have decided to come. After my meeting with that man you can be sure I am in need of some good chatter." She gestured for the back stairs but Margaret was watching the inspector, who stood outside on the pavement writing speedily in his notebook.

"What did the inspector want?" she asked, unable to take her eyes from the man who was determined to prove Jonas's guilt.

"He wished to know about Jonas, of course," Eloise said noncommittally. "Have no fear. I only said that if Jonas killed Professor Frobisher, then he must have had a good reason for it. My Jonas never does anything without cause."

Margaret worked hard to conceal her disgust. How could this woman, who professed to be his fiancée, speak of him in such a way? Did she not realize she was only helping to prove the case against him?

Margaret trailed Eloise into the back room but stopped short of the stairs that would take them to the Locke's living quarters.

"Do you not worry that your assistance may hinder Jonas's case?" Margaret asked.

Eloise's expression was flat even as she took in Margaret's words. "He either did what they say he did or he didn't," she said. "I'm afraid nothing can be done for it now."

"We have an obligation to him," Margaret said. She could feel the panic rising inside her and sincerely hoped it could not be heard in her voice. "We must see that his true character is known. We mustn't give them any reason to believe him capable."

"But we are all capable." Eloise's gaze burned into Margaret. She did not flinch or give any indication that she did not truly mean what she had just said. "Every last one of us is capable of murder given the correct circumstances." Her features alighted suddenly and she reached for Margaret's hand to coax her up the stairs. "Will you come meet Father?"

Margaret was so unnerved by Eloise's sudden change in demeanour that she didn't register her steps until she realized she was at the top of the stairs looking over a long hallway with an ornate bannister guarding the drop of the stairwell.

"We live on the upper floors," Eloise explained, as she adjusted the drapes of a very large window at the top of the stairs. "Father's workspace used to be downstairs but he so rarely ventures down anymore. We had all his equipment brought up here."

"Who oversees the shop?"

"Me, of course. Father taught me everything he knows."

Eloise led Margaret down the hall to a closed door, where she knocked gently. "Father?" She pushed the door in, revealing a large room filled with all manner of jars, tins, and boxes. Drying herbs hung from the rafters and bookshelves lined each wall, some filled with books but most displaying jars of various sizes, each marked with a white label and a handwritten word or two.

Mr. Locke sat in a chair near the window, a pair of half-moon spectacles perched on his nose and an array of mortar and pestles of varying sizes spread out on the table in front of him.

"Miss Margaret Marshall has finally come to see us," Eloise said, stepping out of the way.

Mr. Locke looked up briefly but quickly returned to his work. "Margaret, did you say?" he said in a croaky voice.

"Yes, Father, Margaret Marshall."

He raised his chin to peer at the dropper in his hand through his spectacles. "Forgive me for not coming to the door to greet you … This is a very delicate operation. I must get the measurements exact."

Margaret unwittingly held her breath as she and Eloise watched Mr. Locke deposit three drops of liquid into a slender vial. He slipped the dropper back in its originating bottle and pressed a cork stopper into the open end of the vial.

"I am working on a serum to alleviate pains of the stomach," he explained. He looked to Margaret over his half-moon spectacles. "You don't suffer from pains of the stomach, do you Miss Marshall?"

Margaret shook her head.

"Very well then," he said. "I shall have to find another willing subject." He regarded her sideways and gave a quick, playful wink.

"It's lovely to meet you, sir," Margaret said. "Jonas has told me so much about you and what you've done for him."

The man stopped his work suddenly and looked to her. "Jonas, did you say?"

"Yes, sir. My brother and I are in town—"

Mr. Locke's eyes darted to Eloise at Margaret's side. His disposition changed abruptly when he looked away. His eyes darted over his worktable as his shoulders sank. "The scoundrel. The mutt." Mr. Locke didn't bother to look at Margaret as he barked out the words with disgust.

"Certainly not," Margaret found herself saying. "He is the epitome of righteous character."

"That may have been true once," Mr. Locke said.

"It remains true now." Margaret did not mean to argue. Her words were more a reaction to her surprise than anything else. How could Mr. Locke, who had believed in Jonas's capabilities before anyone else had taken notice of him, suddenly decry him as unworthy? "You may no longer believe in him as you once did, but I will not be so quick to throw him to the wolves." Margaret realized her speech was as much for Eloise's benefit as it was for Mr. Locke's.

Eloise stepped between Margaret and Mr. Locke, her hands ushering her to back out the door. Margaret wouldn't allow herself to be pushed from the room. "Mr. Locke,

Jonas is innocent—"

"Not of what he's done to my daughter and our good name." The man abandoned his measurements and removed his spectacles, tossing them to his tabletop. "I put all I had into that man, even at the expense of my own daughter—"

"Father, there's no need to drum up the past."

"It's true! Had I known he'd turn out such a way ... well, I'd never have done all I did for him. Especially after what he's done to my poor Ellie." He stood then, something which appeared to cause great pain. To ease his movements, he leaned on the tables around him as he inched toward Margaret and Eloise. "Did you know he begged her to come to London last spring? When she showed up he refused to take her about and show her the city. He wouldn't introduce her to his friends. And then he sent her home crying. We all began to wonder if he'd ever set a wedding date, if he ever meant to follow through with his promise. Now I am just thankful that he never did take vows with my daughter."

Margaret found herself utterly confused. She could not find the words to come to Jonas's defence because she knew nothing about any such arrangement. As she understood it, Jonas had never made any promise to Eloise. The old chemist had been thoroughly poisoned against him.

"Father, please."

Mr. Locke ignored his daughter's pleas as he struggled to walk around his workroom. "He's not good enough for her! But Ellie, Lord bless her, still loves the man and won't break things off." He snatched a book from the shelf angrily before retracing his steps with it under his arm. "Now, I'm an old man and I never did see the connection between them. Night and day they are, but what does an old widower like me know about love? Bah!" He fell back into his wooden swivel chair and waved a dismissive hand. "The sooner this trial is done the better, then maybe our shop wouldn't be losing so much business." He slipped on his spectacles and tucked the curved arms behind his ears before turning his attention back to his work.

Eloise donned a saddened face and went to her father. He turned from her, waving off her concern, but she wrapped her arms around his shoulders and hugged him from behind anyway.

"Have no fear, Father," she said, her chin pressed firmly into the top of his head. "The business will recover." She leaned forward and kissed him on the cheek. "We will leave you to your work," she said, "and have tea in the parlour."

Margaret saw Mr. Locke lift his glasses from his cheeks so he could rub tears from under his eyes. She wondered if he suspected he had been lied to or if it was just easier to believe his own offspring even when the things she told him did not sound like Jonas's character at all.

"Come, Margaret," Eloise commanded as she passed Margaret and made her way to the hall.

Margaret didn't follow and instead took a step further into the room. "Sir, it may come to pass that all you have been taught to believe is proven false. It would be best for you to keep an open mind."

Mr. Locke appeared dumbstruck at the thought. His gaze was both sincere and defeated. He looked past Margaret to Eloise, and then back to his work. How often had be done that, Margaret wondered. How often had he dismissed his own judgement to side with his daughter, a woman who had proven herself unsteady and incapable of rational thought?

"Margaret?"

Margaret could feel the gentle tug on her sleeve at her elbow as Eloise tried to guide her away. Margaret met her gaze and found the woman happy, even after all her father had said. Her father's faith lay broken and Eloise found assurance in that. "Shall we take our tea now?"

❧　❦

Upon entering the parlour Margaret was reminded exactly why she had ventured to take tea with Eloise in the first place. The room was adorned with countless photographs and daguerreotypes, all of them framed in ornate tin and wood. Most hung from the walls but many were scattered about on the mantel, the tabletops, and over the piano in the corner.

Margaret's awe at the sight must have been evident on

her face. Eloise giggled slightly. "It was my mother, you see," she said. "She was an amateur photographer."

Margaret leaned in to one framed portrait and immediately recognized Eloise, her father, and a woman who must have been Eloise's mother. "I can see the family resemblance," Margaret said.

"Can you?" Eloise shrugged. "I thought my mother a rather plain woman."

Margaret found her nothing of the sort. She had long flowing hair that displayed near-perfect curls and a striking face with pale, alabaster skin. Margaret noticed a frame at the back of the table and thought she recognized the young boy in the image. Margaret scooped it up without thinking. It was Jonas at about ten years old with long, dirty hair and patches on his knees. A woman, in a plain dress of black, knelt next to him with a hand at his back and another at his stomach to hold the jittery boy still. Her hair was pulled back into a bun at the base of her skull. She looked embarrassed to be photographed but the boy was tickled and smiling broadly.

"I managed to convince Father not to get rid of this one," Eloise said, drawing close.

"Is this Mrs. Davies?"

Eloise nodded. "That's right. She was always so sickly. No pluck, if you ask me. My mother never understood why Father insisted we take them on, but he has a soft heart, you know."

Margaret ran her hand over the small frame and felt the cold glass. She wanted to take that little boy into her arms and shield him from his future. "When did Mrs. Davies pass away?" she asked, without taking her eyes from the image.

"I was twelve, which meant Jonas was thirteen."

"My goodness." Margaret resisted the urge to pull the frame to her chest and hug the boy and his mother. "May I take this to him? It may lift his spirits somewhat." She turned to Eloise, hopeful.

Eloise regarded her suspiciously before finally relenting. "All right, as long as you tell him it was I who suggested it."

Margaret had no intentions of lying but smiled all the same to keep Eloise happy.

"Shall we fetch the tea?" Eloise asked.

"Sounds lovely."

Once left alone Margaret instantly set about to find a recent photograph of Eloise that could be shown to the barkeep. It had to be small, Margaret noted, and less likely to be missed. There was one on the mantel but its prominent place meant its absence would be noticed. Margaret had nearly circled the room entirely before she came to a photograph and frame that could be easily slipped into her reticule. The picture was a few years old but it would have to do. Hurriedly, Margaret pulled at the strings of her bag and listened for any sound that would indicate when Eloise was returning. The frame was almost safely stored away when a floorboard in the hall creaked.

"Would you like a bite to eat as well?" Eloise asked at the door.

Margaret turned, using her body to hide her open reticule on the tabletop. "Sounds lovely." She held the frame tightly behind her so it would not fall from the opening of her reticule and clatter to the floor.

"What have you found?" Eloise stepped through the doorway and came toward her. Margaret struggled to pull the fabric of her bag over the edges of the frame. The drawstring dangled and she could not get a good enough grip on it to close the top of the bag.

"Oh … well, nothing really," Margaret said. "I was just looking at more of these memories."

Eloise came alongside the table, forcing Margaret to turn. She felt her reticule slip from the edge of the table but caught the drawstring just in time. With her one hand held behind her back, Margaret sheltered it with the folds of her skirt.

"Is that little girl you?" Margaret asked, using her free hand to point to a daguerreotype.

The emeralds of Molly's ring caught the light as Margaret reached forward. She saw Eloise's eyes focus on them. Margaret should have removed it before coming. On her ring finger it looked like an engagement ring, something Eloise would believe most likely came from Jonas. Margaret braced herself for the inevitable questions. In the end, Eloise said nothing.

Instead, the woman waved a dismissive hand at the

framed photograph and turned from the table. "Oh, I hate that one," she said. "It reminds me of the sister that was never meant to be."

Margaret raised an eyebrow in curiosity while trying to push the frame behind her back into her reticule with one hand.

"Mother had three still births, you know. All girls." Eloise's face hardened as the memories returned. "Have you ever held a stillborn baby, Margaret?"

The very suggestion startled her. "No. How dreadful."

"Mother made me hold all three so I could have my picture taken with them," Eloise said. She turned in place. "They are here somewhere. I feel them watching me sometimes."

Suddenly, Margaret felt as if she would be sick and resisted the urge to clamp her hand over her mouth.

"You've gone pale, Margaret," Eloise said. "Please do sit down."

Still holding her reticule behind her with the picture frame sticking out of the opening, Margaret followed her to the nearby chair. She carefully sat down and used the chair to conceal her spoils. Eloise left the room, giving Margaret only a few moments to stuff the rest of the frame into her reticule, before Eloise returned a moment later with a tray for tea.

"Here," she said, placing the tray on a nearby table and pouring a cup. "Peppermint settles the stomach."

Margaret could smell the peppermint and desperately wanted something to ease her discomfort. She raised the teacup to her mouth but stopped short of actually taking a sip. Jonas's warnings echoed in her head. The woman was not to be trusted.

"Drink up," Eloise said, using two fingers on the bottom of Margaret's cup to encourage her to drink it.

A horrible feeling had struck her. Her hand shook as the images of the stillborn babies triggered a deep-seated worry in Margaret's mind. Something repressed and clawing to come out.

"Margaret? Is something the matter?"

Margaret lowered the teacup to the saucer and placed it on the table. "Do accept my apologies," she said. "I must be going. I suddenly don't feel so well."

Eloise gave a look of dismay, and glanced to the teacup before donning a devilish smile. "Of course. I'll have John wave down a carriage for you." She moved to stand but Margaret stopped her.

"No, that's quite all right. I can manage." Margaret stood and walked to the table to retrieve the picture of Jonas and his mother. "Thank you for this," she said, hugging it to her.

She did not wait to be excused and simply made her way to the back stairs. She could feel her heartbeat quickening and knew she just had to get out to the street, to safety. She heard Eloise coming down the stairs behind her. Margaret nearly made it to the front door of the shop before Eloise grabbed her arm and pulled her back slightly.

"Bundle up against that wind, Margaret," she said sweetly. She raised both of her hands to Margaret's scarf and adjusted it at her collar. If Eloise saw Margaret's scar beneath the folds of her scarf she said nothing. "It's getting chilly out there." When she pulled away Eloise smiled.

"Thank you, Miss Locke," Margaret said, forcing her next words and praying they sounded sincere. "You are too kind."

Chapter 22

Dr. Waters gave Ainsley a severe look from across the rocking carriage. Despite his agreement to speak about the case, any insight he offered came out slowly, which required a great deal of effort from Ainsley to ask pointed and specific questions.

"We both agree Professor Frobisher was stabbed," Ainsley said.

Waters nodded.

"I counted ten times," Ainsley said.

An amused smile touched the edges of Waters's lips. "Smart man. I can see now why you were recommended for your degree," he said, his amusement morphing into a scowl.

Ainsley chose to ignore the professor's sarcastic remark. "Yet your report mentioned loss of blood at one pint. I thought perhaps this was an oversight. Could you have meant to write seven pints?"

Waters shook his head. "No, young man. There wasn't a sufficient amount of blood at the scene to make that claim. I am not in the business of supplying false details."

"Ten times, though," Ainsley said. "Frobisher was stabbed ten times."

"Yes."

Enough bodies had found their way to Ainsley's morgue in London for the young surgeon to know how the human body responds to wounds such as Professor Frobisher's. Ten stab wounds to the abdomen would have resulted in an extreme loss of blood, not only staining his clothing but pooling around any nearby surfaces. Even as a body lay unconscious the blood will still seep from the wounds, as any liquid would once containment has been compromised.

"How is that possible?" Ainsley's words came out in the quiet tone of contemplation. He wasn't being quarrelsome and it seemed Waters understood this.

Waters shrugged and glanced to the window as the

university came into view. "The body is a mysterious machine," the professor said unapologetically.

The carriage came up alongside the kerb and Waters was quick to head for the door. "I'm sorry for the predicament of your friend, Dr. Ainsley," he said, as he heaved himself from the confines of the carriage. "But those are the facts of the case."

Ainsley found himself not so willing to accept that as an answer. "Could Frobisher's body have been killed elsewhere?" he said quickly before the professor had time to move on.

Judging by the look of puzzlement on Waters's face, it was clear the possibility had not occurred to him. Ainsley shuffled along the seat and came to the doorway to look Waters in the eye.

"If Frobisher was moved from the site of his murder to his office would that explain the lack of blood at the scene?"

Waters licked his lips, a realization donning on him as they looked each other in the eye. "Follow me, Ainsley," he said. "You've reminded me of something."

Dr. Waters led Ainsley to a pair of doors at the rear of the infirmary and then down the cement steps to the morgue. Cecil wasn't there, thank goodness, but Rebecca was. She sat on a high stool at a table next to the entrance doors, a file open in front of her, a pencil in hand. She straightened her posture when Waters and Ainsley entered.

"Miss Stewart, fetch me Frobisher's file."

Rebecca's eyes flashed toward Ainsley before she hopped from her stool and went for an adjoining room.

Waters removed his hat and slid his arms from his coat and hung them both from a pair of hooks along the wall.

"It is possible Frobisher was moved," Waters said at last. He turned to face Ainsley squarely. "What you said just now at the carriage sparked my memory."

Before Ainsley could ask for details, Rebecca returned and presented the file to Waters. The old professor grunted and waved for her to return to her other work. Before she left them Ainsley saw her resentment deepen as the professor turned his back to her.

"He was stabbed ten times, yes ..." Waters opened the file and skimmed his notes. "But six of them looked odd to me when I first looked over them. There was less coagulated blood gathered at the site of the wound." He flipped over the page and pointed to the human body outline sketch where four wounds were indicated on the stomach. "These ones presented the most damage. This is where the most blood was gathered."

"The killer hit Frobisher there first," Ainsley said.

Waters nodded and then he pointed to the other wounds that were separate from the main cluster of entry points. "These ones appear more haphazard and had far less blood clotting inside the wound and on Frobisher's clothes."

"Is it possible Frobisher died because of these four wounds alone?"

"Yes." Waters shook his head and let out a deep breath. "I hate to admit it, Dr. Ainsley, but it is possible my friendship with Frobisher and disgust for what happened to him made me overlook the details." He pressed his lips together and rolled his knuckles on the tabletop.

Ainsley noticed Rebecca had shuffled toward them and was looking down at the paper as well. "But if Professor Frobisher died because of those four wounds, why would the killer inflict six more?" she asked.

Ainsley studied the image as he thought. "Because these were to kill Frobisher, these were done to put the blame on Jonas. They were inflicted after Frobisher's body was moved to his office."

"These were done with Dr. Davies's surgical knife," Waters said, following Ainsley's line of thought. "These could have been done with any knife."

Ainsley flipped the page back. "In your report you say it was all done with the same knife."

"Ah, I said 'it is *probable*' they were inflicted by the same knife. I say nothing with absolute certainty." Waters laughed nervously. "I could not determine the type of blade used from these wounds. They are too close together and involve too much movement up and down. As you can see, I couldn't establish proper measurements because of the elasticity of the skin. I was only able to conclude the murder weapon was Davies's surgical knife because of these two wounds." He flipped the page over and used two fingers to indicate two wounds on either side of the torso.

"This one punctured the liver and I was able to get most of my measurements from that."

"That makes sense, though," Rebecca cut in, pushing her way between the two male doctors. "The murderer staged the scene to make suspicion fall on Dr. Davies. He'd discard the real murder weapon and use Davies's knife for these ones." She pointed to the diagram as she spoke.

Ainsley felt a pain behind his eye as he thought this through and rubbed his forehead. "We can determine that Frobisher was killed somewhere other than his office; that would explain why his state of rigor mortis was so advanced. He wasn't killed that morning."

"Dr. Ainsley, I think it's highly likely, given this new information"—the professor let out a disparaged breath— "that Professor Frobisher was killed sometime the day before his body was found." Waters shook his head in disbelief as he looked over the notes. "And his body had most likely been moved."

Ainsley lifted his gaze to Waters. "Are you willing to testify in court regarding this?"

The older surgeon nodded, with a newfound determination. "Yes, I can explain it as best as I can." He closed his eyes. "I cannot believe I nearly allowed Davies to hang for the sake of my carelessness."

"Do not blame yourself. There is a murderer here who is ultimately responsible for all this."

Waters nodded. "I'll make an amendment to my report," he said, folding up the file and tucking it under his arm. "It's a good thing that you thought to speak with me, Dr. Ainsley. Inspector Hearst comes later this afternoon to discuss my findings."

Ainsley wondered whether such discoveries were enough to free Jonas from guilt. Standing in the centre of the infirmary morgue, his mind played with the circumstances of Frobisher's death. Would the courts and the public accept the fact that Jonas was innocent without having another place to lay blame?

"Don't forget to point out one important thing, Dr. Waters," Ainsley said just before the doctor left the room.

"Yes?"

"The wounds that killed Frobisher were administered

from the front. The professor knew his attacker and had no reason to fear him."

A sober look blanketed Waters's features before the old man nodded and turned from them both. "I'll have this set to rights, Ainsley," he said, waving the file in the air as he walked away. "Have no fear."

Everything Ainsley did of late, however, had been instigated by fear. Fear for Jonas. For Margaret. And for himself. He could not in good conscience allow such a travesty of justice. But was it enough, he wondered, to see Jonas free from suspicion?

"Good work, Dr. Ainsley," Rebecca said from beside him. She was slipping on a tattered coat. "You've proven persistence pays off in the end."

Ainsley shrugged. "I could not live with myself if I did not try. Jonas does not deserve such slander to his good name."

Ainsley saw a sober look flash over Rebecca's face as she buttoned her coat and adjusted her collar.

"How very true," she said, turning to pull a leather satchel from the desk where she had been working.

"It must be difficult working alongside so many men," Ainsley said as he turned for his own coat. He saw a nervous smile wash over her. She was quick to turn away, lowering her gaze to the floor.

"I saw the look you gave Dr. Waters earlier," he explained, taking a step toward her.

She gestured to her workstation, prominently placed amongst the bodies of the dead. The smells must be ghastly in the summers and the cold of the winter would be nearly unbearable. "This is the only way they will allow me to work in medicine," she said. She reached over and folded up a portfolio before tucking it inside her desk. "They pretty much ignore me unless there is tea to be fetched." She turned to face him and then glanced to the office door where Waters had disappeared. "Those were the most words he had ever said to me in a single conversation."

"You side with Dr. Davies then, regarding the admittance of women?" Ainsley asked.

Her features alighted at the thought of women attending lectures freely. "There are many men who are intimidated by the presence of a strong female, those who would see us wither away in poverty than allow us to attain meaningful employment so that we may support ourselves and our loved ones. I would like to think those types of men are few but the reality is the opposite. I've learned as much while working here."

"What do you mean?"

"I've been told countless times that I should try for a nurse," she said. "Fetching tea and copying reports pays a slightly lower wage than mopping up vomit and bandaging festering wounds. Given the choice, Dr. Ainsley, which would you choose?" She glanced about, taking in the sheet-covered bodies. "In truth, relegating me to a mere nurse has more to do with making the doctors around here more comfortable. They behave differently when they notice a female has entered the room. They accuse me of wanting to live like a man but in actuality it's them who don't want to behave like gentlemen." She let out a breath and turned her face away. "Pardon me, doctor, I forget who I am speaking with sometimes." She turned to her desk to gather a small stack of books, taking care to keep her head bowed.

"No, don't apologize," Ainsley said, his mind giddily gathering a thought. "You may be able to help me."

She regarded him cautiously.

"You have been witness to things at the infirmary, things others may not know."

She waited, unable to maintain eye contact.

Ainsley glanced to Dr. Waters's office to ensure they were alone. "I've been told Frobisher was unfaithful to his wife. I thought perhaps—"

Her expression had changed from apathy to angst before Ainsley had even finished his sentence. "Whoever Professor Frobisher was involved with it certainly wasn't me! How dare you accuse me of such a thing?" She hugged her books to her chest and turned quickly to leave the room.

"No, wait!"

Ainsley followed her and was able to stop her before she reached the stairs, pulling back on her arm gently. She shook off his grasp and hit him back with the full force of the books in her hands.

"What in God's name are you insinuating?" She stepped toward him, closing the gap as he took a step back. "The

164

only reason a woman would work in a place like this is if she's having relations with someone? Is that the only thing you men can think of?"

"No, no. Of course it isn't." Ainsley let out a breath and allowed his shoulders to sink. "I only ask because ..." He stopped himself. "Because you are the only person in this building who will give me an honest answer." He ran a hand through his hair. "Men are more likely to protect other men. They will not admit the weaknesses of their sex. Many of them won't even recognize it as a weakness."

Her stance softened a bit at his words.

"You've learned many things while working in the medical field," Ainsley continued, "and so have I. I'm just trying to save my friend from the gallows. I am not making any statements either way about women in medicine."

Rebecca hugged her books closer to her chest. "I can say with near certainty that Frobisher would never lie with a woman who wasn't his wife. That's all I can tell you." For a moment it looked as if she would leave. "We need more men like Jonas Davies, not less," she said. "He does not deserve the accusations against him." Rebecca glanced back to the morgue before meeting Ainsley's gaze solidly. "Will you tell him I said that?"

Ainsley hesitated. "I will if you would like me to."

She nodded timidly and said nothing more before jogging the rest of the way up the steps.

Ainsley lingered for a moment at the bottom of the stairs, watching her skirt then boots disappear into the upper levels of the hospital.

It was entirely within the realm of possibility that Frobisher's maid had been wrong. Frobisher could have found himself so engrossed by his work and unable to pull himself away at times. Such dedication hardly made the man unfaithful. Many men considered themselves married to their work. Ainsley had pictured his own future in such a way, before he met his love. It would certainly explain why Frobisher was found in his office. If he was such a man that room was the most likely place where Frobisher could be found when not at home. Any perpetrator would know this, and it explained why anyone would return Frobisher's body there.

Ainsley emerged out into the light of the afternoon and hunched over against the wind. On the path, he passed a group of three young men rushing to another building and huddling in a similar fashion. Ainsley stopped after they passed. He found himself turning in place, taking in the image set before him: countless men all heading in different directions but all joined together for a common purpose.

What had Rebecca said? Frobisher would never lie with a woman who wasn't his wife. He wouldn't have to lie with a woman ... If Frobisher was having an affair, there was a possibility he was having it with another man.

While the realization should have been empowering, it actually had the opposite effect on Ainsley. Standing in the biting cold, he suddenly realized that he hadn't exactly narrowed down his pool of suspects. In actuality, he had quadrupled it.

Chapter 23

Ainsley arrived at the offices of Humphry and Humphry with convoluted thoughts but hope in his heart. He was certain the information he and Dr. Waters had discovered would be enough to cast doubt on any evidence against Jonas. Ainsley wished they had irrefutable proof but was just happy to be on the right track.

During his walk over he had decided to not worry about the identity, or the gender for that matter, of Frobisher's lover. At least not right then. Instead, he resolved to focus on the evidence that would prove Jonas's innocence, even if they couldn't identify the true killer. He only hoped Margaret had been successful in getting a photograph of Eloise.

The distracted clerk at the front desk directed him up to Samuel's office but did not accompany him. Ainsley peered around the door to Samuel's small office, a broad smile on his face, but found the chair behind his friend's desk empty.

A conversation in a nearby room pulled Ainsley back into the hall. He recognized Samuel's voice amongst the handful of others and followed the sounds two doors down. He rapped his knuckle on the door, which sat ajar, and pushed it open another few inches when the men in the room fell silent. There were three men in total, Samuel, Thomas, and another man who Ainsley recognized as Samuel's father, the other partner of Humphry and Humphry.

"Excuse me," Ainsley said, spotting Samuel just a few feet from the door. "Samuel, I may have found something of interest to our case."

Samuel's expression sank when he saw it was Ainsley. He quickly turned from the others and ushered Ainsley back into the hall.

"Peter—"

"Forgive me," Ainsley said, not allowing Samuel to finish. "I found something and I thought I should bring it to you straightaway. Dr. Waters is revising his report on Frobisher's death. More than half the wounds were inflicted after Frobisher expired."

"He's revising his report?"

Ainsley saw the doubt in Samuel's face.

"How much convincing did it take?" Samuel asked.

Ainsley regarded him, confused. "He mentioned it himself when I sought clarification."

Samuel glanced to the door nervously. "I don't see—"

"We believe, Waters and I, that Frobisher was moved from the original crime scene to Frobisher's office in an effort to cover up the true murderer's identity and set up Jonas. This explains why the estimated time of death doesn't match with the Edinburgh Police's timeline of events. Why are you looking at me like that? At the very least, this casts doubt on the case against Jonas."

The door opened again and Samuel's father stepped out.

"Peter, this is my father, Mr. Humphry. He's just returned from Glasgow."

A look of trepidation overtook Samuel's gaze during his introduction.

Ainsley outstretched his hand to William Humphry and offered a firm handshake. "Good day, sir," he said, channeling the fortified diplomacy Ainsley's own father had been known for. "I was just telling your son about some new evidence that may help our case tremendously."

The older gentleman, red-haired and lean, lowered his chin and cast a wary eye over Ainsley. "You should save your explanations for my next available appointment." He pulled out a gold pocket watch and popped open the cover. "Which won't be today, unfortunately. Have my clerk downstairs schedule you in for some time next week." Mr. Humphry gave a flat-mouthed smile and slid between them.

Ainsley looked to Samuel. "I don't understand."

"He's taken me from the case," Samuel explained in a hushed tone.

"What? But why?"

"As soon as he heard you were the one behind it, he wanted to drop both you and Jonas without notice." Samuel glanced over Ainsley's shoulder as if to make sure his father had gone. "I convinced him to take it on, for

Jonas's sake, even if I can't be involved." His gaze met Ainsley's squarely. "I'm sorry, Peter. That's the best I can do."

Ainsley could sense there was something more behind the man's sudden decision, something Samuel was not telling him. "What was his objection to my name?" he asked. He wondered if it had to do with the scandal of his mother or the recent calamity of his father's condition. There was enough in his recent past to make even the most steadfast friend doubt Ainsley's respectability.

Folding in his lips, Samuel hesitated and his eyes danced about as he tried to find the words to explain. "You've never been in his favour, Peter, so let's stop pretending. Ever since first year, he's bemoaned my friendship with you, but it was that incident involving the apothecary that he objects to the most."

As soon as Samuel said the words the related images flooded to the forefront of Ainsley's mind. It was nearly the end of the second year when, bolstered by drink, Ainsley hatched a plan that he, Samuel, and Jonas should help themselves to some Turkish Opium in the apothecary's stores. Ainsley had assured them they would not be discovered as he had been trusted with the key for some task by one of the professors earlier in the week. They pilfered only a small amount, with the hopes it would not be missed, and went to the morgue to continue drinking. Within an hour Samuel was throwing up. At first, Ainsley and Jonas laughed as their friend emptied the contents of his stomach over the cement floor. It wasn't long, though, before they realized that Samuel was in medical distress, a reaction caused by the inexcusable amount of alcohol they had consumed and the medication they had stolen.

Ainsley remembered the panic he felt, the feeling of hopelessness as Samuel tried to crawl away from the pain that was wreaking havoc on his body. Still in the early stages of their training, neither Jonas nor Ainsley trusted themselves to treat him on their own.

"We have to take him to the infirmary," Ainsley had said once he realized how much danger his friend was in.

"They'll know what we did," Jonas answered soberly. He wasn't against the plan. He was merely saying aloud what they both knew to be true. If they didn't take Samuel to see a doctor, he would die, they knew that much. There was no debate.

They unceremoniously removed one of the cadavers from a nearby stretcher and coaxed a weakened Samuel onto it before racing up the flight of stairs and down the hall, calling for assistance the entire way.

Ainsley closed his eyes to block out the memory of it but quickly realized these embarrassments from his youth would not cease to exist just because he willed them so.

All three of them had narrowly escaped expulsion. All three of them had been the subject of ridicule by faculty and classmates alike. But only one of them had a wealthy family fortune to fall back on if their scholarly ambitions fell through. The situation had been far more dire for Jonas and Samuel than it ever had been for Ainsley.

If the younger Ainsley had been aware of his wealthy privilege, the privilege that allowed him to take bigger risks and not fear serious consequences, he suppressed it easily. To the older Ainsley, the man who now stood firmly in adulthood, the contrast was so striking it nearly knocked him from his feet. He had been the one who beckoned them to join him, the one who guided all their misadventures, the one who would suffer the least amount of consequences should their folly prove disastrous.

"Is this why he has refused to name you partner?" Ainsley asked.

Samuel's jaw clenched but he made no attempt to answer.

Without explanation, Ainsley turned in place and marched down the hall.

"Peter." Samuel followed him. "Peter!"

Ainsley ignored him and was glad he was already four paces ahead. He found Mr. Humphry's office at the end of the hall. A rectangular, brass plaque, etched with the name William Humphry, signaled that he was at the right door. Ainsley went in without knocking.

"Sir," he said, as soon as he spied Mr. Humphry at the bookshelf. "A word with you, if I may?"

Mr. Humphry looked past Ainsley to the door, his expression hardening at the intrusion. "Like I said, you'll have to make an appointment."

Ainsley ignored his words. "I am aware of your contempt for me, sir," he said. "I do not blame you."

Mr. Humphry raised his eyebrows. "Samuel." He nodded toward his son, who stood at the door. "Have your friend removed from the premises."

Ainsley felt a gentle, reluctant hand slide under his arm. He easily sidestepped and pulled his arm free. "Sir, I regret that your son has been slandered as a direct result of my actions." Ainsley felt his heart quicken and his throat tighten.

"Peter …"

Ainsley ignored Samuel's plea. "There was a time when I drank too much and cared too little. My family's position in society allowed arrogance to develop inside me unfettered, a belief that I could do anything without recourse. I was blind to the fact that this wasn't the case for my friends." Ainsley stole a glance to Samuel. "Any misdeeds perpetrated by your son were most assuredly instigated by me. He should not be punished for my reckless behaviour."

Mr. Humphry squared his shoulders to Ainsley and regarded him thoughtfully.

"I'm sure your son and brother have alerted you to my parentage. The very thing I told myself I despised was what I used to avoid my responsibilities. I don't blame you for your reluctance to help me. In fact, I know I don't deserve it. But Jonas, he is a good man. A far better man than I will ever be, and he doesn't deserve to have his name slandered in such a way, not when he has worked so hard."

The room fell silent. Neither Ainsley nor Samuel dared to move as Mr. Humphry slowly lowered the book in his hand to the desk. Ainsley could tell the older gentleman was turning Ainsley's words over in his head.

"That was an impassioned speech, young man," Mr. Humphry said at last, removing his glasses. "But I'm not entirely sure what you are looking for me to do."

Ainsley glanced over his shoulder to look at his friend. "I need Samuel. He has to work this case."

Mr. Humphry chuckled at Ainsley's words. "I do not understand your devotion." The older man licked his lips as his gaze shifted to his son. "I trust you have seen the state of his office. It hardly resembles that of a solicitor of any worth."

"That is only because you insist on squeezing me into a nine-by-nine coat closet," Samuel inserted, before adding a quick "sir" out of respect. His eyes shifted to Ainsley and then back again. He squared his shoulders and lifted his chin. "Perhaps if I were allowed proper desks, cabinets, and shelves, as you and Uncle are afforded, I may impress you—"

"You will never impress me."

The mood of the room, which had only been moderately tense, crashed at Mr. Humphry's words.

"It will take a miracle to impress me at this point." Mr. Humphry placed his spectacles on the top of his desk and slipped his hands into his trouser pockets. "Of all the sons born to me, why was it you who survived?" He regarded Samuel with the hardened feelings of a man heartbroken and floundering. He'd regret his words before long, Ainsley knew this. But in that moment the man seethed with aggression and rage, not necessarily at Samuel but at the world, a world in which promising baby sons met an untimely end and teenage boys rarely met the high expectations of their fathers.

"I had three sons, did Samuel ever tell you that?" Mr. Humphry asked, his attention on Ainsley. "One died in infancy, another drowned at eleven. And yet somehow, by some miracle, Samuel is to be my namesake. My legacy."

Ainsley could see Samuel shrink back, beaten down by the disapproval of his father. It was a calculated tactic that was developed by him at an early age, a method that would keep the peace, but only for so long. Samuel would never meet the approval of his father, not while the old man conjured images of faultless sons who never made it to adulthood.

Samuel reached for Ainsley's arm and gestured for the door. "We should leave," he said, quietly. "I'll help you find another firm."

But Ainsley couldn't bring himself to move. He stood between father and son, two men blinded to each other's pain just as Ainsley and his own father had been before the man was confined to bed and a wordless existence.

"I pity you, sir," Ainsley said at last. "I pity you and all the men like you who refuse to see the potential in their own child. While you mourn the loss of two children, a third lives on subjected to your cynicism and scorn. I had a father like you—"

"That is quite enough, Mr. Marshall—"

Ainsley ignored him even as Mr. Humphry moved toward him. "My father was a man so bolstered by his authority that he never fathomed a day when he would rely upon his children for his very existence."

Mr. Humphry took him up by the arms and began pushing him for the door. Samuel came to Ainsley's aid but only to ease his exit. Despite the two of them entreating Ainsley to leave, he struggled. Their faces inches from each other Ainsley forced Mr. Humphry to look him in the eyes.

"Have you heard the Earl of Montcliff's misfortune? How he can neither eat nor bathe on his own. How his every wish must be interpreted, guessed at by those around him. This once admirable man of the House of Lords, who can neither speak nor write, has been reduced to a shadow of who he once was. You've heard of his fate?"

Ainsley felt Mr. Humphry's grip loosen as he spoke.

"This is my father, the man who rejected me. I would never wish his fate upon anyone but perhaps I would make an exception for you, Mr. Humphry, especially if you insist on punishing Samuel for something done nearly five years ago."

The man, lost in his own thoughts, did not immediately release Ainsley. Finally, he was able to step back and adjust his collar and jacket on his shoulders. "My apologies, Samuel," Ainsley said. "Had I known what I know now I'd never have insisted on cultivating so much trouble."

Samuel took a step back to reveal his uncle at the door. Thomas cleared the way as well to allow Ainsley more room to pass. "I think you should go," Samuel said.

Ainsley did not protest and started for the door.

"Wait." Mr. Humphry's baritone voice merely added to the tension.

Ainsley stopped.

"Why must it be Samuel?" Mr. Humphry asked. "Why my son?"

Ainsley looked to Samuel. "Because no one else would ensure Jonas gets a fair trial, not like Samuel could. It has to be him, because he knows Jonas is innocent and I know he will work as hard as I have been."

Mr. Humphry's gaze shifted back and forth between Ainsley and his son.

"I do not argue for my sake. I have used up all my second chances. This is for Jonas, who no more deserves these accusations against him than Samuel would. They are both innocent of their supposed crimes."

The slightest of smiles touched Samuel's lips. There was a long pause, long enough for Ainsley to question the effectiveness of his argument.

"Mr. Marshall—"

Ainsley stood tall.

"You are in the wrong profession," Mr. Humphry said, his features stoic. "You should have been a lawyer."

Chapter 24

It was some time before Margaret's heartbeat returned to a reasonable pace. She'd made it to St. Giles' Cathedral before she realized the panic she was in wasn't abating. She couldn't explain why she reacted in such a way other than to say there was something dreadfully foreboding about that place and about Eloise in particular. Aunt Louisa would have told her it was her women's intuition, the uncanny ability females had at picking up relatively unnoticeable things.

Margaret paused at the foot of the cathedral steps and leaned against its stone wall. She looked about her before lifting her reticule. Molly's ring caught the light and her heart sank. Eloise had certainly seen it and there was no telling what conclusions she would make regarding it. Margaret opened the drawstrings of her reticule, pulled the ring from her finger, and tossed it inside.

Then, to settle her nerves, she verified that she still had the framed picture she needed to show the barkeep. Sure enough, it was there. Margaret felt a great sense of relief at having done her duty. The discomfort she felt had not been for naught.

There was a flutter in her stomach and she could feel the tightness beneath her corset. Without thinking Margaret touched her lower abdomen over the folds of her skirt. The image of Eloise's dead sister came to the forefront of her mind. A tiny newborn snuffed of life before it had entirely been granted. Margaret closed her eyes and willed the image away. A tear slipped from the corner of her eye.

It had been nearly three months since her courses but she hadn't thought much of it until that moment. And then a panic overtook her as the realization set in. For weeks she had encouraged her own blissful ignorance, denying any correlation between the changes taking place in her body and that one night she and Jonas had shared.

She quickly retied her bag and took a step forward,

nearly colliding with an old woman, the same beggar woman from the train station.

"Lavender oil, my dear," the woman said.

"No," Margaret said, gently pushing the woman's hands from her face. "Thank you."

"Two pence a bottle," the woman said behind a black-laced veil.

Margaret worked hard to conceal her disgust at the smell emanating from the beggar woman's ripped and threadbare clothes.

"No, I must be on my way," Margaret said.

The woman ignored her protests and grabbed for Margaret's hand. Forcing her palm up, the woman poured a tablespoon's worth out and began rubbing it into Margaret's skin. "Makes the lady's skin nice and soft. Calms the mind."

The woman's nails dug into Margaret's skin as she struggled to free her hand.

"Maybe a stomach-soothing draught." She pointed to Margaret's stomach. "For the baby."

Margaret realized she had been holding her stomach protectively and pulled it away.

"No," she said bluntly before snapping her hand back and hurrying away.

The woman called after her but Margaret rushed down High Street. Three blocks later Margaret realized the lavender oil, which had added a sticky feeling to her palm, was still there. In a panic she rubbed her hand on the fabric of her skirt, eager to be rid of it.

As she quickened her pace toward home, she tried to clear her mind of all thoughts. The fear. The panic. The denial. By the time she made it within one block of the house she couldn't deny it a moment longer. The nausea. The fatigue. The tightening of her clothes. It all added up to one thing. She was carrying a baby.

Jonas's baby.

❧　☙

Margaret was so flustered, so shocked, she didn't notice a man standing next to a carriage at the kerb outside

Jonas's house. She was two steps to the door when he called out to her.

"Margaret? Margaret, it's me."

Margaret used the iron railing to steady herself as she turned.

"Blair?"

He flashed an easy smile and then ran a hand through his hair after removing his hat. His congenial manner had not been lost in the last few months, even after the tragedy that struck his family.

He advanced forward and took her hand to help guide her the rest of the way up the steps.

"What are you doing here?" she asked, suddenly aware how out of breath she was.

"I called at Marshall House and was told you and Peter had come to Edinburgh." He lifted the newspaper that was folded in his other hand. "It wasn't until I saw the papers that I knew why you had come."

"Why have you come, though?" she asked.

He licked his lips and gave a half smile. "I've come to see you, of course."

He turned the knob and moved aside so Margaret could enter first.

"I don't fault you and Peter for wanting to come and help our doctor friend," he continued as they filed into the foyer.

"Doctor Davies," Margaret said as a reminder.

"Yes, of course. There must be some explanation. I don't believe the good doctor is capable."

"He's innocent," Margaret said reflectively. She could feel her skin warming in Blair's presence and sweat accumulating on her brow. The flutter in her stomach worsened.

"I know you have come to prove your point, to deliver Dr. Davies from his predicament, but it would be remiss of me to allow you to do it on your own."

Margaret grew warmer as he spoke but she pushed on. "How thoughtful." She could only manage a few words before her throat grew dry. She used the stair bannister to keep herself vertical.

Jonas appeared at the top of the stairs.

"There's the man!" Blair said. "You have my full support,

good sir." He turned back to Margaret and smiled. "Anyone who has won over Miss Marshall has won over me."

Jonas came down the stairs, a look of discomfort on his features.

"Tell me what you need of me, and I shall do it without the hint of hesitation," Blair said.

Eye to eye, they smiled at each other but beneath it existed a challenge, with the winner walking away with Margaret's heart.

Blair's features alighted with an idea. "A character reference, perhaps. I can wire my father directly if you feel the word of a duke has more clout than that of his son." He looked to Margaret apologetically. "I am in no hurry for the position. There are many more interesting things that demand my attention at the moment."

Margaret's stomach tightened at his words. He was so sincere, so smitten, and she had done nothing but lead him on for months. He was a good man who needed no help setting Margaret on a pedestal.

"You don't look well, Margaret," Jonas said.

She waved off his concern. "I'm merely recovering from the cold. The wind is rather biting today." She pulled at the strings of her reticule. "I did succeed in my task," she said. She allowed him a look into her bag but did not bother to pull out the frame. "Is Peter not back yet?"

"Not yet."

She reached for Jonas's arm. "You should know about Mr. Locke."

"Is something the matter? Is it his health?" Jonas looked alarmed.

"No, nothing like that. I believe Eloise may have poisoned him against you."

Jonas's expression was steady but Margaret knew it affected him. She wanted to embrace him and perhaps say more but Blair was at their side. "But she did allow me to bring you this," Margaret said, turning the larger frame over and laying it in Jonas's hands. "I thought you might appreciate having it."

She could feel the surprise emanating from Jonas's body. His jaw tightened and his hands shook slightly as he took it.

"She let you have this?"

"Yes, I asked her if I might take it. She doesn't expect it to be returned."

Jonas nodded stoically but Margaret knew he was overcome.

"Excuse me, just a minute, please."

He disappeared upstairs and Margaret wished she could follow him, to help him through the grief for his mother that he was no doubt feeling because of the picture. She found herself wishing Blair had not come, that such a complication to her life did not exist. Things were becoming complicated enough without Blair surprising her so suddenly.

"Was it a childhood memory?" Blair asked.

"Something of the sort." Margaret closed her eyes against the dizziness that waved over her. "Forgive me," she said. "Do you mind if we sit down?" She guided him into the parlour while taking a few concentrated breaths to slow her rapid heart rate. She could feel her forehead grow cold but the sweat worsened.

Blair was happy to head into the room but turned to her almost immediately. "Margaret, now that we are alone, there is something I feel compelled to tell you." His smile betrayed his nervousness. "I've actually known this for a while but circumstances being as they were ..."

Margaret used the back of her wrist to feel her forehead. She was hot to the touch and growing weaker and dizzier. Thankfully, Blair took her hand.

"Nothing need be done straightaway," he explained. "I just couldn't live another minute without knowing your answer to my simple question."

She could feel her stomach tighten.

"It would mean so much to me to know that you feel what I feel and ..."

The room began to spin and Margaret's vision blurred. She pulled at the scarf at her neck and was thankful for the cool air that reached her skin. When she opened her eyes she found Blair had dropped to one knee.

"Margaret, my darling, would you do me the honour of being my wife?"

Blair waited as Margaret swayed, unable to respond or

speak. She reached behind her for the chair she knew was there but could not find it. She hit the floor with a thud and everything went black.

Chapter 25

Jonas was in his room when he heard the thud and knew instantly something was wrong. He rushed downstairs and saw Margaret's body crumpled on the rug of the parlour, her one arm inches from the chair. Blair was on his knees, pulling her head up from the floor.

"What happened?" Jonas snapped, pulling Margaret's body from him. Something about seeing the man touch Margaret so intimately made his blood curdle like sour milk.

"I don't know," Blair stammered. "She just collapsed."

Jonas placed his hands at her neck, felt her jawline, and then pulled her mouth open to peer inside. The front door opened and Ainsley appeared in the hall.

"Oh, good God! Margaret!"

Jonas pulled back Margaret's scarf and threw it to the chair. He motioned for Ainsley to hold her head.

"I believe she fainted," Blair said, by way of explanation. He looked back to Margaret's motionless body.

"Did she say anything? Anything at all?" Jonas asked.

"Er ... no. She was pale and nervous," Blair said, panic lacing his words. "Is she going to be all right?"

Ainsley held two fingers to her throat. "Her pulse is weak."

"I need my medical bag." Without asking for assistance, Jonas gathered Margaret in his arms and went straight for the stairs. Both Ainsley and Blair followed at his heels. In the hall, Ainsley stepped forward to push open the door to his room. Both Blair and Ainsley stood back while Jonas deposited her on the top of the blankets.

As soon as he let her down, Margaret convulsed. Her back arched and her hand went to her stomach but she still did not open her eyes.

"She's going to choke!" Jonas said. He rolled her onto her side at the edge of the bed.

Ainsley pulled the washbasin from its stand and placed it

on the floor beneath her.

"Mr. Thornton, my medical bag." Jonas snapped his fingers and motioned for him to go to the next room.

Ainsley looked to Jonas in alarm. "Do you think it could be Eloise?" he asked. "Could she have given Margaret something?"

Jonas pressed his lips together in frustration. "I would not put it past her. Her father is a chemist. If anyone knows how to poison someone, it's her."

Blair returned with the bag and clumsily thrust it at Jonas.

Jonas pulled a mercury thermometer from his things and held her head steady so he could place it beneath her tongue.

Drawn to the second floor by the commotion, Mrs. Crane and John peered around the doorframe. The housekeeper gasped when she saw Margaret in such a state. "Merciful heavens!"

"Mrs. Crane, bring some ice from the cellar, if you please. We need to bring her fever down this instant. Mr. Thornton, go with her. I need as big a bucket as you can carry."

The housekeeper disappeared with Blair Thornton at her heels.

"What do you think Eloise gave her?" Ainsley asked, coming along to the other side of the bed.

"I don't know," Jonas answered. He pressed his ear to her chest and closed his eyes. Her heart was behaving erratically and her chest heaved as if it took a great deal of effort to breathe.

His worst fear had been realized. The woman who possessed an unnatural attachment to him had done harm to the woman he loved. He should never have let her go. He'd risk the gallows a thousand times over than have Margaret in such a state.

Without control, Margaret heaved the contents of her stomach into the washbasin. Her body shuddered and then grew cold in Jonas's grasp. Blair returned with the bucket of ice, chipped away from the brick in the cellar, and a clean washbasin. Mrs. Crane filed in behind him with some clean cloths and a pitcher of water.

Jonas dumped some of the ice into the enamel basin and

then poured water over it. He wet one of the cloths, wrung it out and placed it on Margaret's head. He did the same thing again, placing cloths against her armpits and her throat.

"How fortunate we are to have you here, Dr. Davies," Blair said from his unsure position at the other side of the room.

Ainsley left the room and returned moments later with Margaret's reticule. He pulled back the drawstrings and pulled out the small frame with the picture of Eloise. "Damn this blasted thing," he said, tossing it to the bureau without much care.

Jonas mirrored his sentiment. If that photograph had never been needed Margaret would most certainly not be in her current state.

"What's this?" Ainsley pulled a round tin from Margaret's bag and held it up so Jonas could see as he looked over his shoulder. Jonas was quick to snatch it from Ainsley's hand and twisted off the top. The thick lotion was tinted to look like skin colour. Jonas held the tin to his nose and sniffed it, but there were no clues that he could derive from its scent. When he looked back to Margaret, he pulled back the compress on her neck and saw that the dampness of the cloth pulled the lotion away from her skin.

"It's something that penetrates the skin," Ainsley said. He gathered both pieces of the tin, replaced the lid and turned to John, who looked on quietly at the door. "Test this," Ainsley said.

"What am I looking for?" John asked.

"I don't know. Anything that causes convulsions and fever."

For a moment it looked as if John was not willing to take on the task. He looked about the room, taking in the faces of the three men desperate to save Margaret's life and then nodded. "All right," he said.

Shortly after John left, Margaret stirred.

"It's all right, Margaret," Jonas said, snatching her hand and pulling himself closer to her face so she could see him. "Peter and I are going to help you. What happened while you were out?"

Margaret had a difficult time focusing on him. Her eyes

moved erratically as if unable to see what was directly in front of her.

Ainsley drew in close. "Did you eat anything or sip some tea?" he asked.

Margaret shook her head and closed her eyes. "You told me not to," she said softly.

"The ointment. Did she give you the ointment?" Ainsley asked. "Margaret?" He reached out and touched her shoulder, shaking her gently. "Where did you get the ointment?"

"It was behind the counter," Margaret managed to say. "I bought it before Eloise knew I was there." She looked tired and weak, unable to move her arms or lift her head. "I feel so stiff, Peter. Everything hurts."

Jonas forced her head toward him so she would look at him. "Margaret, you've been given something and it's making you very sick. Did anyone give you anything to eat?"

"No." Her voice matched the weakness in her body.

It didn't make sense. Margaret was the picture of health that morning, without any complaints.

"Did anyone touch you or rub something into your skin?"

Margaret's eyes closed and she licked her dry lips. "The ... beggar ... woman." She overturned her free hand to reveal the grease mark on her palm.

Ainsley took her hand and lifted it into the light.

"What is it?" Jonas leaned over to touch her palm. He found it greasy to the touch. "The beggar woman?"

"We met her at the train station when we first arrived," Ainsley said.

"She's harmless," Jonas said. "I've seen her many times myself."

"Could Eloise have bribed her? Could she have given her something and told her to rub it into Margaret's hand?" Ainsley sneered at the thought. He began to pace the room in an effort to control a forthcoming outburst.

"Who's Eloise?" Blair asked from the foot of the bed.

Both Jonas and Ainsley allowed his question to go unanswered.

Mrs. Crane clicked her tongue. "A dangerous woman, I can tell, if she makes Dr. Davies here nervous."

"Would Eloise go to such lengths?" Ainsley asked.

"I told you, she followed me everywhere for a year. Nothing is too great a task where Eloise is concerned."

"She sets you up for murder and then attacks Margaret." Ainsley growled at the thought. He took a long look at Margaret in her sickbed. He pulled the tiny frame and photo from the dresser and looked down at it with disgust. "First thing I am going to do is prove she did it, and then I'm going to hang the woman myself." His vow of vengeance hung in the air as he charged from the room.

"Peter. Peter!" Jonas stood. He couldn't bring himself to go after him, not when Margaret needed him.

As if sensing his internal struggle, Blair stepped forward. "Go with him. If you don't go, he'll do something reckless." He went toward Margaret. "We'll look after her until your return."

Mrs. Crane nodded behind him.

They heard the front door slam, signalling Ainsley's departure.

"Go!"

Jonas nodded and clasped Blair on the shoulder. "Keep her cool. Get her out of those clothes and make sure she doesn't choke." Blair and Mrs. Crane nodded their assurance while Jonas planted a quick but loving kiss on Margaret's hand. "I won't be long," he said softly, before running to catch up with Peter.

                        ❧   ❦

By the time Jonas made it out to the street Ainsley was already at the end of the block. Night was falling fast as dark clouds rolled in over the city, blotting out the last hour of daylight. Jonas ran along the pavement to catch up, dodging puddles as he went. "Peter!"

Ainsley was determined. If he heard Jonas call out his name he made no indication of it. He scarcely even acknowledged his friend as he came running up alongside him. "We have to find out what that woman gave her," Ainsley said, without taking his eyes from the path ahead of them.

"Peter, you're angry. Now is not the time." Jonas tried to

pull him back but Ainsley shook off his grasp.

"Now is exactly the time." Ainsley checked for carriage traffic before darting across a wide road. When Jonas caught up to him he began speaking again. "I'll bet a thousand to one that woman is behind all this. She poisoned Margaret and she got the old woman to do it too. If we can discover what she rubbed into Margaret's hand, we can devise a cure. And after Eloise hangs, you will be rid of her forever." Ainsley stopped, pushed back Jonas's shoulder, and forced him to look him in the eye. "You want that, don't you?"

Jonas hesitated. He hated to think that the daughter of someone so dear to him was capable of such evil. It did not seem right that a man so kind could raise someone so afflicted by madness. "Yes," he said at last. "I want to stop looking over my shoulder."

Ainsley led the way to The White Wolf pub, which was teeming with raucous patrons. He went straight for the barkeep and produced the photograph of Eloise while Jonas held back. A few people glared at him and kept a wide berth, which only served to make him more uncomfortable. He should be back at the house helping Margaret, not risking a public beating like this.

"Was this the woman you saw with my friend?" Ainsley asked, yelling over the din of the room. He leaned into the counter and held the photograph inches from the barkeeps nose.

"Ainsley, let's go." Jonas tugged on Ainsley's arm as the mood in the room grew hostile.

Inundated with patrons, the barkeep pushed the frame to the side but Ainsley repositioned it. "Look at it!"

The man paused begrudgingly but this time Jonas saw him focus his eyes on the image. After a moment, he shook his head. "Nah," he said. "Weren't her."

"Look again!"

"Peter."

"It's her. I know it is."

"I pay attention to everyone who darkens them doors. If it was her, I'd know it. It ain't her. Now get out of my pub before your friend there brings on a brawl." The barkeep nodded to Jonas, eyeing him with distrust.

Jonas nodded his agreement. He was more than eager to oblige.

Ainsley slammed a fist on to the table. "Damn it."

Jonas felt someone push his shoulder and realized a large burly man stood inches from him. Jonas looked the man squarely in the eye and raised his hands up in surrender.

"I have no quarrel," he said.

Ainsley appeared at his side and guided him out the front door of the pub. They both sent out a few curse words into the night; Ainsley for being so sorely disappointed and Jonas for having been nearly pummelled for something he did not do.

"He's probably drunk half the night anyways," Ainsley said, sneering as two more people headed for the front door. "He wouldn't know if the Queen herself decided to take a pint at his establishment."

Jonas paused on the pavement for a moment to give his heartbeat a chance to return to normal. He hadn't been in a fight since school, not even to box, and he wasn't all that eager to start again now.

"Peter, I have to go back to Margaret," he said, skipping to catch up. "John is the only one trained and—"

"I can't go back. I'd just be pacing the floor wishing I were out here doing something to find out who did it to her." Ainsley stopped at an intersection and surveyed the traffic.

As if something were nipping at his heels, Ainsley hastened across the intersection. Jonas felt compelled to follow him, if only to keep a watchful eye and only for a short while. He could not stomach the thought of Margaret in such a state. Only the thought of finding out what had been given to her spurred him forward.

The crowds were thin that night at Waverly Station and the beggar woman was easily spotted. Upon seeing her, Jonas reached for Ainsley's arm, intent on telling him to show caution. They might do better to ask questions in a calm manner than an emotionally charged one. He missed Ainsley's sleeve by half an inch, a mistake that cost them their quarry.

The woman took one look at Ainsley charging for her and

took off at a run, darting between a pair of buildings and turning right as soon as she came to the street. Ainsley followed her in pursuit while Jonas reluctantly took up the rear. It seemed abhorrent to be running after a woman so old and reduced to such circumstances. However feeble, she still managed to lead them on a hearty chase through much of the alleys and crevices of Old Town. Though not speedy, she was nimble, eventually forcing Ainsley and Jonas to split up.

Jonas became increasingly aware of how each turn took him further and further from Margaret's side. As he splashed through stagnant waters and rounded shadowed corners, he thought of giving up the chase and returning to her. At the end of a short street, he spotted Ainsley.

"This way!" he called, circling his arms widely and inviting Jonas to follow him.

When Jonas rounded the corner he found Ainsley already had her blocked off in a dead end, though he hadn't laid a hand on her. All three of them were out of breath. The woman hunched over slightly with her back against the wall, her breaths shallow. Staying against the wall she tried to slip by them as they rested but Jonas took one step over and blocked the way.

"I only have a few questions," Ainsley said, drawing in breaths between much of his words.

"Would a man chase such a feeble soul for just a few questions?" the woman asked, her voice cracking. She kept her head low as she clutched her drooping bag close to her chest.

"You aren't so feeble," Jonas said, propping up his arm on the wall to maintain presence while he struggled to catch his breath. "I know men who would not be capable of keeping up with you."

"Such is the way with many things," she said. "What are your questions then, gentleman?"

Ainsley gave Jonas a look and put his hands on his hips as he straightened his stance. "There was a woman you spoke with today. She was well off."

"Many of the women I approach are. You'll have to be more specific."

"She has brown hair, pale skin," Jonas said, stepping

forward. "She was wearing a blue dress and in the vicinity of Blair Street."

"She is my sister," Ainsley added.

"Ah yes," the woman answered, "The trembling one. A scared little house sparrow."

"Certainly not," Ainsley said.

"Oh yes."

"She's ill," Jonas said.

"I'm sorry to hear it," the woman said. "By the time I found her she was already much troubled."

"By what?" Jonas could stomach no more games. Margaret waited for him. He needed to get back to the house.

The woman shrugged. "I haven't the slightest idea."

"You gave her something, rubbed it onto her palm," Ainsley said.

"Lavender oil. Very soothing in the bath."

"Did anyone bid you give her such an item?" Jonas asked cautiously.

"You believe her illness is the result of something I gave her?"

"Yes, I must get back to her. She is in a bad way."

The woman reached into her bag and pulled out a tiny glass jar. She stepped out from the shadows and handed it to Ainsley. "Here is what I offered her. You both are such learned gentlemen, see for yourself what is contained in such a vial." She moved to step around them. "You will find me innocent, I assure you."

"How did you know we are *learned* gentlemen?" Jonas spied the smooth skin of the woman's jaw in the lamplight and caught hold of her arm as she neared him. She froze as he pulled her veil back from her face.

"I remember you," Ainsley said, stepping closer.

The woman was not old, after all, but rather younger than either of the men. Her hair was the lightest blond, which looked grey in the lamplight. Jonas placed a hand under her chin to allow the subdued light to illuminate her face. "Rebecca Stewart."

She trembled and clutched her bag closer to her chest even as Jonas released his grasp.

"What are you playing at?" Ainsley asked, taking up a

position so she could not run again.

The young woman put up her hands defensively. "I didn't mean any harm," she said, tears pooling in her eyes. "This is the only way in which I may support myself."

"You make a wage as Dr. Waters's assistant," Ainsley pointed out.

"'Tisn't enough! I get paid half the compensation of his male clerks and porters." Her face hardened at her own words, irritated that she would be worth so little.

"There are other positions," Jonas said, "other doctors even."

"But Waters promised to teach me everything he can. None of the others would permit such an arrangement." She pushed back tears from her cheeks and did not lift her head to look at them.

Ainsley held up the vial. "And this?"

Rebecca's shoulders slouched as she exhaled. "When I am not with Dr. Waters, I am peddling salves and lotions of my own creation. I dress as a beggar woman so people will take pity on me," she said. "And I didn't want to run the risk of running into anyone from the school. I wouldn't want Dr. Waters or any of the others finding out." Her gaze bounced between Ainsley and Jonas. "I swear, I had nothing to do with your sister's illness. Have the bottle tested. You will see I am telling the truth."

Ainsley regarded her suspiciously and then looked down at the bottle in his hand. "Where do you make this? At the university? Have you been stealing supplies?"

"No!" Rebecca closed her eyes in an effort to steady her panic. "I make them out of my flat."

"Show me," Ainsley said.

As if knowing it was the only way she could prove she was telling the truth, she relented. "Follow me, then."

She led them back to St. Mary's Street and put a key in a door. They went up one flight of stairs and around the corner before she unlocked another door. As the door swung open a girl, a few years younger than Rebecca, hopped up from her seat on a chair and ran to them.

Jonas saw Rebecca hold the girl's wrists and guide her back into the room. She spoke to her in a soothing tone and kept her face inches from the other girl's. "These are my friends," Rebecca said. "Friends."

The look of elation on the girl's face morphed into uncertainty. She looked to Rebecca a few times for reassurance before finally mumbling the word "friends" and nodding in unison with Rebecca.

"My sister, Mary," Rebecca said to Jonas and Ainsley before leading the girl away from the door.

The place Rebecca and her sister called home was a single room with a bed placed against the wall, and a long table near the window. There were shelves constructed against one wall that housed various vials of ingredients and large jars of her product. After depositing Mary on the bed, Rebecca pulled a small lamp from the table near the window and used it to light another one and then placed it on the end of the table.

Ainsley walked into the room first and circled the table while Jonas closed the door slowly behind him.

"Does your sister have Mongolian idiocy?" Jonas asked, recognizing the facial differences.

Rebecca nodded.

Jonas looked to Ainsley. John Langdon Down had only recently characterized the syndrome as a mental disability, something of which Jonas was aware after assisting a few affected patients in London. Most ended up committed to asylums. The fact that Rebecca hadn't done such a thing was commendable given the lack of appropriate care offered in such places.

"Our mother abandoned us a few years ago. I'm all she has," Rebecca said, as if reading his thoughts. "You'll understand now why I need more than what Dr. Waters is willing to pay me."

The two men exchanged glances and then a feeling of guilt rushed over Jonas. A person willing to care for a mentally incapacitated sibling in such a way was highly unlikely to be involved in a plot to harm Margaret.

"Your compassion for your sister is a credit to your character," Ainsley said, mirroring Jonas's thoughts exactly.

"I don't need your pity," Rebecca said.

"'Tisn't pity, I offer," Ainsley explained. "Praise, perhaps." He stood on the opposite side of the table, looking over an assortment of dried herbs, rose hips, seashells, and leaves.

Rebecca went to the window to open it and remained there while Jonas and Ainsley surveyed her workspace. She was nervous, as anyone would be, and brushed away tears that threatened to spill over onto her cheeks.

"How long have you been doing this?" Ainsley asked, as he picked up a jar of green-yellow liquid and held it to the lamplight.

"Four years," she said. "No one has ever gotten sick. Not that I recall." She pulled the veil from her hair and hung it off the rails of the bed and then began to remove her gloves.

"Who taught you?" Jonas asked, running his hand through some dried lavender buds.

Rebecca didn't answer straightaway. "I taught myself once I realized Mother wasn't coming back."

Jonas knew the feeling well. It had taken him and his mother two months before succumbing to the realization that his father would not be returning home. Like his mother, Rebecca was all alone in the world, with a dependent to support, and this was her only means of survival.

Jonas looked to his friend, his anger extinguished, and his need to head back to Margaret reignited. "Peter, I don't think we are going to find anymore answers here. We can have John test the lavender oil to be sure. Perhaps Margaret contracted something at the train station or in the morgue."

Ainsley bore a look of disappointment. If the facilities were dirty and unkempt, Margaret's sickness could be attributed to some bacteria, perhaps even bacteria, but this room where Rebecca eked out a humble living was kept cleaner and tidier than any lab either of them had ever worked in, and Ainsley knew this.

"We should go." Jonas motioned for the door, eager to return to Margaret.

Ainsley scanned the room and then pointed to Mary. The girl had donned a wig of long, brown hair and was bouncing on the mattress in some internal game.

"What's that?" Ainsley strode across the room in three steps. With a look of panic, Rebecca tried to pry it from him before he turned and showed it to Jonas at the door.

"Where did you get this?" Jonas asked, hoping for an easy explanation.

Rebecca did not answer right away. She looked as if she would cry while she thought of some excuse for having such an item.

"Is this another part of your costume?" Ainsley pressed.

Jonas's hands began to shake as his mind put the pieces together. As a brunette Rebecca would bear a very close resemblance to Margaret. Jonas had no doubt that she had been the one who lured him from the pub that night. He turned from them both and pressed a fist into the wall while taking deep, concentrated breaths.

"I'm sorry," she said, backing away as far as she could. "I didn't know that was going to happen."

Jonas rounded. "Like hell you didn't!" he yelled over Ainsley's shoulder. "My life is ruined because of this." He grabbed the wig from Ainsley's grasp and threw it to the floorboards in disgust. He should leave. He knew if he stayed he'd do something he'd regret and perhaps end up back at Calton.

"I swear ... on my father's grave. I ... I was only supposed to take you from the pub and leave you at the university. That's all I did." Her pleading made her voice crack. "I laid you down on the sofa in Professor Frobisher's office and left. I swear. Please." She looked to Ainsley. "You have to believe me."

Jonas tried to calm down, turning away and walking to the other side of the room to keep the table between them. "And you didn't notice a body lying on the floor?"

"It was dark—"

Jonas scoffed and threw his hands up in the air.

"I could see nothing amiss in the room. As far as I could tell there was no one else there. I have no idea what happened after I left."

"Did you think I was capable of such a thing?" Jonas pressed.

Sheepishly, she shook her head. "You were always so kind to me," she admitted. "I wanted to come forward, after our conversation, Dr. Ainsley, to tell my story but ... he knows where I live. I care nothing for myself, not after what I did, but Mary is innocent."

"Who knows where you live? Who asked you to bring Jonas to Frobisher's office?" Ainsley asked.

"I don't know."

Jonas couldn't keep himself from pacing. The anger he felt seemed to engulf him. The only thing that stopped him from charging from the room was the thought of finally finding out who had done this to him.

"Someone put a letter under my door. It had twenty pounds in it and promised another twenty if I did what he asked. The next day my neighbour told me a boy came with a package for me and the wig was in it."

"A boy?" Ainsley asked.

"Yes, sir."

He turned to Jonas. "A hired intermediary."

Jonas nodded. "An anonymous one at that."

"I'm so very sorry. Twenty pounds. I stole a man's life for twenty pounds!" She sobbed uncontrollably into her palms.

"Do you still have the letters?" Ainsley asked.

Rebecca lifted her head slowly and used her sleeve to wipe her nose. "I believe so." She went to the chest at the foot of her bed, retrieved two letters, and handed them to Ainsley. The first was as she described, the second was blank save for five words, "With my most ardent appreciation."

"This is the one that brought the rest of the money?" Ainsley asked.

The young woman nodded and then she closed her eyes, dropped to her bed, and hid her face with her hands. Mary came along beside her and wrapped an arm around her shoulders in a side hug.

Ainsley looked to Jonas and gave a tiny nod. Jonas suspected she was telling the truth as well, which meant they weren't any closer to finding out who did this to him.

Suddenly, Rebecca let out a deep sniffle and raised her head. "I will go to the constabulary first thing in the morning," she said with conviction.

Jonas kept his gaze on Ainsley. "No," he said.

"Jonas, this proves you didn't do it."

"It only proves how I got to the university from the pub," he said. "At anytime between when Rebecca left and I was found next to the body I could have killed Frobisher."

"I know you didn't do it!"

"We need proof that I either didn't do it or that someone else did," Jonas explained. "Rebecca's confession does not prove either. We are close, Peter, but not close enough."

"It proves that you did not go to the university out of your own volition. There is more at play here," Ainsley said. He turned to Rebecca. "In what state did you find Jonas?"

Rebecca looked at him with confusion.

"Was he inebriated, slurring his words, unable to walk in a straight line?"

She shook her head at each of Ainsley's suggestions. "He was none of those things. He kept saying, 'Margaret, I'm so tired. I'm so tired.' He came willingly. I only had to hold his hand."

Jonas closed his eyes. "What did you put in my drink?" he asked, still unable to look at her.

"Excuse me?" Rebecca stammered, as if unsure if Jonas would lunge for her.

"My drink!" Jonas pounded a fist on the table, rattling the jars on top. "What did you put in it to make me so tired?"

Scared and confused, she looked to Ainsley, then back to Jonas. "Nothing. I never touched your drink."

"Something had to have been put there," Jonas said.

Ainsley pulled Jonas aside. "If it wasn't Rebecca, it must have been Eloise," he said quietly. "Rebecca knows lotions and little else. Eloise knows chemistry. You said so yourself. She must have tampered with your drink or asked someone else to do it."

Jonas shook his head, disbelieving their current circumstances. They had come so far yet lacked all the answers they needed. Already, he felt he had been gone too long. "I must get back to Margaret."

He turned and reached for the door handle.

"Is the baby all right?" Rebecca asked before Jonas and Ainsley could leave.

Jonas stopped. Both he and Ainsley turned to look at Rebecca wearily. "What did you say?" Jonas asked.

"What baby?" Ainsley knit his brow. "There is no baby."

"I just thought ..." She gestured to Ainsley. "You are her brother. That must make you the father of her child."

Ainsley shook his head. "Margaret doesn't have a child."

Rebecca swallowed. "My apologies. I thought you knew." She turned from them, rubbing the back of her neck.

"What were we supposed to know?" Jonas asked, pushing past Ainsley.

Rebecca hesitated. "She's with child. I could tell by the shape of her and the way she touched her lower abdomen. I've seen enough pregnant women to know the look. I thought you knew."

Chapter 26

Ainsley left Rebecca's flat in such a state of shock he could barely put one foot in front of the other. It seemed near impossible that Margaret could be in a state of motherhood. Ainsley knew of their attachment but had been blind to just how close they had actually become. He had been concerned with his own troubles, his own demons, his own feelings of love, that he had not realized exactly how much was at stake. His work to clear Jonas's name went beyond his friend, even beyond the feelings of Margaret. His work to save Jonas from capital punishment meant he was saving the father of his unborn niece or nephew. So much of their future selves rested on the outcome of this investigation.

By the time they reached the street Jonas was running again but he wasn't running home to New Town. He was forging ahead to the one place he had been avoiding since arriving in Scotland, and there was no telling what he might do.

Ainsley caught up to him before he made it to the door, and placed himself between Jonas and the main entrance to Mr. Locke's pharmacy.

"Out of my way, Peter."

"Don't do this," Ainsley said, seeing the rage in Jonas's eyes. He pressed on Jonas's shoulders, pushing him back to the street. He'd push him the entire way home if it meant avoiding a confrontation. Ainsley regretted leaving Margaret's side now. He wished he had stayed, thus allowing Jonas to stay. He wasn't supposed to be roaming the streets anyway, as per his conditions of release, and an assault charge against a woman would most certainly injure their case grievously. "She's not worth it. We need to get home to Margaret," he said, taking hold of Jonas's lapels and hoping he would see reason.

Jonas shook his head and pressed against Ainsley's weight. "She's going to tell me what she gave her." He wanted in that door. He wanted to face the woman he knew had harmed Margaret. "She's going to tell me so I can save my child."

Ainsley wondered if Jonas would hit him, if their friendship, after all they had been through, could withstand such a confrontation.

After a moment, Ainsley released him and held his hands up in surrender. He did not move out of the way and instead turned to try the knob. The door was locked and no lights were on inside. "It's far too late," Ainsley said. When he turned back Jonas was gone.

Ainsley saw a flash of coat fabric at the corner. There must have been another entrance and of course Jonas knew the location of it. This time, Ainsley was not quick enough. Jonas used his body weight and slammed into the door, ripping the trim from the doorjamb.

"Eloise!" He slipped into the darkness of the storeroom.

Ainsley followed, calling Jonas's name in a frantic whisper. They made their way through the dark, following the light to the base of the stairs. Ainsley heard movement on the floor above and moved quickly to prevent Jonas from going any farther. He caught him at the midway point of the stairs.

"Eloise, I know what you did!"

Jonas looked close to tears. The desperation was evident. Both his love and his child were in danger and Ainsley wasn't entirely sure he wouldn't respond in the same way.

"What is the meaning of this?" Mr. Locke appeared in the light at the top of the stairs. His weakened body was hunched over the bannister. "Get away from here, you ... you rabble. We have no more love for you."

Ainsley winced at the man's words and knew Jonas felt the full weight of them as well.

"I have no quarrel with you, Mr. Locke. I love you as a father, nay more so, but your child is a thing of the devil," Jonas said. "Where is she?"

He did not push against Ainsley. Instead, he stood partway up the stairs, looking up at the man to whom he owed his entire existence.

"She is not here," the old man croaked. Even in the dim light Ainsley saw Mr. Locke's eyes flicker to the other end of the stairwell where Jonas and Ainsley could not see.

"She gave something, a poison, we suspect," Jonas said, taking a few steps higher on the stairs, "to the woman I love."

"Love?" The man looked flustered and confused. "Is it not Eloise you love?"

"No, sir. I have never loved that woman. I could never love such a woman. She is the devil and only proved as much today for what she's done to Margaret."

"You promised to marry her out of duty to me," Mr. Locke said, ignoring Jonas's accusations. "Not that I would encourage her to have you, not after what you have done." The man's voice shook as his hand did on the railing.

"I have promised no such thing."

Ainsley slipped past Jonas and caught Mr. Locke's arm.

"Unhand me," he said incredulously.

"Allow me to bring you to your chair, Mr. Locke," Ainsley said, as gently as he could. He imagined his own mother as old as him, confused and weakened.

With a trembling body, Mr. Locke nodded and allowed Ainsley to guide him back to the doorway of his workroom.

"I never imagined in all my life that Jonas would bring such violence, such scandal."

As the man spoke, a shadow moved at the end of the hall. By the time Ainsley looked up, it was gone.

"Don't you think of coming as far as that top step, Mr. Davies," the old man called out, even as Ainsley helped him back into his chair.

"I am not your enemy, Mr. Locke," Jonas said from the stairwell.

When Ainsley looked back he saw Jonas had taken a seat at the stair second from the top and had lowered his face into his hands.

The old man scoffed at Jonas's words and focused his attention on Ainsley. "I gave that boy everything, everything. And see how he repays me." The man gestured widely, punctuating his stress. Ainsley grabbed the man's wrists in an effort to bring his attention to him.

"Mr. Locke, we need your help," Ainsley said soothingly. "My sister, Margaret, is very sick. I am a doctor like Jonas—"

"Yes, yes, I remember you."

Ainsley smiled. "We don't know what has made her sick."

"How am I supposed to know?" He threw up his arms in frustration and leaned back into the cushions of his chair. "Wait, Margaret, did you say? The Miss Margaret who came and had tea this afternoon?"

Out of his peripheral vision Ainsley could see Jonas had lifted his head from his hands.

"Yes," Ainsley answered. "She is my sister."

"Oh, she is a lovely woman. Very kind. I could see as much in her eyes."

Ainsley nodded.

"What are her symptoms?" The old man closed his eyes and folded his hands somewhat in front of him.

"Fever, vomiting, muscle cramps," Ainsley said.

"Erratic pulse," Jonas interjected from the hall.

"Her hands are curled like this." Ainsley demonstrated it for Mr. Locke.

"Is ... is the girl arching her back?" he asked.

Ainsley and Jonas nodded eagerly.

"Yes, that's right," Ainsley said quickly.

"Oh my, my." Mr. Locke shook his head.

"What is it? What has she been given?"

Ainsley looked up and saw Jonas had come into the room. Mr. Locke was so struck by the realization he no longer cared that Jonas was there.

"Strychnine. Oh, that's some powerful stuff." The man's hand shook as he brought it to his mouth.

"Is there an antidote?" Jonas crossed the room and headed straight for Mr. Locke's shelf, where he kept all his potions and ingredients.

Mr. Locke raised a bony hand to the top shelf. "Coniine," he said.

Jonas pushed aside a few small jars, searching for the right one, before finally pulling it from the shelf. "It's here," he said, turning back to Ainsley and Mr. Locke. His elation was short-lived. "Thank you, Mr. Locke."

The old man looked ready to cry and waved off Jonas's appreciation. He kept his eyes trained on Ainsley so he wouldn't have to look at Jonas as he went for the door. "It's hemlock," Mr. Locke said. "She mustn't be given too much.

Only a few drops. Any more than that will surely kill her."

Ainsley nodded and saw Jonas waiting at the door. "Go, Jonas. I'll catch up."

Giving one last look to Mr. Locke, Jonas left, the vial of antidote held firmly in his grasp.

When Ainsley looked back to Mr. Locke he saw that the confusion in the old man had returned. "Mr. Locke, can you help me understand how strychnine is administered? Is it ingested?"

"Oh yes," Mr. Locke said. "Or through the respiratory system. Ingestion takes hold faster but a large enough dose to the mouth and nose will surely kill someone."

Ainsley took the man's hand in his own. "Thank you, sir." He tried to pull away but the old man held fast.

"You think my Ellie did this?"

Ainsley swallowed. "Yes, sir. I do. I don't entirely know how but ..." He allowed the rest of his thoughts to go unsaid. "Thank you for your help," he said, slowly pulling his hands away. "I must return to my sister."

Mr. Locke slowly released Ainsley's hands but did not look at him. Instead, the man sat in the cushions of his chair with his gaze locked on something across the room. As Ainsley circled the top of the bannister he heard the old man speaking to himself.

"Oh Ellie, what have you done to that lovely young woman?" he said, before lowering his face into his hands.

Chapter 27

They jogged the dark, damp streets of Edinburgh, with Jonas in the lead. They charged through ankle-deep puddles and ploughed through standing groups of pedestrians who insisted on taking over the walkways. Only when they had run the better part of a mile did Jonas slow his pace, allowing Ainsley to say what had been turning over in his mind since they left Rebecca's.

"Someone had to have known Rebecca was a young woman, not a homeless beggar," Ainsley called out to Jonas, who was five or six paces ahead of him.

Jonas walked quickly and with a determined purpose. "What of it?" he asked as he looked over his shoulder without slowing his pace.

"It must be someone from the university then," Ainsley said. "Someone who would have also known she was in no position to refuse such remuneration."

"She could have refused," Jonas said, his anger still evident in his tone.

"Could you have?"

When money had been scarce and fees were needed to be paid, both men had gone into the night in search of new cadavers they could claim in the name of science. Jonas would not accept any money from Ainsley, even after learning of his true parentage. His income would be made through his own efforts, he had said, though it need not necessarily be entirely honest. In the end, some conquests were obtained legally, others were highly questionable. Ainsley had done it for Jonas's sake as much as he did it for the thrill.

"I doubt you would have said no, given your position," Ainsley said, shouting against the rainwater that poured from the downspouts and along the gutters.

At Ainsley's words Jonas stopped but did not turn.

"You and I have done worse things. All those late nights in the cemeteries, searching for fresh graves, begging family members of the recently deceased to turn their loved ones' bodies over to us? Was that not done out of desperation?"

Jonas turned, his eyes betraying the true depth of his fury. "Only because I did not have the heart to ask Mr. Locke for a penny more, knowing he could not afford it," he roared back.

"Then you know of Miss Stewart's desperation. She has no one to ask even if she could overcome her pride." Ainsley closed the gap between them.

Jonas waved a hand and charged toward home. "You've become soft, Peter."

"I've become reasonable." Ainsley jogged to reach him and had to quicken his steps just to keep pace. "We have more information than ever before. We are close, Jonas. Closer than we have ever been."

"I cannot afford to be close." Jonas's merciless stance was punctuated by his determined strides. "My child and, God willing, my future wife lay dying and all because of that woman." He growled at the thought of it and Ainsley saw him curl his hands into fists. "I should have ransacked that building, brought her out of hiding, and choked the life out of her while making him watch."

"Why didn't you?" Ainsley asked. "I thought for certain you would have, given the look in your eyes."

Jonas gave a quick sideways glance before refocusing on the path before him. "I couldn't bring myself to do it, not after I saw the look on Mr. Locke's face." Jonas closed his eyes and tilted his head to the side as Ainsley wrapped an arm around his shoulders.

"You are not weak," he said soothingly. "Merely reasonable. Not every problem can be solved with violence. We must pick and choose our battles, and right now Margaret needs us to help fight hers."

Ainsley gave him a quick pat on the back and started a slow jog. He waved for Jonas to follow him. Together, bolstered by the energy displayed by the other, they ran the rest of the way home.

❧   ☙

As soon as they entered the door to the house Jonas

raced upstairs, leaving Ainsley in his wake. Giles stepped out of the dark parlour. He looked pained and concerned, but distant.

"Ezra sent word to me about Margaret. I came home straightaway."

Ainsley nodded.

"John and Mrs. Crane have been standing guard alongside Mr. Thornton, a friend of hers from London, I understand."

"A childhood friend," Ainsley added.

John appeared at the top of the stairs.

"How is she?" Ainsley asked, starting to head up the stairs. Giles fell in behind.

"Very ill," John said. "Her muscle cramps are the worst I have ever seen."

Ainsley paused at the top of the stairs and waited for both men to draw close. "It's strychnine," he said keeping his voice low. He glanced over their shoulders down the hall. He did not wish to alarm Mrs. Crane or Mr. Thornton.

"Strychnine?" John's voice betrayed his disbelief.

Out of breath, Ainsley could only nod.

Giles ran a hand through his hair and pushed back into the wall. "Out of everyone, I believe, I liked her the best."

Ainsley nodded. His friend's comments, added to those made by Mr. Locke, resonated with him deeply. Margaret was the one everyone like best; their parents, their friends, and anyone else they came in contact with.

Ainsley made his way down the hall and noticed John was quick to follow him.

"The ointment was clean," John said.

"It wasn't in the ointment."

"Then—?"

"I don't know."

Ainsley stopped at the door to his room and pulled the vial of lavender oil from his overcoat and handed it to John. "Test this, if you can."

John eyed the jar and held it up to the sconce on the wall. "What do you suspect?"

"Nothing. I just want to be sure." He slid past the threshold and headed into Margaret's sickroom.

Jonas was kneeling at the side of the bed. Blair had

backed away to the bureau, a look of both confusion and trepidation on his face.

"Her body has emptied of all possible liquids," he said to Ainsley. "Mrs. Crane and I have kept vigil." Blair wiped the sweat from his brow.

"You are a good man, Mr. Thornton," Ainsley said, patting his shoulder. "Thank you for all you have done."

"Peter, can you retrieve my medicine dropper?" Jonas asked without turning from Margaret. He had one hand on the back of her neck, readjusting her shoulders on the pillows.

Ainsley went to the bag at the bedside table and produced a small dropper with a red rubber end. Jonas used it to pull a small amount of the coniine out of the bottle while Ainsley moved to the opposite side of the bed. He pulled a chair from against the wall setting it close to the bed, but nearer Margaret's feet.

"How much will it take?" John asked from the door.

"A drop or two," Ainsley said. "Anymore and she will die."

A look of alarm overtook Blair's face. "What is it?" he asked, a slight shake in his voice.

Ainsley raised his eyes to Jonas, who seemed disinclined to answer while he concentrated on perfecting the dosage.

"It's coniine," Ainsley answered. "An antidote."

The entire time, Blair did not move from his place near the door, his face frozen in a state of fear and ignorance. Surrounded by doctors and men of science, he was entirely out of his natural element. "For what?" he managed to croak.

Ainsley hadn't wished to answer. Telling him what Margaret had contracted meant that he as a brother had been derelict in his duties. He had grossly underestimated how much danger she had been in.

"Strychnine," Ainsley answered matter-of-factly.

The mood in the room was raw. Any movement, even the slightest shift, seemed to send a shockwave through the space. Jonas moved with purpose, as if ignoring everyone else in the room. John hovered, more in the hall than in the actual space, while Blair looked on helpless. And Ainsley was happy to work as intermediary if it meant taking his mind off the poison they were using to cure his sister.

"What if it doesn't work?" Blair asked, swallowing hard.

Upon hearing Blair's question, Jonas's eyes lifted to Ainsley before bringing the end of the dropper close to Margaret's open mouth. They were both happy to let Blair's question hang in the air, unanswered.

No one knew exactly how long it would be before the antidote took effect.

If it took effect.

Ainsley rubbed his hands over his face as Jonas pulled back the dropper and slid it back into the tiny bottle. Three drops; that was all he had given her. Any more might be fatal.

Mrs. Crane appeared at the door with a pitcher of water and fresh towels draped over one arm. When she saw Ainsley and Jonas she let out a sigh of relief. "Oh thank heavens," she said, entering the room. "She's been asking for ye."

"Has she?" Ainsley perked up at the thought of her having some sort of consciousness.

Blair nodded and slipped his hands into his trouser pockets. "She's been asking for Jonas, mostly. Or perhaps just repeating his name, I'm not sure. It's barely audible."

Ainsley nodded. He knew why Margaret would call for Jonas but to Blair she could have been merely worried about his present legal troubles.

Mrs. Crane deposited her offerings on the bureau. "I'll make ye boys a tea," she said.

Finally, Jonas turned to the room, shaking his head and raising a hand in protest. "Please don't, Mrs. Crane," he said. "I could not stomach anything at the moment."

"But ye have to eat something," she said.

Ainsley shook his head as well. "Thank you kindly, Mrs. Crane. Jonas and I will be fine."

She pressed her lips together as her gaze bounced between the two of them. "All right then," she said after a time. "If ye need anything ..." She did not finish her sentence and after a moment left.

A moment passed before Ainsley turned to Blair.

"You should go rest as well," Ainsley said. "You've already done so much."

Blair seemed surprised at the suggestion but after a

moment's thought he nodded. "She has both of you to watch over her now," he said, reaching for his jacket on a hook behind the door. "Shall I check back in the morning?"

With a quick glance to Jonas, who was still not acknowledging anyone else in the room, Ainsley nodded.

Blair hesitated at the door, perhaps unsure if it was the right thing to do, before slipping into the hallway.

After a time, a new wave of convulsions began just as the hectic pace of the house was settling. Margaret was throwing up clear liquid now, everything else having vacated her body hours before. Her empty stomach did nothing to end her agony, however. Her body wished to eject everything and anything that may be causing her illness.

Ainsley looked to the vial on the bedside table. "Should we give her a drop more?" he asked.

Jonas gave a silent nod and passed over the vial to Ainsley.

"You should do it," he said. "My hands are shaking too much."

Ainsley administered one drop before sealing off the coniine for good.

No one said anything as Ainsley and Jonas made small bundles of ice and cloth before placing them at her underarms and neck. Jonas used the remaining ice in the washbasin. He dipped a towel, wrung it out, folded it, and placed it gently on Margaret's sweltering forehead.

Ainsley could not stave off remembrances of another woman he had helped through such a time. It was a suspected poisoning then, and he could not help but think the same method was at play here. In the bed, Margaret's face morphed into Lillian's and then back again. When she began to moan, Ainsley only heard the piano music Lillian had played for him once, which haunted him still. He had feared for Lillian then, but the terror he felt for Margaret was even more pronounced. She was and would remain the only person in his family whom he truly loved and cared for. She mustn't die. He would do anything to avoid such an outcome.

"Dr. Waters is revising his autopsy report," Ainsley said without taking his eyes from his sister.

"Peter, I don't need you bribing everyone involved in my case."

"I didn't bribe him." Ainsley shrugged. "I asked him a few questions and he pointed out some irregularities he found. I offered some possibilities."

Jonas rubbed his forehead and scrunched up his face as if he were in pain.

Ainsley hopped to the edge of his seat and looked directly at his friend. "We can prove the body was moved. Frobisher wasn't killed in his office. That is proven by the lack of sufficient blood at the scene."

"It certainly didn't look like a lack of blood," Jonas said.

"We are getting close, Jonas. Don't you see? Your case will be dismissed and, if what Rebecca said is true ..." Ainsley looked back to his sister. "Everything will be fine." The final words he spoke lacked the same level of conviction evident in his previous arguments.

Jonas would say no more. He sat there, with Margaret's hand in his, and waited.

An hour went by, the ice long since melted, when Margaret began to shiver uncontrollably. Jonas and Ainsley's vigil became a race for blankets and layers, anything to help her body retain her core temperature. And so her illness continued vacillating between fever, convulsions, and chills before she fell into a deep, otherworldly sleep.

"You should go to bed."

Ainsley started in his chair and caught the wall to steady himself. He had not realized he had fallen asleep. "You need sleep as well," he said to Jonas, rubbing his eyes.

Jonas mirrored none of Ainsley's current state. He sat holding Margaret's hand as if it were noon and no later. "I will be fine," he said. "You should get some rest."

Unenthusiastically, Ainsley stood up from his chair, pulled his jacket from the footrail and made for the door. He paused for a moment, said an uncharacteristic prayer for Margaret's recovery, and then went for the attic stairs.

⤳   ⤸

The servant's quarters were just as desolate and grey as

Ainsley remembered. He had never wanted Margaret to sleep there, and certainly not after he had learned about the room's former occupant. Suicide made a young person's death all the more tragic. It did not have to be that way. Even though Ainsley did not know the woman, much less her reasons for committing such an act, he still felt empathy for her. He felt the loss as he turned the key in the keyhole and then placed it on the windowsill.

Barely able to keep his eyes open before he entered the room, Ainsley found himself wide awake and his senses heightened in the darkness. A noise on the other side of the wall indicated John was still at work in his laboratory, most likely chasing Ainsley's phantom poisons.

He sat down on the bed without bothering to remove his shoes. He reached into the inside pocket of his jacket and pulled out the letters Rebecca had given him and laid them on the bedside table. A small paper square floated and fluttered to the floor. Ainsley bent over and picked it up. It was his ticket from the train. He turned it over in his hand and held it to the light. *York to Edinburgh* with the date and times of their departure and arrival noted beneath. He was about to put it with the letters when he noticed the discrepancy. The ticket should have said London to Edinburgh.

Ainsley shook his head at the ticket office's mistake, tossed it to the letters, and draped his jacket over a nearby chair. Moments later he dimmed his lamplight and crawled into bed.

How he wished Margaret had left on the train as she was supposed to. Jonas had warned him and would probably blame him once he had a chance to think about it. He should have put his foot down when it came to her. Had she not been so headstrong and reckless. Had he not been so convinced of her fortitude. Had she not gone to Eloise Locke's house in the bloody first place.

Angry at himself for not being able to diagnose her, Ainsley slipped away into sleep. He dreamed of blue medicine bottles, bloodstained laboratories, and waking up in a pool of Frobisher's blood.

And then he heard the door of his room open. Impossible. He glanced to the windowsill and saw the outline of the black iron key in the limited moonlight. He froze and listened as the floorboards next to his bed groaned. Then whatever it was stopped suddenly. Ainsley listened intently, holding in his own breath so as not to confuse himself. The thing in his room was breathing and was most definitely a person.

Ainsley sprang to his feet, lunging into the darkness, assured that whoever was in his room had flesh and a heartbeat. He let out a visceral growl when his hand hit a person, most definitely a man, and then threw him into the wall behind him. He used his arm under the man's chin to hold him in place at the collar. "Who are you and what is your business in here?"

"Don't hurt me, Peter," said a scared voice.

"John?"

Ainsley was reluctant to release him, unsure if his mind was playing him for a fool. He still could see very little, but in the darkness he could feel the man was slightly shorter than him and far less muscular. His prey trembled under the weight of Ainsley's arm pressed into his chest. And then he began pulling at Ainsley's forearm, entreating him to let him go.

Ainsley felt him double over when he went for the lamp. A few seconds later, with the lamp lit, he was finally able to see that it was indeed John, bent over and gasping for breath.

"What in God's name are you doing here in my sister's room?" Ainsley charged.

"Nothing."

Ainsley stepped forward, doubtful. "Have you been coming each night?"

John's eyes widened in horror at the suggestion. "For goodness sake, Peter!" He cringed at the thought. "I would never ..." He looked nervous and Ainsley sensed there was more. John pulled at his collar with one finger. "I didn't know anyone would be here. I'm merely looking for something."

"Looking for something? At two o'clock in the morning?" Ainsley glanced about the room and saw that the second door, the one which they had been told no longer had a key, was ajar. "Is this how you got in?"

Ainsley went to it and opened it to look at John's laboratory on the other side. The shelf he used to hide the door was askew, but other than that everything looked as it should.

"How long have you been doing this?" Ainsley asked, trying hard to dampen his disappointment and frustration. "How long have you been coming into this room uninvited?"

"I only came tonight because I thought Miss Margaret was in your room," he explained. "I was coming for the lamp when you came at me."

Margaret told him someone had been coming into her room each night.

"Have you come in here before?" Ainsley asked, wearily.

"Peter!" John looked indignant. "I would never. This was my first time since your and Lady Margaret's arrival." He paused from breath. "I told you," John said. "I am only looking for something."

"What would that be?"

John hesitated. He pressed his lips together and looked away. "A ring. It's a family heirloom." He grew agitated by Ainsley's continued questioning.

Ainsley shook his head and gestured to the sparse furnishings. "What would make you believe it was in here?"

"Because I gave it to Molly before she died," he snapped. "Satisfied?" The man's lower lip trembled slightly before he managed to turn away.

"John, were you"—Ainsley's throat grew dry at the thought of what he was about to say— "taking advantage of Molly?"

"We loved each other," John snapped. "Something you would know nothing about."

Ainsley recoiled, angered by John's spiteful assumption.

"I loved her and wanted to marry her desperately. I asked her to marry me. I gave her the ring as a promise. But, my research ... you see. I needed to finish my research."

Ainsley swallowed and tried not to imagine the young girl, compromised and alone. He wouldn't have been surprised to find out she was with child when she died. "How long?" he asked, not really wanting to hear the answer. "How long had you two been involved?"

"I did not know what she planned to do. I did not know

she intended to take her own life." John turned from him, weeping. "I did not know ..."

"How long?"

"As long as I've lived here."

"John—"

"I know! It's horrible. To keep her waiting so long. I had no choice, Peter. The college was threatening to pull funding. I had to remain focused."

Ainsley spied the crucifix on the wall above the bed. Molly had been Catholic. His heart sank. "Do you realize what you have done?"

"No worse than you or Jonas!" John used his handkerchief to wipe his nose as he sniffled.

"What is that supposed to mean?"

John appeared hesitant to say more but then rolled his shoulders back in a show of defiance. "You know exactly what it means! You may be the son of a gentleman but I've always known you to be a rake, nothing more."

Ainsley laughed at the absurdity of his words.

"You used many women for your own carnal desires—"

"And they used me! I didn't have to sneak into their rooms at night."

John took two steps to Ainsley, angered and venomous. "At least I loved her! And ... and I didn't throw her away after the first night." What was born from frustration and rage now morphed into shock and grief. He lowered his head as the tears spilled from his eyes. "I loved her," he mumbled through grief-stricken tears. He fumbled backward and collapsed into a simple wooden chair.

The tragedy was not lost on Ainsley, who himself had taken up a relationship with one of his family's hired help. At first he hadn't given their class divide much thought until his feelings for her grew and he realized he had a bigger role to play to ensure her reputation wasn't compromised. In the end he decided she was the one who needed to be in charge of their relationship. If she decided it needed to end then, as devastated as Ainsley would be, he knew, because of his position in society, it was what needed to happen.

John had been Molly's superior in class and in the running of the house. She probably felt she couldn't refuse him, even if she wanted to.

"It wasn't like that," John said suddenly, mirroring Ainsley's concern. "I gave her the ring. That should have been enough."

Ainsley shook his head in disbelief. John had never been very personable. He kept mainly to himself. Ainsley couldn't imagine John having a lengthy conversation with anyone, least of all a woman. He felt sorry for the girl and wondered if it truly was the heartfelt relationship John professed it to be.

"Margaret has your ring," Ainsley said, unable to look at his friend.

"Margaret has it?"

"She found it in the chest and wanted to return it to its rightful owner. You can retrieve it in the morning." Ainsley placed a hand on his forehead and closed his eyes. It had been a long day and he needed sleep desperately.

John stopped at the door. He had a look of regret in his face. "I'm sorry for saying those heartless things about you," he said.

"Don't apologize," Ainsley said, shaking his head. "It was all true once." Ainsley looked up and met John's gaze. "But we all change, John. We learn and we change. Whether we realize it or not."

Chapter 28

The hours passed by and thankfully Margaret slept until the promise of morning kissed the distant sky. The entire time Jonas remained vigilant at her side, startled by any slight movement or moan she made. There was nothing more he wanted than to erase her pain. He shouldn't have let her go, but how could he stop her? Expecting such obedience was akin to caging a songbird, something he refused to ever do, least of all to Margaret.

How he loved her. Her tenacity. Her strength. Her courage.

Absentmindedly, he began to stroke the curve of her hand and saw how much darker his skin was compared to her pale tone. We are two very separate beings, he caught himself thinking, from two very separate worlds. He reached to her face to move her hair from her cheek. As he did so, the scar at her throat and collar was caught by the lamplight behind him. Though completely healed the jagged line was still raised and the colour dark pink.

The image made him cringe. He blamed his lack of skill that had marred her skin permanently. It did not matter how many lives he had saved before or since. Hers was the only one that truly mattered; hers and the life she carried for both of them.

During the hours he spent at her bedside he prepared his heart and mind for what he must do for Margaret's sake, and now for the sake of their child. He must release her from their promise to marry. It was a solution that had occurred to him within his first hour at Calton and it had been toying with him ever since. She'd not be subjected to jealous and vindictive women like Eloise and her reputation would not be tainted by her association with him, an accused murderer. She'd have no more scars for the rest of her days. She deserved a better life than he could give.

It was an imperfect answer to an imperfect predicament. He'd been prepared to do it even before Blair showed up at his doorstep. He reasoned that even if the charges against him proved unfounded he'd still be subject to mockery and ridicule for the rest of his days. His career would never entirely recover and he'd never be able to provide the lifestyle she had been accustomed to. Blair Thornton, on the other hand, could provide that lifestyle and more, for Margaret and their child.

"You should marry Blair," he found himself saying, despite a screaming frustration that burned in his gut. "As soon as you can." If she married Blair soon, he'd have to accept the child as his. If Jonas went to the gallows both Margaret and their child would have the second chance they deserved.

He had been so close to calling her wife, and now he was glad she had been delayed and could not join him. Oh, the misery it saved her from.

The echoes of Rebecca's last words to him resounded even now, as he looked over Margaret's overpowered and injured body.

"Is the baby all right?"

Jonas could see the woman's tearstained face even then as he stroked Margaret's hand.

Is the baby all right? Will Margaret survive? Is the baby all right?

God he hoped so.

The words had repeated themselves countless times in his mind as he made the excruciatingly long walk home back to Margaret. How this illness would affect the unborn child remained a mystery. He wondered if Eloise had known. Had she guessed? Any such revelation would have made Margaret an easy target for her vindictive attacks. Eloise was the epitome of madness, able to function and appear normal all the while acting out on her absurd and deluded wishes without anyone being the wiser. Even her own father had fallen under her spell.

But how? How had she gotten to Margaret, the woman who swore she would not eat or drink anything? How had Eloise broken through their defences?

Jonas went for the door and made his way down stairs. He stood in the foyer for a moment, before heading into the parlour. Margaret's silk scarf was draped over the back of a chair. He pulled it toward him and looked at the delicate fibres in the light.

"Got you."

❧　❧

John startled awake and nearly jumped from his bed as Jonas tapped his shoulder. "What? Is it Margaret?" he asked, squinting at the lamp Jonas placed on the bedside table.

Jonas held up the scarf. "Test this." He dropped it in John's reluctant hand and retreated to the door.

"Now?"

"Now!"

An hour later the remaining members of the house were up. Jonas paced the floor in Margaret's room, biting the edge of his thumbnail. The only thing that pulled him from his agitated state was a noise Margaret made, groaning from discomfort, and a shifting under the sheets.

"Jonas ..." Her words were hoarse and quiet. Another round of convulsions ensued as sweat dripped from her forehead and glistened on her skin.

He felt her pulse at her wrist and found it quickening. With her eyes closed, she ripped her hand away and placed it at her stomach as another round of convulsions took hold.

"Peter!" Jonas yelled as he held the washbasin and guided Margaret to it.

Seconds later, Ainsley and John raced in from the hall. "We've got her," they said in unison.

"Strychnine?" Jonas looked to Margaret.

Ainsley nodded. "Yes. Mr. Locke said it can be inhaled. I think Eloise touched her scarf."

Jonas looked back at Margaret, who appeared weak and fading. "I think we need to give her another dose," he said.

"She's already had four drops."

"She vomited out the first three." Jonas's eyes trailed Ainsley as he came alongside the bed. "One more, Peter. We just need one more."

Ainsley looked over his sister in the bed and gave a heavy sigh. "What about the child? We don't know what it could do—"

"None of that matters without Margaret!" Jonas reached over and grabbed Ainsley's hand. "Please, we have to save her."

Chapter 29

"How is the patient doing?"

Ainsley lifted his head from his hands and saw Blair at the door, hopeful.

Jonas had administered one more dose, just a drop, about an hour before and they had been waiting on bated breath ever since. They had exchanged few words and even fewer glances as the minutes ticked by. It was starting to occur to Ainsley that he should send some sort of word regarding Margaret's illness to Marshall House in London. A wire would suffice. The exact wording of the missive eluded him, though; so did the energy required to move him from his spot at her side.

Ainsley shot a glance to Jonas on the opposite side of the bed and saw that not even the words from Blair had stirred him from his vigil.

"We are waiting," Ainsley said apologetically. "She did speak, but neither of us could make it out."

Blair entered the room and hovered near the foot of the bed. His gaze seemed focused on Jonas, no doubt confused by the attention he paid Margaret. Ainsley's distress was understandable, but Jonas would have had no reason to be so distraught.

"She smiled," Jonas said, without moving his hands from in front of his mouth.

"No doubt she is glad for the attention you both have showered upon her," Blair said, reluctantly pulling his attention from Jonas and redirecting it at Ainsley. "Perhaps we should bring her to the infirmary," he suggested. "There will be other doctors. We can draw from their expertise."

"We aren't moving her," Jonas said. When he turned his head he looked to Ainsley across the bed. "Just a little while longer," he said. "We will know after a little while longer."

After the last dose, Ainsley was quick to seal the bottle of hemlock and tuck it away in the bureau. While it had sat on the nightstand, it beckoned to be used, an antidote to

Margaret's troubles but also an invitation for death if not used sparingly. They would feed her no more, and putting it away was a symbolic gesture on Ainsley's part to signify the end of its use.

Beyond the door Ainsley caught sight of Ezra passing in the hall, a deep scowl on his face. A second later John passed by in pursuit. Ainsley stood up from his chair. Blair's eyes followed him as he circled the bed and went for the door.

"Feel free to sit down, Blair," Ainsley said as he reached the door and peered down the hall. "I just need a minute."

By the time Ainsley reached the stairwell he could hear the two friends arguing.

"You're a better friend to him than I," John said. "Don't tell me you don't know where he is."

"I don't!"

Ainsley rounded the bannister and saw them standing on the landing just below.

"I know you are involved in something," John said. "Tell m—"

Ezra looked up and spied Ainsley.

"What do you need, Peter?" he asked, his expression hardening.

John looked far more hospitable. "Is everything all right with Miss Margaret?"

Ainsley gave a quick nod. "Jonas believes she is on the mend."

At that moment he was not thinking of Margaret, however. His attention was equally divided between the two of them. Ezra, normally even-tempered, looked ready to pounce. His gaze was stern and his stance unmoving. John looked far more embarrassed than angry. Jonas had long maintained that someone in the house had been behind Frobisher's murder and that the same person had manoeuvred against him. Ainsley certainly hoped it had not been Ezra all this time.

"Who is missing?" Ainsley asked, watching Ezra's reaction closely.

Ezra's eyes rolled to the ceiling but before he could say anything John cut in.

"Giles. He left shortly after you came back last night."

"I told you, he's probably working in his office," Ezra cut in, rubbing his temple, obviously frustrated that he was forced into having this conversation.

"For the entire night?" John turned to Ainsley. "Something about this doesn't feel right to me—"

Ezra gave John a slight shove, forcing him to back away from Ainsley. "It's quieter, all right? You can't blame him for wanting peace and quiet with all the ruckus going on here lately." Ezra looked incredulous. "Why does it matter to either of you?"

"It matters because one professor is dead and another is accused of murder," Ainsley said.

"Peter!" Blair's panic-stricken voiced reached them at the stairwell before the man hurried down the hall and looked down the stairwell. "Come quick, it's Margaret."

Ainsley ran up the stairs, pushed past Blair, and rounded the doorframe to the room. He found Jonas hovering over Margaret's body, his hand at her neck checking for a pulse.

"What happened?" Ainsley asked, coming along the opposite side.

"She went limp and she stopped breathing." Jonas's voice betrayed his panic. "Margaret. Margaret!" He began slapping her gently on the side of the face.

Ainsley searched for a pulse. "She's cold. Margaret!"

Blair and John came into the room but stayed near the door

Jonas pulled back the covers and put his ear to her chest. "She has a heartbeat." He placed a hand on her cheek, tapping lightly. "Breathe, Margaret. Come on, breathe." He pulled the pillow out from behind her head and tossed it aside. With his ear to her mouth and nose, he listened for a second before placing his mouth on hers and blowing air into her cheeks.

"What are you doing?" Blair moved forward but John coaxed him back.

Ainsley reached over and pinched Margaret's nose. "Do it again," he said.

Jonas did it again and this time they saw her chest rise.

"Doctors do this to newborn babies who don't start breathing straightaway," John explained.

A panicked gasp filled the room. Jonas and Ainsley pulled back as Margaret began coughing wildly.

"Sit her up. Sit her up." Ainsley grabbed the pillows and began placing them behind her back as Jonas pulled her body forward and then laid her down on them in a semi-reclined position. Her eyes fluttered for a moment.

"Margaret." Her name escaped Jonas's lips as he held her hand to his chest. "Are you awake?"

Ainsley could see her chest rising and falling with regularity.

Then they all watched in awe as she raised her other hand to her head and felt her face. "Everything feels like pins and needles," she said quietly.

"It's all right," Jonas said, trying to keep his enthusiasm at bay. He stroked her hair, pulling it back from her face. "You're going to be all right."

When Ainsley looked away from the bed he saw that Ezra as well had entered the room and was standing alongside Blair and John at the footrail.

"How did you know to do that?" Blair asked. "How did you know it would work?"

Jonas turned his head to look at him. "At that time what other option did I have?"

Outwardly, Ainsley smiled, but inside he had a sinking feeling in the pit of his stomach. Margaret looked to be on the mend once and for all, but no one had seen Giles since the day before.

❧   ❦

Ainsley knew he was being followed but went into Ezra's room anyway.

"What are you doing?" John asked when Ainsley reached the centre of the room.

He motioned for John to close the door. "Has Ezra left?"

Apprehensively, John pushed the door into place. "He's gone for at least an hour. I don't think we should be going through his things."

Ainsley ignored him and opened the top drawer of Ezra's desk. "John, I think it's time you accept the fact that one of your housemates is involved in Frobisher's murder and I don't mean Jonas."

John stood back and watched as Ainsley riffled through a few papers. Nothing caught Ainsley's eye. All the handwriting was small, too small and too short, to do a proper comparison.

"I won't believe it's Ezra," John said. Despite his reluctance, he still watched as Ainsley went through each drawer and book systematically.

When Ainsley moved to the bedside table he found what he was looking for almost instantly. He moved it to the light of the window and pulled the letters Rebecca had given him from the inside pocket of his jacket. His heart sank. He stood near the light for some time, reading over each word, cross-comparing it to the others to be sure, before finally folding up both pages together and tucking them away in his jacket. He would not let John see it, and was glad he had not been looking over his shoulder.

"Peter, what is it?" John asked, as Ainsley passed him for the door. "Where are you going?"

"To the telegraph office," he said opening the door. "I have a friend with the Yard who might be able to help us."

Chapter 30

Never before had Margaret felt so stiff. Pain radiated from each of her limbs, culminating at her neck, which felt constricted and swollen. She had vague memories of illness, of heat and pain, vomiting and arguing. And Jonas. He had been talking to her, almost crying. Had he been afraid she would die? Judging by the way her body felt perhaps she had died.

With some struggle she opened her eyes to find Blair seated at her bedside. The image of him was blurry, but she could make out enough to know he was there and no one else.

"Where's Jonas?" she asked groggily. "And Peter?"

Ignoring the pain in her muscles, she tried to pull herself from the pillows to look about the room. Blair was quick to coax her to lie back down. "Jonas is resting," he said, "I don't know where Peter ran off to."

"But Jonas was here," she said confused. "So were you." The last few hours flashed through her mind but there was no chronological sequence to her thoughts. Everything had melded into one finishing with memories of her and Jonas in the parlour. He had gone down on one knee.

No.

Margaret stopped herself and closed her eyes. It was not Jonas. It had been Blair.

When she opened her eyes again she found Blair had moved closer and was now cradling her head with his hand. He used his thumb to stroke the side of her cheek as he smiled. Had her eyes been closed for a minute or had more time passed than that?

"When I thought you were dying I ..." His voice trailed off in uncertainty. "I just didn't want to contemplate it. We've only just reacquainted ourselves." His smile was genuine, as were his feelings for her, but her feelings for him were not as pronounced. It took a moment, but then she remembered what Jonas had said. He wished her to marry

Blair, to remove herself from the scandal of Jonas's current situation. To save their child from lifelong guilt by association.

"Don't look so frightened." Blair drew her attention back and she realized her expression betrayed her thoughts. "However this happened to you, I promise it won't happen again. Not while I am here."

His assurance fell flat. She had no desire to be protected by anyone but least of all him. It was true, he had saved her life and was a dear childhood friend, but she could not in good conscience marry him, not when she knew she carried Jonas's child.

Slowly, she grabbed Blair's wrist and gently pulled his hand away. "I have something I wish to say," she said.

"It's all right, Margaret," he said softly, perhaps wishing she would not have the words to refuse him. "Now that you are on the mend, we have the rest of our lives to say things to each other."

Margaret's gaze followed the movements of Blair's lips. It took a few moments for her to realize he had finished talking. When she looked up to his eyes, she found him tearing up.

"That is *if* you accept my hand." Blair raised her left hand and touched the underside of the ring moving it side to side slightly. The diamond sparkled against the dampened light streaming in from the window. He must have slipped it on while she slept off the lingering effects of her illness.

"Oh—"

"Say yes," he pleaded. His expression looked less confident than it had a day or two before. Perhaps he held on to the hope that he had been the one to ask her first. But it was clear he was shaken and anxious for her official acceptance.

"I can't."

"Margaret—"

"My heart breaks for you, but I just can't." Seeing the distant look in his eyes, Margaret reached for him but he pulled away. "You are a good man," she said, watching him straighten in his chair. "Anyone would be blessed to call you husband."

"Your heart belongs to another," he said quickly, saving her from having to utter the words.

Margaret nodded. "I am so very sorry. It was never my intention to lead you on in such a way. You saved my life."

He smiled and finally met her eyes again. "I have never met a girl who found herself in peril so routinely," he said with a laugh.

"Yes," she said, "I will admit to that. It seems to be an affliction I suffer from."

Despite the jovial speech, a sombre mood had befallen the room. Realizing this, Margaret slowly pulled the ring from her finger and placed it in the palm of Blair's hand before closing his fingers around it. "You are a very special man, Blair Thornton," she said, "and you deserve to be with someone who only has eyes for you."

Blair nodded but his expression reflected his broken heart. He stood up from his seat next to the bed and stepped toward the door. He stopped short, paused for a moment, and then turned to face her one more time. "I had meant to stay on until this business with our doctor friend had been resolved," he said. "I'm not so sure that would be ... prudent, given the circumstances."

How could he stay, knowing his suit had been denied and that the man he was helping to keep from the gallows was the man who had ultimately won Margaret's heart?

"Peter and I understand."

"Perhaps I may compose a letter, speaking of his excellent character," he offered, with a hopeful look. "It could be used in his defence. I could convince my father to write as well."

Margaret forced a smile, even though her insides churned with panic. What had she done? If Jonas went to the gallows and she was indeed with child, everyone would know of their fornication. A quick marriage to Blair would disguise such a scandal.

As he slipped out into the hall she resisted the urge to call out to him, to take back her refusal. In the end, she knew he did not deserve to have someone use him in such a way. Any illegitimate child born to her was her burden to bear alone.

She listened to the sound of him heading down the stairs

and noted the slow, melancholy way he opened the front door and left.

With the house quiet Margaret slipped her hand under the blankets and felt her lower stomach. A small mound existed, hardened and unmistakable. It hadn't been a delirium-induced desire. It was real. She was pregnant and she had known for the past four months. Her preoccupation with her father's illness and her heartbreak at having to postpone her elopement with Jonas had served as great distractions against the many changes taking place in her body. Her tender breasts, her excessive fatigue, her relentless nausea had all been warning signs of a larger situation, one she had been content to ignore but could no longer deny.

Marrying Jonas without the consent and blessing of her family had been a simple choice four months before compared to the hardships they faced now. Their lives were no longer simple. Had she not been such a spineless coward, had she left London with him as they had planned, none of this would have ever happened.

❧   ❦

Margaret could not fight the sleep that engulfed her for another hour or two. When she finally woke again the sun was almost set and cloud cover hovered over the city. She could hear the drops of rain hitting the windowpane. It was a cold rain. Rain always had a different sound when it was cold.

She opened her eyes and saw John just outside the door. He peered around the doorframe. "Are you awake?" he asked. Margaret could see him silently chiding himself for asking a question with such an obvious answer.

Margaret pushed herself higher on her pillow. "Yes, it's all right."

He held out both hands as he entered the room. One held a glass of water, the other a white pill. "Jonas bid me give you this," he said, "for the pain, should you have any."

Indeed, Margaret did. Never before had she felt such pain in every crevice of her body. She took the medicine offered to her and greedily drank the entire contents of the glass.

"Shall I get you some more water?" John asked.

"Please."

He smiled, gave a slight nod, and moved to exit. He stopped himself before he reached the door. "I should offer my deepest apologies to you," he said as he turned, "for not making you aware that I had a key to your room."

At first Margaret was confused, unsure of what he was trying to say.

"I only had it because of Molly. She had become very dear to me."

Margaret nodded. "Is it your ring I found?"

"My mother gave it to me before she passed," he said. "I had given it to Molly, as a promise, but I guess she didn't see it that way."

Margaret spied her reticule on the chair at the side of the bed. It took a moment for her to pull at the strings enough so that the top would open. At the bottom she found the emerald ring and presented it to John. He took it in his free hand and stared at it a moment.

"I feel responsible for her decision. Perhaps I should have made it known how deeply I cared for her. I should have married her months ago or at least made her know of my intention to do so." His face began to show the pain he obviously felt. He collapsed in the chair at the side of the bed and threw his hands up to his face.

Margaret reached over and placed a hand on top of his. When he looked to her she made a point to keep his gaze trained on her. "Love is too great a feeling to be associated with something as lowly as regret." She squeezed his hand. "Her choice was hers alone. You loved her. Many don't get such a gift."

A silence befell them for many minutes until finally John nodded. "Thank you, Miss ... I mean, Lady Margaret. Your words are a comfort."

A moment later, after his tears had dried somewhat, John stood. "I'll get you that water now."

Chapter 31

Ainsley hadn't expected anyone to be about when he returned to the house. When he entered Margaret's room he saw that she was standing in the centre of the rug while John and Jonas stood close by. Overcome with relief, Ainsley went straight for her, wrapped his arms around her and nearly lifted her from the ground.

"Oh thank God," he said, closing his eyes.

"It would take far more than that to do me in," Margaret said, returning his tight embrace.

When they parted Ainsley pointed back at the bed. "What are you doing out of bed?"

"I'm merely stretching my legs. You can see I am well supervised." Margaret turned gingerly, keeping her steps short and calculated. "Everything feels so stiff. I am beginning to wonder if I ever will be able to get on normally again."

"You will. Give it time," Jonas chimed in. The smile in his words was unmistakable.

Ainsley helped guide Margaret back to bed, giving her something steady to lean on as she sat down.

"I've taken your scarf to the Edinburgh Police," Ainsley said.

Margaret's eyes shot up and then went to Jonas. "My scarf?"

"Did Eloise touch your scarf at any time during your visit?"

"Well … yes. She pulled it higher around my neck before I took my leave," she said, her hand suddenly going to her bare neck.

"John found traces of strychnine, which can be inhaled rather than ingested," Jonas explained. "We had to use coniine to counteract the poison."

"Hemlock," John said by way of explanation.

"She was trying to kill me." Margaret looked to Jonas in panic.

"What did the constables say, Peter?" Jonas asked.

"They said they will send an officer around to take statements and they may need to seek independent test results of the scarf."

John perked up at the door. "It shouldn't be a problem," he said. "There was more than enough left on the scarf for further testing."

"The man and boy who work for her, they saw her touching my scarf," Margaret said.

Ainsley nodded. "Exactly. I believe her jealousy prevented her from thinking through her deeds clearly. She wasn't worried about getting caught, it seems."

"Is she behind what's been done to Jonas?"

Ainsley took a breath. "Not the way I understand it. She's dangerous but not guilty of that. Margaret, I didn't just go to the constabulary." He looked to Jonas. "I've had a hunch about who might be behind all this."

Jonas straightened his stance as Ainsley spoke.

"I wanted to be certain before I got anyone's hopes up. I think—"

They heard the front door open. "Help! Someone, please, come help!" It was Ezra. Ainsley, John, and Jonas went for the hall but Ezra had already run up the stairs.

"You must come. It's Giles!" The man gasped for breath.

"You found him," Ainsley said.

Ezra nodded. "He's on the roof of the infirmary. I think he plans to jump. You must come and help me."

Jonas and Ainsley both turned to Margaret, who was trying to stand up from bed. "I'm all right," she said quickly. "Go. Help your friend."

Ainsley nodded and pulled Jonas, entreating him to follow them.

"Mrs. Crane is here to help me. You need to go!" Margaret repeated.

Finally, Jonas nodded and the four men ran for the stairs.

"Mrs. Crane!" Ainsley went to the kitchen and propped open the door. Mrs. Crane had already been heading toward them, most likely drawn by the ruckus and noise.

"What is all this 'ollering about?"

"Keep watch over Margaret, yes?"

"Of course, Dr. Ainsley. Where are the two of ye heading off to?"

Only then did Ainsley notice that Jonas was standing beside him.

"There's no time to explain," Ainsley said, pushing Jonas away from the kitchen and guiding him toward the front door. "Keep the doors locked and don't let anyone in or out, yes?"

Mrs. Crane followed them to the foyer, a frightened look overtaking her features. "Yes, doctor. Of course." Ainsley heard the click of the lock behind them seconds after they left and instantly felt better about leaving Margret in such a hurry.

Ezra had a carriage waiting at the kerb but before they reached it, a young boy appeared at the walk.

"Excuse me, Mr. Ainsley, sir?"

Ainsley waited as Jonas filed into the carriage with John and Ezra.

"A message, sir. From the wire service." He held out a folded piece of paper for Ainsley.

"Come on," Ezra called half hanging out of the carriage window. "We have to go!"

Ainsley pulled a fistful of coins from his pocket and placed them in the boy's free hand before he snatched the paper. "There's a good lad," he said before jumping in the carriage and taking his seat amongst the others.

"What is it?" Jonas asked as the carriage jerked into motion.

"It's a message from Simms," Ainsley said, "I believe."

He took a moment, ignoring the anxious fidgeting of Ezra on the opposite bench to read over the telegram. "I knew it," he said before he could stop himself.

"What does it say?" Jonas asked. Ainsley handed him the note just as the university came into view.

"Giles had not visited his sister recently," Ainsley said. "In fact, I'm willing to wager he wasn't even in London as he claims."

Ezra and John exchanged glances.

A look of confusion on Jonas's face prompted Ainsley to continue. "When Margaret and I first met him he had said he was returning from London where he had been visiting his sister and his newly born niece." He reached into his pocket, pulled out his train ticket, and inspected it. "Simms, my friend with the Yard, has paid her a call. She hasn't seen her brother in many months."

"Some other business then," Ezra offered.

"No," Ainsley shook his head. He smiled and reached across the seat to hand Jonas his train ticket. "Margaret and I had only met him on the platform. We never saw him at Kings Cross, or at any other time in the journey. He switched my ticket after knocking them from my hand and dropping his newspaper in a puddle. Mine now says I was departing Edinburgh and arriving in London, but it should say London to Edinburgh. It wasn't a mistake by the train company, like I thought. This is Giles's ticket. He took mine."

With the ticket in his hand, Jonas smiled and then raised his eyes to look at Ainsley, who nodded.

"Peter, you aren't making any sense," John said as the carriage pulled up to the front of university. "Why would he go through all this trouble to convince us he was in London?"

"To create an alibi in case any of this fell back on him." Ainsley turned to Jonas. "And I have the letters." Ainsley reached into his inside pocket and pulled out the folded papers.

"What letters?" Ezra looked terrified as Ainsley revealed the few pieces of key evidence they would use to prove Jonas was innocent.

Ainsley kept his eyes trained on Jonas. "I found this in Ezra's room." He opened the folded pages to reveal a letter addressed to Ezra. He trailed his finger down the page to show Giles's signature.

"This is written in Giles's hand. I used the letters Rebecca gave us and compared them to a letter I found in Ezra's room." Ainsley pulled the letters from Rebecca out from behind the letter addressed to Ezra.

With a look of half disbelief and half elation, Jonas took the pages in his own grasp.

"The handwriting is clearly a match. Don't you see, gentlemen?" Ainsley could hardly contain his excitement. "It's Giles. It's been Giles this entire time. He's the one who set Jonas up. He killed Frobisher and wanted Jonas to take the fall."

Chapter 32

With the men gone, the house fell into an oppressive silence. As much as Margaret told herself to rest, she couldn't. An unease took hold of her that she was unable to shake. She couldn't tell if her worry was for Giles or Jonas or something else entirely. Darkness descended, forcing her to put on her lamp. She had heard Mrs. Crane's humming, wafting in from the kitchen, earlier but for the last half hour Margaret had heard nothing. An insatiable thirst brought her to her feet and forced her to walk to her door. There she stood for a moment listening for any sign of the housekeeper.

"Mrs. Crane," she called out. "May I bother you for a glass of water?"

Margaret's heartbeat quickened when there was no immediately reply. Like a good mother hen, Mrs. Crane had been doting on her since the beginning of her illness, but now Margaret realized it had been a good while since Mrs. Crane had ventured to the second floor. If the woman had gone out, even for a brief period of time, she would have announced it. And Margaret had no doubt Peter wouldn't have left knowing Margaret would be all alone. One of them would have stayed just in case.

In case that woman comes—

Margaret froze at the thought, unsure of the root of it. Was Eloise capable of such a thing? Poison was such a sterile method of murder, so very distant compared to other devices. Could Margaret imagine the woman coming to the house?

In that instant her concern for Mrs. Crane doubled. Margaret walked the length of the hall and stood at the top of the stairs. She listened and heard nothing. No humming, no movement, no creaks of any kind. A carriage passed by on the street, casting a shadow on the window of the front door. For a moment Margaret thought it could be her brother and Jonas returning.

Margaret felt a cold draft on the landing and decided to return to the room to retrieve a shawl or blanket to cover her night shift before she ventured any further from her room. As she walked she saw a brief movement of light that streamed from her room and she stopped midstep. After five minutes standing motionless in the hall there were no further movements or sounds.

A figment of your imagination, she told herself. *My, what a cynical old goat you have become, Margaret.* With this internal chiding ringing in her ears, Margaret walked the rest of the way to her room and rounded the doorframe.

Eloise stood at the bureau. A small box sat on the top. In her other hand Eloise held a ring.

Margaret froze.

"Isn't this lovely?" she said, without pulling her gaze from the gem as she inspected it in the lamplight. "I was there when Jonas picked it out for you. He never knew it, of course."

"How did you get in here?" Margaret asked.

"I've been coming here for months, darling." Eloise's voice was steady and unnerving. "I've been following Jonas a lot longer than that."

Margaret took a step back and felt the wood of the doorframe through her shift. "Get out," she said. "Get out of here or I'll summon the constables."

Eloise didn't acknowledge anything Margaret had said. Not once had she moved her eyes from the ring. She flexed her fingers and slid the gold band down her ring finger. "So pretty." It was then that Eloise turned her head, revealing a rage in her eyes Margaret had never seen before. "It's a pity you won't ever see it on your finger."

Margaret recoiled and fumbled into the hall. She ran for the servant's stairs. Two flights. Could she make it two flights of stairs and lock herself in the maid's room? Her head was heavy with exertion but she was determined to try.

At the top of the stairs she slammed the door, but Eloise had been right behind her and was pushing her way in. With her weak body pressed against the door, she tried to reach for the two keys on the nightstand. One was for the servant's stairs door, the other ... Margaret looked up and saw the door to John's laboratory. But which key?

She could feel herself growing tired. Her will to live would only take her so far in her weakened state. She could make it. She had to. After a steady inhale of breath, she ran deeper into the room, snatched up both keys as she passed the bed, and ran for the second door. Thankfully, the shelf on the other side was still pushed to the side and Margaret could squeeze her way in. Again she slammed the door and fumbled with the keys, slipping one into the lock. There was no way to know if she had chosen the right one. They both looked identical.

As she turned it in the lock she heard the mechanism latch followed by incessant pounding from Eloise on the other side a second later.

Satisfied it was locked, Margaret ripped the iron key from the keyhole and slowly backed away. She scrambled around in the darkness. All of the windows in John's laboratory were covered. No ambient light penetrated to the attic room, leaving Margaret in the pitch dark. She did her best to manoeuver his maze of tables and experiments, and was thankful when she reached the main door, expecting it to be locked. It had been secured when he had first showed the room to her. His experiments were too previous. His work too vital to leave vulnerable.

She twisted the knob to check and the door opened. Opening the door a crack, she groped on the other side for a key, but found nothing. She knew she could not hold the door against Eloise, not after her illness. There was no telling how long Jonas and Peter would be away. Two choices existed for her: hide or run.

The pounding at the door in the maid's room ceased. In that instant there was no choice. If what she had said was true, if she had been coming to the house undetected Eloise would eventually find her way to John's laboratory. If Margaret was going to run, she couldn't wait another minute.

She barrelled down the stairs to the third-floor landing, skirted the bannister and ran the next flight as quickly as she could. One more flight, she told herself. One more flight and then she could run for the front door and scream for help. Someone would be passing by, someone would answer her screams.

As she rounded the bannister on the second floor, she felt a nudge from behind, a quick push on her back that sent her off balance. She felt her feet tangle beneath her. Her arm hit the bannister rail, but she could not catch hold. Her cheek hit the stairs, and then her shoulder and her back as she tumbled, finally landing with a thud.

"You can't hide from me," Eloise said evenly as she descended the stairs.

Margaret couldn't move for the pain. She feared her arm was broken, her back felt even worse. With one eye open she could see Eloise coming for her, slowly taking each step, a self-assured smile on her lips.

"I know every rusty door hinge and every hiding place," Eloise said as she drew closer. "I know every creak of every floorboard." To emphasize her point she lowered her left foot to the next step and then moved it to the far right. Her movements gave no sound. It was if she wasn't actually there.

Margaret rolled from her side and began backing away, moving toward the front door. She felt the door behind her but could not stand. She reached above her head with her good arm for the doorknob but could not get a grip.

"I know everyone's secrets," Eloise continued, coming to the bottom of the stairs. She was standing right over Margaret when she bent down low, bringing her nose level with Margaret's. "And now you know mine."

Margaret fingered the iron boot scraper at her side and steadied her breathing. She curled her fingers around the iron before swinging it upward with all her might. The unwieldy cast iron implement struck Eloise on the side of the head, knocking her over. Margaret pulled herself from under and scrambled to her feet. She ignored the pain, but was unable to push past the weakness of her body. She fought the need to close her eyes and used the wall to hold herself upright as she went for the kitchen.

The kitchen was the only lighted room in the house, other than Jonas's bedroom, but Mrs. Crane was nowhere to be seen. A large, unlabeled bottle sat uncorked at the kitchen table with a tumbler at its side. Margaret looked to the doorknob and found no lock. She pulled one of the chairs from the table and wedged it against the doorknob and listened. She heard nothing in the hall and thought for a moment that maybe she had successfully knocked Eloise unconscious.

She breathed a sigh of relief before the doorknob began to shake violently. A resounding thud rang out as something heavy hit the other side of the door. And then hit it again. And again.

Margaret backed away. She circled the table, looking for anything that could help her but found nothing. The butcher's block was empty, the sink as well.

The chair at the door moved with the third pounding and Margaret began searching for the door to the back of the house. There was a darkened archway and three steps down to a landing with a door to the outside, a closet, and more stairs to the cellar.

Margaret leaned on the wall again to support herself, taking each step carefully, hissing from the pain in her ankle. Before she reached the landing she felt a hand at her hair, tugging her backward. In desperation, Margaret grabbed for the doorknob but somehow she had been turned around and ended up opening the closet. Mrs. Crane stared back at her, eyes wide, sweating and gasping for breath against the fabric that was used to gag her mouth.

But Margaret couldn't help her. With a viselike grip, Eloise guided her back up the steps to the kitchen, knocking a mop from its place along the wall. Eloise deposited Margaret beside the table on the floor. From her position on the floor, Margaret saw a stream of blood trickling down the side of Eloise's face where she had hit her.

"I've made you a little drink," she said, straddling Margaret, who tried to crawl away. She held Margaret's chin up with one hand and brought the glass down from the table with the other. "This ought to take care of our little problem."

Margaret's sense of urgency doubled. Was she intending to harm the baby? Margaret wriggled and pushed against the weight of her captor as the glass came closer to her mouth.

"No!" she screamed. She managed to get a hand free from under her and began pulling at Eloise's arm and then she knocked the glass out of her hand. The shards of glass burst outward upon impact with the floor, sending the clear liquid splashing all over. Margaret reached for the mop and used the handle to jab Eloise in the chest.

The woman gasped and tried to grab hold of the wooden handle. Margaret turned it horizontal and used it to keep her attacker at bay. She could feel the shards of glass cutting into her as she backed away, sliding across the kitchen floor a few feet before being able to use the wall to brace herself. With a quick twist, Margaret brought the mop handle upright and hit Eloise on the cheek. Eloise fell over, clutching her face, and Margaret gathered herself from the floor. The glass that clung to the fabric of her nightgown and folds of her skin cascaded to the kitchen floor.

Margaret was tired of running. She knew Eloise would just keep chasing her. She wasn't just protecting herself anymore. She was protecting the life of the tiny being inside her. Her baby. Jonas's baby.

With a renewed sense of determination, Margaret brought the end of the mop handle in front of her and thrust it into Eloise's ribs. The impact sent Eloise to the floor again, crying out in pain. Then Margaret hit her again. And again. A sudden burst of anger took over Margaret as she watched the woman who wanted to kill her baby trying to crawl away from the onslaught.

Margaret grabbed one of Mrs. Crane's aprons hanging on a hook next to her. She could still hear the poor housekeeper's muffled screams through her gag. The fabric ripped easily in Margaret's hands. Once she was sure she had enough, she pushed Eloise's body over with the heel of her foot. Eloise looked up horrified as Margaret stood over her, her newly formed rope in her grasp.

"Give me one more minute, Mrs. Crane," Margaret said to the muffled screams coming from the landing. "I'm nearly finished."

Chapter 33

Ezra led Ainsley, Jonas, and John up three flights of stairs to a maintenance hatch with an iron ladder fastened to the wall.

"He's up there," Ezra said, pointing to the opening in the ceiling.

Ainsley and Jonas exchanged glances, both equally unsure if they should proceed. Ainsley half expected Giles to be riddled with guilt for the deed he had done. The other half knew that if someone were as cunning as to manipulate evidence of a murder they were just as cunning to manipulate an emergency. By the time Ainsley had made up his mind not to go, John was already climbing toward the night sky. It was too late to stop him and they couldn't expect him to go alone.

Jonas paused at the bottom of the ladder and looked to Ainsley. After a moment of thought, Ainsley gave a nod. They couldn't let a man like Giles get away with framing Jonas and then killing himself. They needed to put the pieces together enough so Jonas could clear his name.

A cold, Scottish wind whipped across their faces as they left the shelter of the building. Once Ainsley reached the flat portion of the roof he realized Giles was nowhere to be seen. A wide chimney with five stovepipes jutted up alongside where the roof peaked and connected to the other, newer section of the building.

"He's not here," Jonas proclaimed after surveying their landing.

John rushed to the edge and looked over the knee-high wall that signalled the end of the roof. Jonas did the same on the other side. He gave a shake of his head to Ainsley with a look of worry on his face.

"We should go," Ainsley said, turning to the hatch.

Before they reached it, Giles appeared on the ladder. He produced a small handgun, black and shiny in the moonlight, pointing it at them with a determined purpose.

"Don't move another inch," he said, abruptly repositioning the barrel of the gun at Ainsley.

Ainsley put his hands up in front of him and slowly backed away. He knew enough to bide his time and wait for the right moment if he ever expected to overpower a man with a gun.

"What is this, Giles?" Jonas asked, yelling against the wind that threatened to put icicles on their noses.

Giles tilted his head toward Ezra. "He did a good job, didn't he? He actually convinced you that I was preparing to take me own life." He gave an amused laugh. "He knew it was me all along, didn't you, Ezra?" He stretched out his arm to point the gun at Ezra. "He was the one who convinced Jonas and John to go drinking that night. He knew exactly which pub to take you to."

Ainsley's eyes darted to Jonas. "Your drink," he said quietly.

"That's right." Giles smiled. He looked far too pleased with himself. "Do either of you gentlemen know where I procured such a concoction?" When no immediate answer came, Giles took a step forward. "I'll give you a hint. The woman who made it is quite talented, as you well know." His smug smile faded. "Who am I speaking of, Jonas?"

"Miss Locke," Ainsley answered quickly in an effort to save Jonas from having to say it.

"That's right. I doubt she would have given it to me had I explained to her my true intentions for it. She is quite smitten, you know. She'd do anything for one of your housemates."

Jonas's expression remained unchanged, but Ainsley could tell a seething anger boiled just below the surface. He had known Jonas long enough to know the calculations that were quickly being performed in his head.

"How's Lady Margaret, Peter? Is she well?"

Ainsley stiffened at the mention of his sister. "She's on the mend."

"That's a pity. I would hate to have to do something to set back her progress."

His hands balled into fists, Jonas stepped to Giles, but Ainsley raised an arm to keep him back.

"You wouldn't dare touch her," Jonas growled over

Ainsley's shoulder.

With a slight shake in his hand, Giles raised the gun higher as if to remind everyone who was in charge. "You're right," he said, "Perhaps I'll leave that to Eloise. I'm fairly certain she's already devising a brilliant way to take out her greatest competition. I won't need to lift a finger."

Ainsley felt Jonas pushing on his hands. "I swear to God, Peter, let me go." His voice was low but his words were strong.

"Don't play into him," Ainsley cautioned quietly. "He's trying to bait you."

"What's that you are saying, Peter? Speak up so the rest of the class can hear," Giles said.

Ainsley felt Jonas relax somewhat and decided to step aside. He raised his hands again in a submissive gesture toward Giles.

"I'm so sorry, Jonas," Ezra said from a few feet away. "I didn't know what he intended to do and once I realized the part I played I couldn't stop it, not without ..." Ezra's voice trailed off in doubt.

"Not without exposing his deepest, ugliest secret," Giles said. "A few weeks ago, I caught him fondling the breasts of a patient."

All eyes turned to Ezra, who looked abashed and ashamed.

"She was dead," Giles added before chuckling at the shock on Ezra's face.

"Stop," Ezra growled through gritted teeth.

Giles raised his shoulders in a shrug. "You didn't actually expect me to keep my promise once we got to this point, did you? A woman died and this man, who hasn't bedded a girl in his life, took it upon himself to get acquainted with the opposite sex."

"Stop it!"

Ainsley saw a pool of tears glistening in Ezra's eyes. He had been coerced, that much was clear. The young professor could not afford any such blight on his record or stain on his character.

Ezra took tiny steps toward Ainsley and John, brushing tears from his eyes. "He made me do it," Ezra said, openly crying now. His shoulders shuddered and he nearly doubled over. "He was going to tell on me. I have a perfect record. He was going to take away my perfect record. What would I have said—?"

BANG!

Ezra's knees buckled and he dropped to the ground. His weeping was replaced by a look of despondent disbelief. A circle of blood appeared on his chest as his body involuntarily writhed in agony. Jonas, John, and Ainsley moved toward him. Giles let John pass him, but then turned the gun toward Jonas and Ainsley. "Not another inch."

A moan escaped Ezra on the ground. He wasn't dead yet.

"He's dying!" John yelled from his place at Ezra's side.

"Use your research. Grow him another heart or lung or whatever it is I hit," Giles answered mockingly. "Years wasted in the laboratory for what? You can't even save your friend."

"You took an oath, Giles!" Ainsley reminded him. "Do no harm!"

Giles squinted at him, titling his head to the side as if confused. "I can't seem to recall. Refresh my memory, Peter. I was never a very good pupil."

Ainsley said nothing. He kept his gaze unwavering and his stance strong.

A muted chuckle escaped Giles as he looked over his two hostages. "You remember those late nights when you both tried to help me with my studies? I just never could understand why the subjects came more easily for you than they did for me. Do you want to know what helped me in the end? It wasn't late-night studying, I'll confess to that."

Ainsley and Jonas waited as Giles paced, circling around them with the gun pointed at them.

"Frobisher. He and I came to an arrangement. He wanted to help me ... if I helped him with one minor life detail."

"He wasn't attracted to his wife." Ainsley said the words and knew instantly what it meant. Giles had been Frobisher's lover.

"That's right. She had money and he didn't. Her family connected him to other important people and so began a career of prestige and worth. They don't knight random surgeons, even ones who save the lives of important people in parliament." He gave a marked look of disdain to Jonas. "Frobisher couldn't bring himself to, you know, consummate, you could say. Twenty years married and no children. Why do you think that was?" Giles smiled. "It wasn't her fault. He couldn't bring himself to do it and I don't blame him."

"Is that why you killed him?" Ainsley asked.

"In part. I loved him, but he refused to leave his dove of a wife. After months spent begging him and then threatening to expose him he tried to rid himself of me. But that was the last thing I would ever let happen."

Ainsley saw a hint of remorse in Giles's eyes as he spoke.

"What are you going to do? Kill us all? Here? Like this?" Jonas asked.

If Giles came a few inches closer, Ainsley could have grabbed for the gun and would have gladly risked getting shot if it meant Jonas and John could leave unscathed.

But Giles did not come closer. He kept a perfect distance from both Ainsley and Jonas and offered little concern for John, who was still panicking over the state of Ezra. His stance may have been flawless, but his eyes betrayed his lack of confidence.

"I've been thinking of this for the last few days when I realized the charges were most likely going to be dropped. You weren't supposed to be here, Peter. Jonas was supposed to be put on trial and hang."

"My apologies."

"Always the hero, aren't you?" His face hardened as his gaze fell on Jonas. "Although I appreciate the sentiment of Peter's loyalty, I can't risk having you live. This is the way it's going to happen, in a fit of rage you kill them all and then, seeing what you did, you jump."

Ainsley forced a laugh. "You think anyone will believe that? I have a Scotland Yard detective looking into this right now. The charade won't last long once he hears of my death, I can assure you of that."

Giles's confidence waned. His eyes went between Ainsley and Jonas. "I can't let him live," he said, as if trying to convince Ainsley. "He's a pariah, don't you see, Peter? He's going to take away everything you and I have worked so hard for."

Ainsley didn't bother to hide his confusion. "How? How can what he does affect you or I?"

Giles shook his head. "So intelligent, yet so blind—"

"You filed the complaint against me," Jonas said. "It wasn't Frobisher."

"He would have agreed with everything I wrote."

"But he didn't even know about it because he was already dead by that time." Ainsley could feel the pieces coming together. During an argument, Giles stabbed Professor Frobisher, killing him, and hid the body until he could file the complaint, bribe Rebecca, and stage the scene. He made a few more wounds to make it appear as if Jonas had done it in Frobisher's office that night.

"Why me?" Jonas asked through gritted teeth. He pointed a finger at the ground. "You owe me an answer—"

"I owe you *NOTHING!*" Giles screamed. "God, you two are so alike. Conceited. Arrogant. Not deserving of anything providence has given you. I was not surprised in the slightest when Peter told us he was heir to a great fortune. Did you know, Peter, did you know we all took bets in school to see who could find out who your patron was and whether or not you were fucking her for your fees?" A tiny laugh escaped him. "Then we all heard about little Margaret. Beautiful, smart, aspiring doctor Margaret."

Out of the corner of his eye, Ainsley saw Jonas stiffen at the mention of her.

"Don't you see? We can't have her at this school, or anyone like her. Women aren't suited. They don't have the temperament. Their minds aren't as strong. Their stomachs are even worse." Giles regarded Jonas with disgust. "The way you talk about them you'd think we should just give them degrees for walking through the doors."

"That's not what I said," Jonas answered.

"You don't have to say it. I know you and all the other men like you. Women get what they want because you all want to get them in your beds. I had to fight for my degree and you ..." Giles marched toward him. "You would have them taking classes, attending lectures, and acting like men." He took Jonas up by the collar, with the gun still in his grasp. "When I needed someone to frame for Frobisher's murder you were the most natural choice I could make.

One less *woman* to worry about."

Jonas raised his arms to push Giles from him and knocked him to the ground. The gun skidded across the surface of the roof and came to a rest at the short wall. By the time Ainsley reached the gun Jonas was on top of Giles, holding him up by his shirt and punching him in the face. After only a few hits Giles's nose was covered in blood and so was Jonas's hand.

"Jonas, stop!" With the gun safely in his possession, Ainsley ran back to Jonas and tried to pull him away.

"You took my life away from me!" Jonas yelled as he fought Ainsley's attempt to break them apart. Jonas tried to land another punch but missed. Then he turned on Ainsley, pushing him away and doubling his efforts to get at Giles. Before he could reach him Ainsley cocked the gun and pointed it right at Jonas.

"I told you to stop!"

Jonas straightened his stance as Giles moaned in pain on the ground, covering his face with his hands. "You wouldn't kill me, Peter," Jonas said.

"I would shoot you in the arm to keep you from the gallows," Ainsley said. "I'm warning you, though, my aim isn't that great."

"I think Ezra's dead!" John yelled from the other side of the roof.

Jonas closed his eyes at the news and then both he and Ainsley turned their attention to their friend. Ainsley came alongside Ezra and laid the gun down on the ground before reaching for a pulse. He didn't need to get too close, however, to see that John was right. Ezra had lost too much blood.

"Oh God!" John clutched the side of Ezra's jacket and cried with his head lowered.

There was a scuffling sound near Giles. When they looked up, he was through the hatch and climbing the ladder into the building. Ainsley watched as Jonas snatched up the gun and ran after him.

"John," Ainsley said, trying to pull him from Ezra's body. "John!"

Finally, the man looked up.

"There's nothing we can do for him now," Ainsley said. "I

have to go after Jonas. I need you to get out of the building as quickly as you can and fetch someone from the Edinburgh Police."

John moved to stand.

"Quickly!"

With a renewed purpose, John nodded.

Ainsley crept down into the building first and ran down the first flight of stairs to the main hall. At the far end he could see Jonas sprinting in the darkness, only illuminated by the pale moonlight streaming in from the arched window at the end of the hall.

John appeared behind Ainsley. "Go now," Ainsley mouthed, motioning for him to keep heading down to the ground floor. He watched for a moment as John ran down the flight of stairs, and hoped that help would arrive before Jonas made an irreversible mistake.

"Jonas!" Ainsley ran after him, trying to stay in the shadows at the side of the hall. "Jonas!" If Jonas heard him, he made no indication. Ainsley could just see him at the end of the hall, a black shape sliding further and further away. There was another corridor that joined with this one that would lead to the lecture halls. The shadow of Jonas disappeared at the corner.

Ainsley arrived at the corridor just in time to see Jonas, gun in his hand, duck into the operating theatre.

"Jonas!" Ainsley kept his voice low but the panic was real. Giles could have been anywhere and he had already proved he was capable of killing without a firearm.

Ten feet further down the hall, Ainsley paused and listened for a moment. What was that noise? Breathing.

Ainsley felt a sharp object at his throat and the forceful grasp of Giles behind him, pulling him through a doorway. Ainsley squinted against the brightness of the gaslights above the examination table. Once his eyes adjusted, Ainsley saw Jonas on the other side of the room amongst the spectator railings. A long counter separated them with an assortment of bell jars and scientific apparatus on top. Giles pulled Ainsley further into the room, ensuring the empty examination table was positioned between them.

"Fancy us all meeting here again," Giles said from behind Ainsley.

Ainsley swallowed and felt the surgical knife pressing into the skin at his Adam's apple.

"I guess this narrative works too," Giles said. "Ainsley confronts you. You kill him in a rage. Then Ezra follows you to the roof and you kill him. All before killing yourself. Not my first choice, but still effective."

"Let Peter go," Jonas said carefully.

Giles clutched him tighter. "Why? Because he's your best mate?"

"Because he pleaded for your life. Up on the roof. He told me not to kill you."

"Another benevolent move, I must say," Giles said from behind Ainsley.

Ainsley felt himself pulled backward as the knife eased into his skin.

"Giles, Giles, wait." Ainsley raised his hands another inch to reinforce he was not a threat. "Don't do this. We've been through too much together. All of us."

Jonas did not lower the gun. Ainsley could see him with both hands up, cradling the piece of metal while keeping Giles squarely in his sights. He could not see Giles but he could feel the man loosen his grip slightly as Ainsley spoke.

"Remember"—Ainsley swallowed—"remember that time when we went drinking when we were supposed to be studying for our chemistry exam. Remember that?"

"Peter, now is not the time." Jonas eyed them.

Ainsley stood a single finger up on one hand. "This is good, Jonas. Hear me out. Do you remember, Giles? You and I got so drunk we didn't know what year it was, let alone the date." Ainsley tried to turn his head to the side to look at Giles and was reminded of the blade at his throat. He looked to Jonas, who shook his head slightly in warning.

"You don't remember?" Ainsley took on a positive tone in his voice. "We remember, don't we, Jonas? We remember." He gestured with his hand back and forth between them.

Jonas nodded his understanding of Ainsley's meaning and raised the gun half an inch.

Ainsley felt Giles's grip loosen slightly. "Jonas here was so pissed at me. I don't remember what I did, maybe I said something, but he was coming for me. He tried to hit me, you remember that? But I ducked out of the way and he hit—"

Ainsley elbowed Giles in the ribs. Once the knife was away from his throat, Ainsley hit the floor and a single shot rang out.

When Ainsley looked up he saw Giles pushed back into the chalkboard. Jonas had hit him squarely in the chest. As the blood gathered in the fibres of his shirt, Giles looked at Jonas with wide, unfocused eyes. The surgical knife dropped from his hand and then he collapsed on the floor.

"You, Giles. I ducked out of the way and Jonas hit you."

Jonas was at Ainsley's side. Blood was coming from his neck. He raised a hand to his throat to feel the wound. The cut wasn't very deep. "A flesh wound," he said, wincing against the pain as he touched it.

Jonas helped him get to his feet. "Nice story," he said. "I don't remember any of that."

"Because I made it up." Ainsley looked to Giles on the floor. "It worked, didn't it?"

As the fight-or-flight response lessened in the minds, they surveyed the scene. Ainsley tried not to replay the events over again in his mind, especially since he knew he'd not be able to help himself from focusing on the alternative outcome. Ainsley closed his eyes and took a breath. When he opened them again he saw the look of horror in Jonas's eyes as they stood over the body.

"You had no choice," Ainsley said. "I would have done the same for you."

They locked eyes for a moment, the worry and fear evident in both of them. Would anyone believe their story or would Jonas have to now pay with his life for the deeds of a madman?

❧ ❦

By the time Inspector Hearst showed up Jonas and Ainsley were seated on a pair of stools far from the body of Giles. While they waited, Jonas had disinfected Ainsley's throat wound and applied a bandage. A pair of constables filed into the room after the inspector.

"Check him," Inspector Hearst said, pointing to the body.

"The gun which shot him is right there," Ainsley said,

gesturing to the weapon that sat on the examination table directly in front of the policeman.

"Who shot him?"

Jonas stood. "I did, sir."

The inspector looked taken aback by Jonas's easy confession.

"He saved my life, sir," Ainsley said and gestured to his bandage.

The friends had been careful not to touch the knife, which remained inches from Giles's hand.

"He may have used such a knife to kill Professor Frobisher two days before his body was found," Ainsley said. "There was so little blood in the professor's office on the night Jonas was found there because the body was moved there."

"We have a witness as well," Jonas said, "who will tell you how I came to be at the university that night."

The inspector looked at them with astonishment. "You figured this all out on your own then?"

Ainsley chuckled slightly and looked to Jonas. "Yes, Inspector, we did."

A young officer ran into the room and stopped suddenly before he collided with the inspector.

"There's been another murder, sir," the constable said, out of breath.

"Where?"

"In New Town, sir. Heriot Row."

Jonas and Ainsley looked to each other. "Margaret!"

Chapter 34

Mrs. Crane met them in the foyer as they raced in from the carriage. "Where is she?" Jonas asked, walking past her and the constable next to her.

"The kitchen," Mrs. Crane said, near to tears. "She's in the kitchen."

Ainsley followed closely at his heels as Jonas pushed open the kitchen door and saw Margaret on the floor. Her back was against the cupboard door but Ainsley could see the streaks of blood that dotted her nightgown and the scraping wounds that littered her exposed skin. She hugged her knees close and stared at something on the other side of the room. When they entered she looked up, revealing a tearstained face and quivering lower lip.

"She came for me," Margaret said, shaking. "She attacked Mrs. Crane and then came for me. She was trying to kill the baby."

On the other side of the room was Eloise, eyes wide and breathing heavily through a gag fastened around her head and face.

"I wanted to kill her so badly," she confessed. She looked to Ainsley with wide, expectant eyes as he came to her side. "After everything that has happened, after all we have been through, I never wanted to kill someone so thoroughly."

"But you didn't, Margaret," Ainsley said. "You possess the strength I never had." He took her hands in both of his in an effort to stop the shaking.

"Are you hurt?" Jonas asked, kneeling at the opposite side.

"Just my arm," she said, "but I don't think it's broken."

Ainsley pulled out her arm for inspection and felt through the flesh. He shook his head. "It's not broken."

Jonas scooped her up in his arms, readjusting his grasp of her once he was standing.

"We still need to conduct our interview of the witness," a constable at the door said.

"You may do so from the comfort of her room," Jonas snapped. "This woman is still recovering from a terrible sickness, poison by that monster on the floor."

Eloise closed her eyes upon hearing Jonas's disgust for her and began crying uncontrollably. Ainsley walked across the room and helped the officer lift her to her feet.

"Is it true?" the young man asked, as Inspector Hearst entered the room. "This woman is the perpetrator of a poisoning?"

Ainsley looked between both officers. "I personally dropped off the scarf to your offices this afternoon and we have the names of the men who witnessed her touching the scarf," he said. He reached for the gag to untie it.

"Leave it on," Inspector Hearst said, raising a hand to stop him. "It's no less than she deserves."

☙　❧

Three days passed before Margaret was strong enough to travel. On their last evening in Edinburgh, Margaret insisted that Ainsley take her for one final walk around the neighbourhood before they were to head home on the train the next day. Ainsley was careful to ensure Margaret was warm enough and every few hundred feet he asked if she would prefer to head back.

"Just a little further," she said, clinging to his arm and guiding him forward somewhat.

Ainsley knew they could easily hail a hansom but he worried nonetheless.

"What an interesting little adventure we've had, wouldn't you say? A new round of stories to add to all the others," she said.

Ainsley chuckled at the thought. The last year had not been boring, in the slightest way. They had come to a stone wall, with dark green ivy trailing over the top.

"What do you make of it all? Have the Marshalls been cursed for some unknown deed in days past?" she asked, walking slowly.

"Cursed?" Ainsley shrugged. "I wouldn't believe such things. A little adventure never hurt anyone."

She gave him a sideways glance.

"Well, a scar or two doesn't change much," he said.

"Now there is where you are wrong, dear brother." Margaret stopped and turned to him. "We have changed considerably. We aren't the people we were twelve months ago and we are all the better for it."

Ainsley couldn't help but smile. Her optimism hadn't been tarnished one bit since her ordeal.

"Come," she said, pulling at his arm, beckoning him to follow her. "Let us see how today shall change us." She led him a little further down the pavement and then turned through a stone arch in the wall. Ainsley's smile faded when he realized they had entered a churchyard and were headed for the front door.

Inside, a gathering of people waited for them expectantly at the end of a short aisle. Jonas stood slightly off-centre of a vicar in a freshly pressed suit with a small flower attached to his lapel.

"What is this?" Ainsley asked.

"Our happiness is better served when we endeavour to follow our own hearts and minds, isn't that what you said to me?" Margaret smiled.

Ainsley was too dumbstruck to answer.

John stood next to Mrs. Crane, who cried softly into a lace handkerchief. Mr. Locke came into view at their side with a posy of flowers he presented to Margaret.

"Peter, it would be an honour for both of you to walk me down the aisle," Margaret said, as she removed her shawl and laid it over the back of a pew. She met his gaze and tried hard to supress her delight in having bested him.

"I ..." Ainsley struggled to hide his emotions. He surveyed the scene before them. Three days had passed and no one had said anything to him. "Of course."

Ainsley moved to her left side as Mr. Locke took his position on the right.

"One more change to round out the year," Ainsley said.

A sudden look of fear came over Margaret as they paused at the end of the aisle. "Do you think Father will mind that I didn't have him here?" she asked.

"To hell with what he minds," Ainsley said rather loudly. "This is about you and Jonas, finally."

After a moment's thought, Margaret nodded and replaced

her doubt with a cheerful smile. "Are you ready?"

Ainsley nodded. "Are you, dear Margaret?"

Epilogue

The next day Ainsley returned to London alone and found Marshall House quiet and dark upon his arrival. Aunt Louisa spied him from the second-floor landing as he climbed the stairs wearily.

"Where's Margaret?" she asked.

"She elected to stay in Edinburgh," Ainsley answered as he reached the top, "with her new husband."

At the news, Aunt Louisa raised her chin and gave an indignant look. "I should have known something was up when I heard that Mr. Thornton had returned to London so quickly. I doubt it would have been the case if she had accepted his proposal like I instructed her too."

Ainsley did not bother to hide his sigh of disdain. "Aunt Louisa, we Marshall children are the products of our mother and father alike. We cannot be ordered to do anything we don't already have a mind to do." He passed her in the hall and went straight for the nursery, where he knew Lucy would be sleeping.

He was surprised when he found Cassandra seated at the rocking chair coaxing the babe to sleep. "Hello, my love," he said quietly as he crossed the room.

Cassandra smiled as he came to her and knelt in front of the chair at her feet.

"How is my heiress?" he asked, picking up her small hand and planting a gentle kiss over her knuckles.

"Very well, I suppose," she said. "With many thanks to Mrs. Louisa Banks for sneaking me here most nights so I can rock her to sleep."

Ainsley stole a peek at the sleeping Lucy, wrapped up in a few blanket layers.

"How has Father been doing?" he asked. "Difficult as ever, I imagine."

Cassandra's face fell at the mention of the invalid down the hall. "He is not doing well, Peter. The doctors have warned us it won't be long now."

Two weeks later, the doctor's warnings came to fruition. Two days after that, the family was gathered around the newly dug grave at North Western Cemetery alongside the gravestone of Lady Charlotte Marshall. Margaret and Jonas had taken the train to London the day before to be there, but the eldest brother, Daniel, refused to look either in the eye. He was the first of the family to leave the graveside, beckoning Evelyn, his wife, to follow.

"Give it time," Ainsley said reassuringly to Margaret as they watched him leave.

"How long do I have to endure this before you too join me in the ranks of shunned Marshall children?" Margaret gestured to Cassandra, who walked a cemetery path alongside Aunt Louisa. "I can't be the only one casting a long shadow on the great Marshall name." They kept their voice low so no one else gathered could hear them.

Ainsley smiled. "Not long, I should hope. I wouldn't fret about it too much. Daniel has only spoken ten words to me since the Edinburgh papers announced the true nature of my trade, in all its gory details."

Margaret laughed softly. "Oh, how I would have loved to witness him reading that."

After a few moments of laughter, Margaret and Ainsley noticed the crowd had thinned and they were the only ones left at the graveside.

"What do we do now?" Margaret asked solemnly.

Gently, Ainsley grabbed her wrist and placed her arm under his and guided her away. "We live as we always have, to the best of our ability."

"You mean by the skin of our teeth," she teased.

Ainsley shrugged playfully. "That too."

About Tracy L. Ward

A former journalist and graduate from Humber College's School for Writers, Tracy L. Ward has been hard at work developing her favourite protagonist, Peter Ainsley, and chronicling his adventures as a morgue surgeon in Victorian England. She is currently working on a new mystery series. To find out more about Tracy's books follow her on www.facebook.com/TracyWard.Author or visit her website at www.gothicmysterywriter.blogspot.com